K. Edler

Caitlin gasped. "You!"

Mac sighed. "Yes, it's me."

Shock mingled with confusion. She'd woken up to find Mac here. If she hadn't been in so much pain, she could almost have believed this was all a bad dream. "Why are you here?"

"To help."

"I don't need your help."

"Oh, I think you do. And if I wasn't sure before, I am now," Mac said.

Caitlin knew as she asked that she wasn't going to like his answer, but she asked it just the same. "Why?"

"Because a few minutes ago, someone came into your room. I don't think he expected me to be here."

Her heart skipped a beat.

"In a truly riveting story, Ms. Sala draws you in from the very beginning."
—*Romantic Times* on *Butterfly*

SHARON SALA

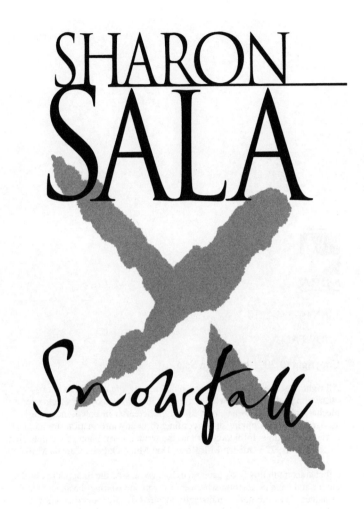

Snowfall

MIRA®

MIRA®

ISBN 0-7394-2210-3

SNOWFALL

Printed in U.S.A.

When we are born into this world,
we do not choose the family we are given,
only the friends we yearn to keep.

Throughout my life there have been many,
some fleeting, some steadfast,
who stood, not by me, but with me,
through the proverbial thick and thin.

I cannot name you all, but you know who you are,
and I cherish my place in your life. You have
unselfishly given me both your presence and your time.

I can only hope that, in return,
I did not fail to return the favor.

One

You will suffer for the sin.

Caitlin Bennett took a deep, shaky breath as she re-read the letter in her hand. No matter how many times she read it, the warning didn't change. It was the latest in a chain of hate mail she'd been receiving for the past six months. Each one she received was worse than the last.

When they'd first started coming, she'd chalked it up to nothing more than a disgruntled fan. As C. D. Bennett, bestselling mystery author, it wasn't the first weird fan letter she'd ever received. But when the second, and then the third, came, each with a similar message of retribution, she began to get nervous. Public figures were often murdered with less provocation.

Deciding to err on the side of caution, she had called Boran Fiorello, an old friend of the family and a detective with the 45th precinct. When she showed him the letters, he was most understanding but didn't consider them truly threatening, and as she looked back, she could understand his reaction.

The first three letters were almost ambivalent, written in an "I don't like you because" style. It was no wonder he wasn't impressed. Fiorello had sent her home with a pat on the back and a promise to take her out to dinner sometime soon.

But the letters kept coming, each one a bit more threatening than the last and renewing her anxiety. Certain that Fiorello would take these more seriously, she called him again. That time his response had been brief, almost distracted. He'd told her that there was no law against not liking what she wrote and no law against telling her about it. Short of receiving an actual physical threat, which she had not, he didn't think she had anything to worry about. Feeling suitably chastened, she'd given up, even though the tone of the letters continued to darken.

Now she had just over two dozen, and all very obviously from the same person. The last one had come this morning. The bright crimson of a felt tip pen on white paper was eye-catching; part of what the writer most likely intended. But it was the perfect bloodred drops added to the bottom of each word that gave her chills. The letters appeared to be seeping blood, and where there should have been a signature, there was an accumulating pool of blood instead. It was the perfect visual assault—horrifying without striking a single blow.

She was scared—as scared as she'd ever been in her life—yet there was nothing but words on which to base her fear. She'd never been accosted, never received a threatening phone call, never had one moment when she'd experienced physical danger.

A small clock on her desk began chiming the hour, and as it did, she jumped at the sound. Dismayed by the time, she put the letter in the file with all the others and then hurried to her bedroom.

In less than an hour, a car would arrive to take her to DBC Studios. Kenny Leibowitz, her publicist, had arranged her personal appearance on the *Live with Lowell* show to promote *Dead Lines,* her newest release. She didn't like the publicity part of the business, but she dealt with it. Doing television was her least favorite thing, especially when it was on the DBC network. She began a mental countdown of the interview as she put on her makeup.

Inevitably the host of this particular show seemed bent on bringing up the fact that her father was Devlin Bennett, who, among other things, had founded Devlin Broadcasting Company. After that, he seemed compelled to mention that when her father died, he'd left all his millions and his holdings, which included DBC, to Caitlin. Doing television meant she had to cope with the one-liners about owning the network and buying her way into fame. It didn't seem to matter to the glib talk-show host that her books had an average eighty-five percent sell-through, which was phenomenal in and of itself. All Lowell was looking for was the laugh. She didn't like his snide remarks, but she dealt with them in a witty and urbane manner, giving the host as good as he gave. To his credit, he loved it—and her. He didn't know that Caitlin was cringing inside, or that she would much rather have been home watching videos of old movies and having her favorite snack, a peanut butter and dill pickle sandwich. To too many people in the world, she was a poor little rich girl who played at being a writer. Although her father had been dead for almost five years, Caitlin had been forced to accept the fact that she would forever live in his shadow. Not for the first time, she was wishing for a man in her life, and maybe children. She wasn't just afraid, she was lonely. But wishing didn't produce results.

Her makeup finished, she rummaged through her closet, snatching the first warm black outfit she came to, and began to dress. One good thing about being a writer—nobody expected you to look pretty. You just had to be smart. By the time her car arrived, she was ready and waiting.

"So…Caitlin…may I call you Caitlin, or should I say Ms. Bennett? After all, you are my boss."

Caitlin smiled what she hoped was a forgiving smile and tried not to wince. God. Where did they get those people? Ron Lowell was an attractive man, but his brain seemed stuck on Rewind. This was the fourth time in as many years that she'd been on his show promoting a book, and he always started her interview in the exact same way.

"I don't care what you call me, as long as you buy the book," Caitlin quipped.

The audience roared, and Ron Lowell beamed. The interview was getting off to a good start. He picked up the book and made a pretense of flipping through the pages, although his focus was definitely on the swell of her breasts beneath the black knit dress she was wearing.

"So the new book is called *Dead Lines.* Tell us about it."

Caitlin leaned forward. "It's a murder mystery, Ron."

He grinned. She'd fed him the perfect line.

"Which means you're not going to tell us anything juicy?"

Another round of titters floated up from the audience. Although Lowell couldn't see them, he thrived on the sound.

"I didn't say that," Caitlin said. "I will tell you that it has nothing to do with meeting a deadline. Picture this, if you will. A beautiful inn in the Adirondacks filled with people who've come for an enjoyable weekend. An early winter storm drops two feet of snow on the mountains, making the roads impassable and snowing everyone in. All the utilities go out. No phones. No electricity. No communication with the outside world. Then people start to die...and not from natural causes."

"*Oooh,* I get it," Lowell said. "Dead lines of communication.'' Then he began wiggling his eyebrows in mock fright. ''And the killer must be one of the guests, because no one can get in or out, right?''

Caitlin just smiled.

Lowell beamed back. ''I know. I know. Read the book.''

''Ah...brains to go with all those good looks,'' Caitlin said.

The audience laughed again, and Ron Lowell glowed in appreciation.

Minutes later they broke for commercial and Caitlin got up to leave. Lowell stood to shake her hand, and when he did, held it a little longer than usual.

''How about some dinner after the show?''

Caitlin smiled as she slipped her hand out of Lowell's grasp.

''Ron, I would love it, but another time, okay? I'm on a *real* deadline with my next book, and I need to work. Thanks for a wonderful interview, though, and I hope you enjoy the book.''

She was so smooth he never knew he'd been brushed off. By the time she got off stage, she was sick to her stomach from nerves.

''Caitlin, darling! You were marvelous, as always.''

Caitlin made a face at Kenny as he helped her into her coat.

''Next time you better ask me first before you book one of these things. I need more warning.''

Kenny kissed the side of her cheek, then winked. "Of course," he said, straightening her coat on her shoulders. "It's cold as a witch's tit outside tonight. Looks like it might even snow."

Caitlin shivered at the thought and ignored the fact that he hadn't promised anything regarding her scheduling. She sighed, reminding herself that he was only doing his job, then shivered. She hated winter. If it weren't for the promotions Kenny had set up here in the city for the new book, she would have gone south weeks ago.

As she began to button up her coat, Kenny caught her hands in his own.

"Let me, dear," he said. "Your fingers are almost blue. Didn't you bring gloves?"

"I think I left them in the car."

"Poor baby," Kenny murmured, as he buttoned her up, then clasped her hands in his, pretending to warm them.

What he wanted was to hold her hand, and Caitlin knew it. He had been making delicate passes at her for some time now, and it was all she could do to fend him off without ruining their working relationship.

"They're warmer now. Thanks," Caitlin said, and stuck her hands into her pockets as one of the producers led them through the backstage maze to an exit door.

The limousine was waiting just outside in the alley.

Kenny opened the door before the driver could get out. Caitlin stepped into the interior, settling into the luxurious leather and bone-melting warmth with relief.

"*Oooh,* this heat feels so good," she sighed. "Why on earth do they always keep those studios so cold?"

"Money, honey," Kenny said, and slid as close to her as he could get. "Here, put on your gloves. I don't want my best girl to get sick."

Caitlin slid her fingers into the soft, creamy calfskin and ignored the "best girl" remark. After that, they rode through the busy streets in silence, and as they did, Caitlin's thoughts returned to the letters.

A part of her wanted to tell someone, but her close friends were few and far between. Finding the right person to tell secrets to without having them wind up in the morning papers was a caution she'd learned at an early age. She glanced at Kenny, considering how he would take the news, and then discarded the idea. She didn't trust him not to use the letters as some sordid hook to sell more books. She could see it all now: Mystery Writer Fields Own Death Threats.

She sighed again, and as she did, Kenny leaned over and cupped her face with his hand.

"What's wrong, honey girl? And don't tell me nothing, because I know you too well." When Caitlin remained silent, Kenny persisted. "You can trust me."

She smiled. "Nothing is wrong, Kenny, other than that I'm cold and tired."

"Do you want some company tonight?"

Her smile felt as cold as her hands. Some men were so dense. How many times would she have to say no before he got the message?

"Thanks, but I just want a quiet evening alone. You understand."

Leibowitz's eyes glittered with a frustration he never verbalized.

"Sure, honey. No problem. Maybe you'll feel better in the morning." Then he glanced out the window as the limo began to slow down. "And it looks as if we've arrived."

The driver got out and opened their door. Kenny stepped out first, then steadied Caitlin as she exited the car.

"Have a good night," he said softly, and kissed the side of her cheek.

Caitlin waved goodbye and, as soon as the doorman opened the door, bolted inside the building. The security guard looked up from behind his desk and smiled.

"Good evening, Miss Bennett."

"Good evening, Mike. How's the family?"

Mike Mazurka grinned. "Good, good. My youngest boy, Tom, just had his first child. I'm a grandpa again. Can you believe it?"

Caitlin laughed. "How many does that make?"

"Seven. But who's counting?" Mike said.

She waved goodbye as she continued toward the elevators. But when she got inside and slid her key card into the slot, apprehension returned. She wouldn't feel safe until she was behind the locked doors of her own apartment. Even though this elevator took her straight to the penthouse without stopping on any other floors, she felt her vulnerability all too acutely.

She exited quickly, dashing across the foyer outside the elevator to her door. A quick turn of the key in the lock and she was inside, slamming the door and turning the dead bolt behind her. Slumping with relief, Caitlin leaned against the door, her heart pounding, her skin clammy. The longer she stood there, the more disgusted with herself she became.

"I will not live like this," she muttered, and headed toward her bedroom to change, turning on lights as she went.

But who to tell? She thought of calling Fiorello again and then dismissed the notion. He hadn't believed her the first time, and he'd blown her off the second. She wasn't in the mood for more of his derision. Yet as she readied herself for bed, she accepted the fact that something had to be done, and the resolution had to come from her.

The steady rise and fall of a pair of scissor blades cast a shadow across Buddy's newspaper, separating the article about C. D. Bennett from the rest of the page. He tacked it to his bedroom wall beside all the others, then stepped back.

Bennett pens another winner.

He sneered. Bennett had been a winner the day she was born.

A gust of wind rattled the windows, reminding him of the bitter cold outside, but he had no fear of freezing. The rage inside his gut would keep him warm.

His belly growled. He hadn't eaten since noon, and it was almost midnight. Technically tomorrow was already here, but he was hungry now, and it was too long to wait for breakfast.

With the job that he had, regular meals were sporadic at best. Half the time he ate on the run; the other times, when he managed to sit down at a table, something or someone managed to interfere. God. He didn't belong at this job—always at the beck and call of others. He should be the one calling the shots, not the one always being paged.

He glared at the wall, scanning the pictures and clippings. Caitlin Doyle Bennett. What the hell was she playing at, taking up shelf space in bookstores? There had never been a day of her life that she had needed money. She didn't know what it was like to wonder where her next meal was coming from or if she would still have a roof over her head next week. If she had half a conscience, she would step aside for those more deserving.

His belly growled again, breaking his concentration, but when he strode to the refrigerator, the sight of food turned his stomach. He slammed it shut with a frown. He didn't want to eat, he wanted to forget, and the best way to do that was a couple of drinks. The bar on the corner didn't close for another couple of hours. That was what he needed—a drink or two, maybe some pretzels or nuts and a little conversation.

Grabbing his coat, he patted his pockets to make sure his keys were inside. The bulge of his switchblade was in his right pocket, the jingle of his keys in his left. The knife was a holdover from his childhood, one he was reluctant to leave behind. As a youth, it had saved him more than once from being beaten half to death, and as an adult, he found it a comfort against a possible mugging.

He let himself out the door of his fifth floor apartment and took the stairs down to the street. The first bite of wind took his breath away, but he began to acclimatize as he walked, relishing the frigid cleansing.

Despite the hour and the cold, the bar was noisy. He entered with a grin, and when someone called his name, he nodded and waved as he slid onto a stool and ordered a drink.

"Looks like I'm not the only cold fool in the city," he said, grabbing a handful of pretzels from the closest bowl.

The bartender laughed. "Cold weather is always good for business," he said. "What'll it be?"

"How about a lager?"

"Any particular brand?"

"Just something dark and smooth."

Moments later, the bartender sat a tall glass of brown liquid in front of him, which he used to wash down the pretzels. The cold bite of the brew tasted of yeast and hops and something wonderfully strong. He liked the scent almost as much as the taste as it slid down his throat. Glad that he'd come, he leaned forward, resting his elbows on the bar and closing his eyes, letting the anonymous camaraderie of the place seep into his soul. For this moment, it was easy to pretend he was among friends.

An hour had passed when he got up to leave, tossing a handful of bills onto the bar then waving goodbye as he left. The cold seared his eyeballs, making them tear as he walked outside. It had gotten colder in the short time he'd been inside, and he quickly put on his gloves and pulled the collar of his coat up around his ears.

He paused, looking up at the sky and wishing he could see the stars. But in a city the size of New York, you couldn't see night past the streetlights. A spurt of longing swept through him as he thought of his mother's house on the outskirts of Toledo. Unwilling to go to bed with old ghosts, he turned in the opposite direction from his apartment, hoping to walk off the mood.

The sidewalks were almost deserted, although the street traffic was fairly constant. After a while he got weary of squinting against oncoming headlights and took a left onto a side street. There, in the lee of the wind, exhaust fumes from the traffic seemed suspended within the cold, and he wrinkled his nose in disgust. Now and then he caught a glimpse of himself in the windows he passed and was reminded that while he hadn't been born rich, he couldn't complain about his physical appearance. He was above average height, muscular in build, and had more than his share of good looks. With a little luck, he should have at least a good fifty years more on his side before he left this earth. He walked without aim, enjoying the power of his stride and the knowledge that he was Man, the superior animal.

The window displays were well-lit and cheery, even though the stores were all closed. They reminded him of the days when he was a boy and his mother had taken him into the city to look at the holiday decorations.

Look at that one, Buddy. Isn't it marvelous?

He smiled to himself. His mother had been fond of superlatives. He used to tease her about them. Now he would give anything just to have her back. Losing her to cancer had been hard, but losing himself had been harder. She was the only one who'd called him

Buddy, and he missed hearing it said. Everyone else knew him by another name, but in his heart, he would always be Buddy.

Lost in nostalgia, he was almost past the bookstore before it dawned on him what he was seeing. The elaborate display of C. D. Bennett's latest release sent his thoughts scattering out of control. He started to shake, his fingers unconsciously curling into fists. Wasn't there a single goddamned place in this city that didn't bow at her feet?

Long minutes passed as he stood unmoving. By the time he came to his senses, he was freezing. Rage was hot in his chest as he turned away from the store. Tucking his chin against the cold, he began to retrace his steps toward home. It wasn't until he heard the sound of women's voices and then the heartbreaking tinkle of feminine laughter that he came out of his fugue.

On the stoop of a brownstone across the way, two women were hugging each other and then waving goodbye. As one of them came down the steps and started across the street, he stepped back into the shadows. He had no desire to speak, not even in passing.

He watched as the woman jumped the curb and passed under the streetlight, giving him a clear view of her face. She walked with her head up, her shoulders straight, as if she didn't have a care in the world, her slim, youthful features framed by thick straight hair the color of chocolate.

She looked familiar, and he stared intently, wondering if he'd met her through his work. It wasn't until she passed beneath the second streetlight that recognition hit. She looked enough like Caitlin Bennett to be her twin.

Breath caught in the back of his throat as he watched her approach. Bile rose in his mouth, as bitter as his thoughts. Without thinking, he stepped out of the shadows and grabbed her by the throat. He had nothing against her beyond the fact that she resembled the wrong woman, and introductions seemed unnecessary, since he'd made up his mind to kill her.

Choking off her screams, he encircled her throat with his fingers and dragged her out of the light into the shadows of the alley. About twenty yards from the street, he stopped and then let her fall.

With her larnyx crushed, she lay sprawled on her back like a small, broken doll, too traumatized to move. A thin trickle of blood oozed from the corner of one eye, where his ring had cut the flesh. Her gaze was wide and terror-filled as she struggled to breathe, but drawing air past her damaged throat was almost impossible. When she saw him unzip his pants, she closed her eyes and prayed to die.

The assault was brutal and his cleansing was great. The more she bled, the less pain he felt. By the time he was through, he was euphoric. He staggered to his feet, inhaling deeply as he pulled much needed oxygen into his adrenaline-charged body. His mind was blank, his body strangely relaxed. She was dead now, but he couldn't bring himself to walk away.

He glanced at her again, as if seeing her for the very first time, then smiled in satisfaction. He'd taken that smug look off her face. But the longer he looked, the deeper he frowned. Her eyes, dark brown and still brimming with tears, were wide-open in silent accusation.

"Don't look at me like that," he snarled.

In a last act of violence, he pulled the switchblade, slashing her face in two intersecting diagonal strokes. The flesh parted beneath the knife, aptly quartering her features as if he'd cut up an apple. He wiped the knife on her coat, then carefully closed the blade and walked out of the alley as if nothing had happened.

Within the hour he was home. Later, he dreamed of Christmas and his mother standing by the stove stirring gravy, and smiled as he slept.

It was morning before Donna Dorian's body was found, and by the time the police arrived, it had started to snow.

Two

"Hell's bells, this snow is really coming down," Sal Amato said as he rolled his substantial girth from the passenger seat of the car, while his partner, Paulie Hahn, got out from behind the wheel.

A couple of patrol cars were already on the scene, and even at this early hour a crowd was beginning to gather behind the yellow crime scene tape.

Hahn turned up the collar of his coat and tugged on his gloves as he circled the car, wincing as he caught sight of the body in the alley, a short distance away. A uniformed patrolman lifted the tape as they ducked under.

"Hell of a way to start a shift," the patrolman muttered.

Amato settled his hat a little more firmly on his nearly bald head and then glanced into the alley. Even at this distance, he could tell it was going to be brutal.

"At least you're still breathing, Knipski. Do we have an ID on the victim?"

"Yeah. Her purse was about ten feet from her body. Name's Donna Dorian. Her mother reported her

Title: SNOWFALL
Condition: Good
Location: Row 3 Shelf 4 Bay 3 Item 703
Description: **PLEASE READ** The dust jacket shows some shelf
wear FAST shipping, FREE tracking, and GREAT customer
service! We also offer international and EXPEDITED
shipping options.

Source: KC   General Book 4/23/2020
SKU: 3D7E2G000TKD
ASIN: 0739422103
Code: 0739422103
Employee: chelsea

missing this morning. Said she went to the movies with a girlfriend. Didn't come home. Thought she was spending the night with the girlfriend and called over there this morning before she went to work, only to find out they'd parted company some time after 1:00 a.m. That's when she called it in."

"Who found the body?" Amato asked.

"Some jogger." The officer turned around, scanning the crowd, then pointed. "That's him. The one in red and black sweats, throwing up in the gutter."

"Yeah, thanks," Amato said. "Come on, Paulie."

"I feel like joining that jogger," Paulie said.

"We'll wait until he's through puking before we try and talk to him," Sal said.

"Good idea," Paulie said, and took his handkerchief out of his pocket as his nose began to run.

Paulie Hahn's throat was sore and his head was pounding. He blew his nose and then tilted the brim of his hat just enough to keep the snowflakes from drifting into his eyes. Damn flu. It wasn't even Christmas, and he was already sick. But when they reached the body, he wished he'd called in sick this morning like his wife had wanted.

"Jesus Christ," he muttered, and then crossed himself before taking a deep breath of the cold air. "Sal, how many years we been partners?"

Amato frowned. "Since my second year as a detective, which I guess is about seventeen years now. Why?"

Paulie pointed at the body in disgust. "In the old days, people used to just shoot each other. You know...a nice clean kill. A couple of bullets. Some neat holes. Bang, you're dead. So what the hell is with this mutilation shit? What kind of perverts do we have on our streets that feel the need to do this kind of thing? Ain't it enough that he killed her?" He looked down at what was left of the young woman's face and wanted to cry. "He didn't have to butcher her like that."

Amato's frown deepened. "She was probably dead when it happened."

"How you figure that?"

"The cuts are even and clean. You know...no struggle."

Paulie took out his handkerchief and blew his nose again, then waved down another patrolman.

"Anybody called the Medical Examiner yet?"

"Yes, sir, on the way," the officer said.

"Here come Neil and Kowalksi," Paulie said.

Amato turned, nodding a hello.

The smile on Detective Trudy Kowalksi's face slid sideways.

"Well, hell," she muttered, as she glanced at the body and then looked away. "I hope she had some ID, otherwise it's not going to be easy to get an identification."

"The perp was kind. He left her purse," Amato said.

J. R. Neil, Trudy's partner, stood without moving, staring at the body.

"Obviously it wasn't about her money," he said. "From the looks of her, he was pissed. Anybody know if she had a boyfriend or a husband?"

"We just got here," Amato muttered. "But since you're so interested in helping, there's a jogger puking up his guts at the mouth of the alley. Why don't you go find out what he knows? And while you're at it, take Red, there, and canvass the apartments above this alley and across the street. See if anybody heard anything last night."

Trudy Kowalksi tossed her copper-colored curls and then winked.

"You're just jealous because I have hair and you don't," she said, then nudged her partner. "Come on, J.R., you do the jogger, I'll start on the apartments above the alley. That way Amato and Hahn can stand here looking important when the M.E. arrives."

Neil grinned at the two older detectives and then walked away with his partner, laughing at something she said as they cleared the alley and parted company in the street.

Amato frowned as he watched them walking away. He liked Kowalksi. She was short and stocky and fiery as her hair, but she gave as good as she got. But he had to admit, when he was being honest with himself, that he didn't like Neil all that much. It was hard to like a man who was tall, good-looking and still had all his hair.

Then a cold gust of wind whipped down from the sky, funneling the falling snow like smoke from a chimney. Paulie blew his nose again, while Amato squatted down beside the body, careful not to disturb any evidence until the crime scene unit had come and gone.

"As cold as it is, I'm betting they send the new assistant from the M.E.'s office," he said.

"I'm not taking that bet," Paulie muttered. "Because I'll bet you're right." He looked back at the body, guessing the victim was close to his daughter's age, then glanced up at Amato.

"You know what I never get used to?"

"What?" Sal asked.

"The fact that we can't cover them up. This kid is nude from the waist down and her face is in pieces. Goddamn. We oughta be able to at least cover them up."

Amato stood and clapped his partner on the back. "But what if it messed up the evidence we needed to catch the son of a bitch who did this to her?"

Paulie sighed. "I know. I was just thinking out loud, okay?" Then he glanced at the area again. "As for evidence, it's not going to be easy, what with the snow and all."

"Yeah," Sal said, then turned to look toward the sound of arriving vehicles. "Looks like the M.E.'s here.'' When he saw a tall, skinny black woman get out of the car and then heft a large black case from the back of the station wagon, he started to grin. ''Looks like I would have won that bet. It's Booker.''

''Good morning, gentlemen,'' Angela Booker drawled, as she set down her case and then opened it up.

Sal had seen the contents of such cases a thousand times, and they still made him think of the science kit he'd gotten for Christmas one year. Lots of little instruments and slides that he never did learn how to use. ''Got anything hot in there to drink?'' Sal asked, as he watched her trading driving gloves for surgical gloves.

''Get lost, Amato. My hormones are raging and I'm not in the mood.''

They grinned at each other and moved back toward the mouth of the alley. It was time to start the business for which they'd been hired.

Caitlin woke with a start, her heart pounding, her eyes wide with fright. It took her a few moments to realize that her fear came from the nightmare she'd been having and not from within her own home.

But the dream had been too real for her to want to go back to sleep, so she swung her legs over to the side of the bed and got up, grimacing when she realized it was only fifteen minutes after six.

By the time she emerged from the bathroom, she

was wide-awake. Slipping into her favorite house shoes and her oldest robe, she combed her fingers through her hair and then made her way to the kitchen, telling herself that as long as she was awake, she might as well get an early start on the day.

As she entered the kitchen, she glanced toward the windows and saw snow swirling down on its way to the streets below. Thankful that her job did not take her beyond the warmth and familiarity of her own home, she ambled into her office and switched on the computer. While it was booting up, she went back to the kitchen and began scrounging through the cabinets. When she realized she was out of cereal and eggs, as well as milk and tea, she put a couple of ice cubes in a glass and poured it full of Pepsi. Half a glass later, the caffeine in the pop was starting to kick in. Toast was browning in the toaster, making her mouth water, but it wasn't until she thrust a knife into a jar of peanut butter that she remembered the dream.

He'd come at her with a knife. Even when she spun and started to run, she knew she would not get away.

She shuddered, then took a deep breath and looked at the knife. In a defiant gesture, she pulled it out of the jar and licked it clean before thrusting it back into the peanut butter, coming up with another thick dollop, which she spread on her just-done toast. Adding a spoonful of orange marmalade to a second piece of bread, she slapped the two together, put the sandwich on a plate and tossed the cutlery in the sink. After topping off her glass of Pepsi, she ambled into the living room to eat.

She turned the television on out of habit, rather than from a need to know what was going on in the world. When some on-the-spot reporter began talking about a midnight murder, she grabbed the remote and channel-surfed until she found one showing cartoons. By the time she was through with breakfast, the Road Runner had dispatched Wile E. Coyote three times and her mood had been lifted.

After setting her dirty plate and glass in the sink, she headed for her office, promising herself she would get dressed as soon as she checked her e-mail. Hours later, she looked up to realize it was almost noon. Not only had she answered the mail, but she'd written ten good pages of the current chapter, as well. Hitting Save, she leaned back with a smile and was still grinning when her telephone rang.

"Bennett residence."

"Caitlin, it's Aaron. Are you decent?"

Her smile widened. If she had to pick a best friend, her editor, Aaron Workman, would be on the top of the list. The fact that he was also gay just made everything easier. Besides the books she wrote, the only thing he wanted from her other than friendship was her shoes.

"What do you think?" she asked.

She heard him sigh and knew he was probably rolling his eyes.

"I think you haven't even brushed your hair, let alone your teeth."

Caitlin laughed. "You know me too well."

"Come have lunch with me," Aaron said.

Caitlin groaned. "It's cold and snowing outside."

"It stopped snowing an hour ago, and you own a coat. Get dressed and meet me at the Memphis Grill at one-thirty. We need to talk."

"Are you buying?" she asked, and heard him snort.

"Don't make me come up there," he muttered.

"Okay, okay, I'll be there."

"I've already called your driver. He'll pick you up at one o'clock."

Now Caitlin was the one snorting beneath her breath.

"What if I'd told you no?"

"But you didn't, did you? Now be a good girl and get out of those horrible clothes and into something sexy."

Caitlin grinned. "Sexy? Aaron, is there something you want to tell me...like have you had a change of heart?"

There was another faint snort in her ear, and then Aaron answered. "Hardly. However, one of these days you might actually meet the man of your dreams. I want you to be ready."

Caitlin frowned. "You better not be trying to set me up again. You don't know how close I came to ditching your ass when you tried to set me up with Mac.''

"How was I to know that my two favorite people in the whole world would hate each other's guts? It's not my fault that you and my stepbrother don't get along.''

"We don't get along because Connor McKee is six feet four inches of pure testosterone and an attitude that won't quit. I'll be there at one-thirty, and you better be alone.''

"If I'm not, the other guy at the table will be with me, so go make yourself pretty. I'm already hungry.''

Caitlin smiled as she hung up the phone. Even though it was miserable outside, a decent lunch with Aaron sounded like a good idea. Afterward, she would stop off at the market and pick up some groceries before she came home. Suddenly the day had become an adventure.

Kenny Leibowitz reached into the humidor on his desk, removed a long, thin cigar, then strode to the window, looking out as he lit up. Despite the snow, the streets were teeming with holiday shoppers, their arms laden with colorful bags brimming with purchases. When the end of the cigar was glowing, he took a slow puff, savoring the sweet bite of tobacco on his tongue. With careful precision, he puckered his lips and blew four perfect smoke rings into the air.

Watching them dissipate, he smiled to himself, remembering the long, rainy weekend of his sixteenth birthday and how sick he'd gotten smoking his first cigar. He'd come a long way since then. Although he'd sampled other vices since, he was thankful that none of them had stuck.

As he stood, he caught a glimpse of his reflection and absently combed a hand through his hair, settling the thick, wavy strands back in place. He considered himself fortunate that he was more than attractive, with few vices and no addictions.

Then he amended that thought. He wasn't addicted to anything, but he was to someone. He had a thriving public relations business, with six very high profile clients and seven up-and-coming. He was good at what he did, and he knew it. The only problem was, he wanted more from Caitlin Bennett than her business. But she couldn't see past their working relationship, and it was driving him nuts. He dreamed about her nightly and fantasized about her during the day, imagining what her naked body would look like and the way her eyes would go all sleepy as she lifted her lips for his kiss.

"Son of a bitch," he muttered, and then took another puff on the cigar. This time, the perfect smoke rings gave him no joy. He knew what he wanted—what he'd needed for a long time now. Caitlin. She had everything he coveted. Money. Prestige. A name that people remembered. She belonged to him—to do with as he wished. All he had to do was make her see that. One day she would realize that she needed him for more than just to publicize her books.

In frustration, he turned away from the window and strode back to his desk. He flipped the page of his day planner and sighed. Nothing. No one wanted to plan anything around the holidays, which basically meant he might as well go on holiday, too.

He looked around his office and frowned. *So why am I here?* Impulsively he picked up the phone. This was the perfect time to ask Caitlin to lunch.

He dialed her number, smiling to himself in anticipation as he waited for her to answer. After fifteen rings and no pickup, he hung up in disgust. She hadn't even turned on the answering machine. He flipped through his Rolodex until he found her cell number and dialed it. After being transferred to her voice mail, he slammed the receiver back onto the cradle without leaving a message and stubbed out his cigar. This was ridiculous.

Frustration replaced his good mood as he headed for the door. His secretary looked up and smiled as he came out of his office.

"Susan, I'm taking an early lunch."

"Yes, sir. Do you want me to make a reservation for you?"

"No. I'll take my chances."

Shrugging into his overcoat and tossing his scarf around his neck, he exited the office with purposeful strides. If everyone seemed hell-bent on getting into

the holiday spirit, then it was time he did, too, with
or without his favorite client.

Caitlin smiled at her driver as he helped her out of
the car. If all things were equal, she would have been
the one helping him. Although John Steiner was almost seventy and suffering with arthritis, he took of-
fense if anyone offered him help. He'd been with her
father for more than twenty years, and at Devlin Bennett's death he had taken it upon himself to work for
her instead of retiring. Although she didn't often use
the family car, the fact that she owned it kept John
Steiner happy and employed.

"Thank you, Uncle John. You don't need to wait.
I'll catch a cab home."

John frowned, causing his unruly eyebrows to un-
dulate like fuzzy caterpillars.

"Now, missy, it's too cold to be standing out in
the street trying to hail a cab. I'd better wait."

"That's exactly why you're going home. I'm
lunching with Aaron, and you know how he is.
There's no telling how long we'll be. Besides, Aaron
had no business calling you in the first place, so won't
you please go home…for me?"

John tried another frown, but it didn't quite make
the grade. Caitlin Bennett was the daughter he'd
never had. He loved her to distraction and had yet to
tell her no and make it stick.

"All right, then, if you're sure?"

Caitlin kissed him on the cheek, as she would have her father. "Thank you, Uncle John. Drive safely, and we'll talk later."

Then she waved goodbye and watched him drive away. Once inside the restaurant, she made her way through a small crowd of people waiting for tables. When she reached the hostess, she smiled.

"I'm Caitlin Bennett. I'm having lunch with Aaron Workman. Has he arrived?"

The hostess smiled. "Yes, Miss Bennett. Please follow me."

Caitlin wove through the tables, waving across the room to a couple she knew as she followed the hostess.

Aaron saw her coming and stood, greeting her with a kiss on each cheek.

"Darling, you look gorgeous! Is that outfit new?"

"You know it's not. The last time I wore it, you told me it made my skin look green, so what are you up to?"

Aaron ignored her as he pulled out her chair.

"Do sit down, Caitlin. The least we can do is get comfortable before you start yelling at me."

Caitlin smiled at him sweetly.

"I don't yell at you. Ever." She picked up her menu. "I'm starving. What are you having?"

The change of topic suited Aaron. There was plenty of time to discuss why he'd called after she'd had a good meal and some stimulating conversation.

"I'm thinking about grilled salmon and one of their wonderful little salads."

She wrinkled her nose. "I don't like fish."

Aaron rolled his eyes. "I know that," he drawled. "But I do, and the question was...what am I having, not what do I think you should have."

She laughed as she leaned across the table and gave Aaron's hand a quick squeeze.

"You're so right, and I apologize for being such a beast."

Mollified once he'd made his point, he grinned as he returned to studying the menu.

They ordered within minutes, and a short while later their food arrived. They ate as they talked, discussing print runs and the cover of the book on which she was working. It wasn't until their waiter had taken their order for dessert and served them some coffee that Caitlin brought the cozy little scene to a halt.

"Okay, I've been fed and petted, and now I want to know why it was so important that I leave the comfort and warmth of my home to come have lunch with you. Not that your company isn't great," she added with a smile.

Aaron smoothed both hands down the front of his vest and then leaned forward, lowering his voice as he spoke.

"It's regarding some fan mail we've been getting about you at the office."

She felt suddenly sick.

"What about it?"

Aaron frowned. This wasn't the reaction he'd expected from her. She was pale and trembling.

"Are you all right? If you're not feeling well, we can continue this discussion at another time."

She brushed off the question with one of her own. "What about the fan mail?"

He sighed. He knew Caitlin well enough to realize that she would talk only when she was ready.

"Okay...but before I start, I want you to know that Hudson House Publishing is behind you one hundred percent."

"Aaron...please get to the point."

"Right. Within the last couple of months, we've received about a half dozen letters condemning us for publishing your books."

Caitlin tried to laugh it off. "Probably some frustrated wannabe who got a manuscript rejected and is taking it out on me."

"They don't think so."

"Why?"

"It's not complaints. It's threats."

Caitlin stiffened. "What kind of threats?"

Aaron sighed. "The last one was a bomb threat." He watched the blood draining from Caitlin's face and wished they were not in such a public place. He could tell she was on the verge of tears. "I'm sorry, darling, but we felt you should know...just in case...well, so you could be forewarned. Understand?''

''Oh my God.'' She looked around at the restaurant and the people in disbelief. How could they be carrying on in such a calm and happy manner when her world was falling apart?

''Caitlin. Darling. Talk to me.''

She looked back at Aaron, her gaze wild and unfocused.

''What do you want me to say? Oh darn? Oh well?'' She reached for her purse. ''You don't understand. I've got to get home.''

Aaron grabbed her arm. ''Listen to me. I think you're overreacting. It's not like the letters came directly to you.''

Caitlin gave him a frantic look and then laid her napkin on the table and shrugged out of his grasp.

At that moment, understanding dawned. She saw it in his eyes.

''Oh my God! You've been getting them, too!''

Caitlin pushed her chair back, but Aaron grabbed her arm again. Short of making a scene, she was stuck.

''Let me go,'' she whispered.

''Not until you answer me. Have you or have you not been receiving threatening letters?''

''Yes. I have.''

Her voice was just above a whisper, but Aaron heard everything, including her fear.

"For how long?"

She sighed. "I don't know...maybe six months."

"My God! Have you lost your mind?" he yelped. "Why didn't you tell someone?" Then he lowered his voice and tugged gently at her fingers. "Why didn't you tell *me?*"

It was all she could do not to cry. Aaron looked so hurt, and that was the last thing she wanted.

"I don't know," she muttered. "At first they didn't amount to much. Just the typical 'I don't like what you're doing' type of things. You know the kind. And I did seek advice. Twice."

Aaron touched Caitlin's face with his forefinger, then swiped a small tear from her cheek with his thumb.

"From whom?" he asked.

"Boran Fiorello. He's a detective with the NYPD and an old friend of my father's."

"What did he say?"

Caitlin shrugged. "He told me not to worry, that it wasn't against the law not to like what I wrote or to tell me about it. When the letters got worse, I called him again, and he pretty much blew me off. After that, I just kept them to myself."

Indignant on Caitlin's behalf, Aaron reached for his cell phone.

"What are you doing?" she asked.

"Calling that know-it-all detective and telling him his testosterone is sadly misplaced."

Aaron's exaggerations never failed to make her smile, and this was no exception. She shook her head. "No, please don't. It won't do any good. Besides, you're the one who has the most to worry about. My letters are full of vague threats like making me pay, which, unlike a bomb threat, is pretty non-specific. Has someone called the police?"

"Yes, but they are, of course, keeping it low-key. The last thing we need is to light a fire under every nut case in the city."

Caitlin nodded, then covered Aaron's hands with her own.

"I'm sorry," she said.

He made a face at her and then smiled. "Forgiven."

She glanced at her watch. "I need to get home."

"And I have an appointment in half an hour, or I'd take you there myself."

Caitlin shook her head. "About my behavior...that was nothing but panic. I'm really okay."

"Good girl. However, don't assume anything. Be careful, and I'll call you tonight. We'll make a plan then."

Caitlin grinned. "I'm trying to finish a manuscript. That's my plan."

Aaron canceled their dessert order, tossed some bills onto the table and helped her into her coat before following her out of the restaurant.

Outside, the bitter wind lifted the scarf around her

neck and blew it into her face. She caught it, tucking it down inside her collar before pulling on her gloves.

"Wait here. I'll hail you a cab," Aaron said.

"No, you take the cab," she said, then pointed down the street. "I'm going to walk down to that market and buy some groceries before I go home."

He frowned. "Are you sure?"

"Well, I had Pepsi and peanut butter for breakfast and there's no other food in my house."

Aaron rolled his eyes. "Good Lord! Go, go! And while you're at it, buy some fruit and vegetables. And some milk. Buy some milk. The next thing you'll be telling me you poured Pepsi onto your cornflakes."

Caitlin grinned. "It's not so bad."

Aaron covered his ears, as if pretending he couldn't bear to hear what she was saying.

"You eat like a teenager," he moaned. "Don't tell me any more."

"There comes a cab," Caitlin said, and gave him a quick kiss goodbye as the driver swerved to the curb. "Thanks for lunch, and for the words of encouragement."

"Just watch yourself until we figure out what to do," he warned, and then he was gone.

The streets were still slushy, but the sidewalks were clear. Caitlin immediately turned to face the wind, ably dodging the heavy flow of pedestrians as only a true city dweller could do. She knew the neighborhood. There was a nice market on the corner only a few blocks up. She would buy her food there and then take a cab home.

By the time she got to the end of the block, the light had turned red, and she, along with a good ten or fifteen people, hovered on the edge of the curb, waiting for permission to walk.

As she waited, she began a mental grocery list, smiling to herself about Aaron's demand to buy milk, which, of course, she would do. She'd never had Pepsi on her cereal in her life, but she wasn't going to tell him that and ruin his image of her bohemian habits. She liked being thought of as a bit of an eccentric instead of the heiress to the Bennett fortune.

She glanced up at the light, her thoughts still on shopping, and heard a truck downshifting gears. She saw it coming from the corner of her eye and could see that the driver was trying to make the light before it changed. She turned her head, wincing as the truck hit a puddle of slush, and knew she was going to get splashed.

And then, out of nowhere, she felt a hand on her back. Before she could react, she was shoved headfirst into the street. Instinctively her arms flew outward as she braced herself for the fall. It wasn't until she heard squealing brakes that she remembered the truck. In the split second before impact, she saw her own reflection in the truck's chrome bumper and screamed. She was unconscious before she hit the ground.

Three

"Miss... Miss...can you hear me? Can you tell me your name?"

Caitlin moaned. Someone was yelling in her ear when she needed to sleep. Aaron. It had to be Aaron. He was the only friend she had who was rude enough to wake her like this.

"Go away," she muttered, and then winced as something sharp pricked her skin.

"Get a neck brace on her. Dave, bring the spine board before I start this IV."

Suddenly she realized she wasn't in bed. Before she could focus, someone began pulling at her arms, then her clothes, running their hands up and down her body in an intimate fashion. Panic sliced through her pain like a knife as she flailed blindly.

"Easy, miss, I'm a paramedic. My partner and I are trying to help you. We're going to take you to the hospital and get you checked out, okay? Just relax and let us do our job."

Caitlin flashed on the bumper of an oncoming truck, and then another wave of pain dashed her thoughts as the paramedics rolled her from her face onto her back. Somewhere in all the chaos, she realized she was being put on a stretcher.

"Wait...wait," she begged, trying to remember what she needed to say.

"Easy, Miss," the paramedic said. "We're taking you to the hospital."

"Can't go," Caitlin muttered. "I'm out of milk." The medics chuckled as they lifted her into a waiting ambulance.

"You can get that later," the second one said.

She wanted to argue with them, but the words wouldn't come. Doors slammed, shutting out most of the street noise. Now there was only the occasional question from the man who was sitting at her side.

"Let's roll," he yelled.

Moments later, the ambulance began to move. Then came the sirens, and Caitlin winced and tried to cover her ears, only to find she couldn't move her arms.

"My arms," she muttered, trying unsuccessfully to open her eyes. "I can't move my arms."

Someone touched her hand briefly, letting her know that he was there.

"That's because we buckled you onto the stretcher so you wouldn't fall off. Just relax."

Caitlin's body went limp, but her mind was in a panic. They didn't understand. She couldn't relax. She couldn't be unconscious. It was too dangerous to sleep. Someone wanted her dead. She tried again to open her eyes, but the pain was too great. In the midst of her fears, the sound of sirens began to fade. Mercifully, she slipped into unconsciousness. When she woke, she was being transferred from the stretcher to a gurney.

"Miss, can you hear me?"

Caitlin moaned. "Yes."

"Can you tell me your name?"

"Bennett. Caitlin Bennett."

She heard a gasp, then a woman's voice saying, "Oh my God. It's C. D. Bennett. You know, the mystery writer."

Before she could respond, they began cutting off her clothes as someone else put a hand on her forehead.

"Caitlin, I'm Dr. Forest, and you're in the emergency room at New York General. Don't fight the nurses. We need to check your injuries. We're only trying to help."

She moaned. The last thing she remembered was being put into the ambulance. Someone slid a stethoscope onto the middle of her chest. She gasped when the cold metal touched her flesh.

"Sorry, was that cold?" the doctor asked.

She nodded.

"Can you tell me where you hurt?"

"My head...shoulder."

"Do you remember what happened?"

"Someone pushed me. They wanted me to die."

There was a brief moment of silence, as if everyone was absorbing the implications of what she'd just said, then the same doctor spoke again.

"Are you sure?"

"Yes, I'm sure," Caitlin said, then reached toward her eyes, wanting to feel her face, trying to figure out why her eyes wouldn't open.

"Don't move," the doctor said. "I'll clean your eyes in just a moment. Someone call the cops," he said. "And get a portable X-ray machine in here."

Caitlin sighed with relief. She didn't have to worry anymore. The doctor was in charge.

"Caitlin, Nurse Carson is going to clean the blood from your face and then flush your eyes, so relax, okay?"

Immediately afterward, something cold touched her forehead, and she flinched.

"Miss Bennett, you need to hold still. You fell face first into the snow. The streets had been salted, and I suspect some of that is in your eyes. That's why they hurt, and that's why you don't want to open them."

Caitlin's panic receded. Answers. That was what she needed, answers.

"Caitlin, is there someone you'd like us to call? Maybe a member of your family, or a friend?"

Caitlin answered without hesitation.

"Aaron Workman."

"Is he family?"

"I have no family. He's my editor."

She thought she heard someone mutter "poor little rich girl," and then everything went black. When she woke up again, they were transferring her from a gurney to a hospital bed. Pain shot through her body from her head to her toes. She held her breath, willing herself not to scream until the feeling had passed. When she dared to move, she saw the nurses leaving and Aaron standing in the doorway, his face a study in disbelief.

"Caitie! Darling!" He kissed her forehead and patted both cheeks, as if he needed assurance that she was truly all right. "How did this happen? They told me you got hit by a truck as you crossed the street."

Caitlin frowned. "No. No. I was standing at the curb. Someone pushed me."

Aaron stilled, an odd expression on his face.

"You mean...you were jostled in the crowd, right?"

Caitlin grabbed his hand and started to cry.

"No. I was pushed."

"How do you know? I mean...isn't it possible that someone inadvertently bumped you and caused you to fall?"

"No, it isn't. I know because I felt a hand in the middle of my back, and then I felt a distinct push." Her chin began to quiver. "Please...Aaron, if you don't believe me, then how—"

Aaron's eyes glittered as he yanked a cell phone

out of his pocket. "I'm calling the police. This could be linked to the letters."

"What letters?"

The sound of the man's voice was startling. They looked toward the door. A tall man and a short, stocky woman were just entering the room.

The man pulled out a badge as he spoke. "I'm Detective Neil, and this is my partner, Detective Kowalksi. Are you Caitlin Bennett?"

"Yes."

"We got a call that someone tried to murder you. Is this true? And what letters are you talking about, and how are they connected?"

"Someone pushed me in front of a truck."

Neil frowned slightly as he began to make notes. Then he looked up at Aaron, taking note of the fact that he and the woman were holding hands.

"You, sir. What's your relationship to Miss Bennett?"

"I'm her editor, and a very good friend."

"Mr. Workman, if you don't mind, we'd like to speak to Miss Bennett alone," Kowalski said.

"No!" Caitlin cried, clutching Aaron's hand before he could move. "He stays." Panic was thick in her voice as she turned to Aaron and pleaded, "Don't leave me."

"As if," he said, then took off his overcoat and laid it on a nearby chair before sitting on the foot of her bed. The look he gave the detectives said he wasn't budging.

Neil shrugged and came closer, his partner following.

Aaron glared at the man, reading his body language and not liking what he saw. The detective was too handsome for his own good, and from the way he moved, he knew it.

Caitlin suddenly moaned. "I'm going to be sick."

Kowalksi grabbed the wastebasket, thrusting it under Caitlin's chin as she leaned over the side of the bed.

"Get a nurse," Kowalski ordered.

Neil bolted out the door, while Aaron ran to get a washcloth. Moments later, Caitlin's nausea had passed and Aaron was gently wiping her mouth. J.R. came back into the room, followed by a nurse, who took quick stock of the situation and ordered everyone out.

"Miss Bennett has suffered a concussion, and she needs her rest. You people need to leave."

"No," Caitlin begged. "Please. Not until I talk to the police."

Neil and Kowalksi identified themselves to the nurse, and she reluctantly relented.

"Tell it quick, or tell it to them tomorrow," she said, and pointed at the trio around Caitlin's bed. "After that, please leave."

Neil eyed the burgeoning bruises and the scrapes on her forehead and chin.

"Miss Bennett, are you sure you're up to this? We can come back."

She took a slow breath and then exhaled softly.

"No. Please stay."

He smiled at her before turning his attention to Aaron. "Are you and Miss Bennett a couple?

Aaron's fingers gently curled around Caitlin's ankle beneath the covers, and then he patted her leg.

"No, but I like to believe I'm her best friend. Since her father's death, she doesn't have any living relatives."

Neil glanced at Caitlin. "You have no one? Is this true?"

She nodded, and as she did, she moaned again and grabbed her head.

Immediately Aaron was at her side.

"Honey, are you feeling sick again?"

"No. It just hurts."

"We'll be brief," Neil said. "Mr. Workman, where were you when this incident occurred?"

"We'd just had lunch together. I took a cab back to the office, and Caitie was going down the block to do some shopping."

"I see," Neil said, taking notes. Then he looked back at Caitlin. "Is there anyone you can think of who has a grudge against you?"

Caitlin groaned. "I don't—"

"Let's get this over with quick," Aaron said. "And I'm going to start the ball rolling by telling you that our company has already filed a complaint with the police. They've been receiving hate mail for publishing her and, most recently, a bomb threat. Caitlin told me today that she's been receiving similar letters for almost six months. Now this," he said, waving his arms in the air. "Something has to be done."

Trudy Kowalksi moved to the foot of Caitlin's bed. "Miss Bennett, can you tell me exactly what happened today that led you to believe this wasn't an accident?"

"Yes. I was standing at the curb, waiting for the light to change, when a large delivery truck came around the corner. It was going very fast, and I knew as it passed I was going to get splashed with slush. At that moment, I felt a hand in the middle of my back and then a distinct push. After that, I have only vague memories of falling and of seeing my own reflection in the bumper of the truck."

Aaron shuddered in disbelief, unable to take his gaze off her bruised face.

"It wasn't an accident," Caitlin said. "It was on purpose."

"Can you think of anyone who would have a reason for doing that to you?"

"No, of course not. I've never hired or fired anyone in my life. I just write my books and mind my own business."

Trudy continued. "About your books. I have to admit I haven't read them, but is there anything in them that would incite this kind of anger in a reader?"

Caitlin sighed. "I wouldn't think so, but who knows?"

Neil had been silent the entire time his partner had been talking, just watching Caitlin's face and listening to the panic in her voice. Suddenly he found himself caught in her wide-eyed gaze. The contact was brief, but startling. Almost immediately, he turned away, focusing his attention on Aaron.

"We'll need to see the letters Miss Bennett has been receiving, as well as the ones your company had gotten."

"I'll get Caitlin's tomorrow," Aaron said. "And check with your bomb unit. Someone there already has Hudson House's copies."

"Right. We'll check," Neil said, then took a card from the inside pocket of his overcoat and handed it to Caitlin.

"Miss Bennett, if you think of anything...anything at all that might help us in this investigation, then give me a call." His voice dropped. "Anytime. Day or night."

He watched Caitlin read his name and number and then look up, studying him in a most uncomfortable way. He hesitated, as if he wanted to say something more, then nodded and left, leaving his partner to follow.

Caitlin heard them speaking briefly together in the hall, and suddenly she just didn't care what they thought. She sighed and laid her forearm across her eyes.

"Aaron, be a dear and turn out the lights, will you? They're making my headache worse."

He did as she asked, but when he returned to her bedside, she seemed to have fallen asleep. He stood for a moment, absorbing the scope of her injuries. The darkening bruise on her left temple was horrific, as were the stitches they'd put above her eye. He kept thinking how close he'd come to losing her today and gently leaned over the bed rail and kissed the side of her cheek.

"You rest, Caitie. I won't be far."

He strode into the hallway, his cell phone in his hand.

Connor McKee stepped out of the shower and reached for a towel. It was the first full day of his vacation—the vacation he'd been promising himself for the better part of six years.

Wrapping the towel around his waist, he strode out of the bathroom and across the warm, carpeted floor of his bedroom to the windows overlooking the ski slope below. Colorado was a beautiful state, but in the winter it could be stunning. He'd owned this chalet in Vail for three years, bought with the first large profit his private security system had turned, but this was the first time he'd used it. Last night he'd christened it with a bottle of Cabernet and a cute little redhead he'd met at the lodge the day before. Now the redhead was gone, the bottle was empty and all he wanted was to fly down that powder until his feet were numb and his mind was free.

With a satisfied sigh, he undid the towel, drying himself off as he moved away from the windows. He had to admit, he felt pretty damned good. It had been a long, uphill struggle—going from a burned-out Atlanta cop to owning his own business and being responsible for the welfare of six employees. The first two years after he'd gone into business, he'd often wondered if he'd made a mistake. Then, a little over three years ago, everything had turned the corner. One of his security systems had been directly responsible for preventing the kidnapping of a child, who happened to be a member of one of Atlanta's most prominent families.

After the media attention and the father's public accolades for McKee Securities, Mac had known he was going to make it. Occasionally he still felt guilty that his success had come at the cost of a traumatized child, but he knew what would have happened had the system not been in place.

Tossing the wet towel onto the floor, he moved to his closet. It was time to get dressed, get some breakfast and then hit the slopes while the powder was still fresh.

Just as he was pulling a sweater over his head, the phone began to ring. Still thinking of the little red-head, he grinned as he picked up the receiver.

"Hello?"

"Mac, it's me."

Mac smiled. His stepbrother Aaron had been the first to call him Mac, and the nickname had stuck.

"Aaron, how are you?" Then he laughed. "How the hell did you track me down? I told my secretary not to tell anyone where I was."

"I told her it was a matter of life and death," Aaron said.

Mac laughed again, remembering the drama with which Aaron went through life. He'd been the first person to know Aaron was gay and had accepted it without a second thought.

"Don't you think that's a little dramatic, even for you?"

But Aaron wasn't laughing. "This isn't a joke. We're in trouble, and I don't know where else to turn."

Mac frowned. "Who's *we,* and what kind of trouble are you talking about?"

"Caitlin Bennett. Someone is trying to kill her."

At that moment, a thousand things went through Mac's mind, including the urge to hang up. Ever since their first meeting three years ago, he had alternated between the desire to shake Caitlin silly and the equally strong urge to strip her naked and take her to bed. More often than not, the latter thought usually won out, which in turn made him mad. He didn't want to be attracted to any woman beyond a one-night stand, but the sudden thought of her dead made him ill.

"What the hell do you mean?"

"I'll explain it all when you get here," Aaron said.

Mac exhaled sharply. "Damn it, Aaron, this is the first day of a vacation I've been promising myself for six years."

"She's in the hospital."

The floor tilted beneath Mac's feet. "What happened?"

"Someone pushed her in front of a truck."

Shit. "It couldn't have been an accident?"

"We received a bomb threat, promising to blow the place up if we didn't stop publishing her, and she's been getting threatening letters for over six months."

Mac was still locked into the image of her lying beneath the wheels of a truck. It took him a few moments to realize Aaron was no longer speaking.

"How bad is she?" he asked, then realized Aaron was crying. "Damn it, Aaron, talk to me."

"Bad bruises, some cuts and a concussion. She was lucky. This time."

"I don't believe in luck," Mac growled. "Give me

a few hours to get packed and catch a flight. I'll be there by tonight.''

Aaron sighed. ''Thank you, Mac.''

''You knew I would come,'' Mac muttered. ''But you're gonna owe me big time on this one, little brother. Caitlin Bennett and I don't exactly get along.''

''I didn't ask you to like her,'' Aaron said. ''I just want you to save her life.''

Mac stepped off the elevator carrying his suitcase and the strap of his carryall slung over his shoulder. His stride was long and swift, his gaze steady as he counted off the room numbers he was passing. Caitlin Bennett's image had been in his mind ever since he'd gotten Aaron's call. His gut was in knots. *Please God, just let her be all right.* When he reached Room 420, he paused, then took a deep breath and walked in.

Almost immediately, he saw Aaron on the other side of the bed. When their gazes met, Aaron stood abruptly, his finger to his lips to signify quiet. Mac stepped inside and set his bags by the door, then glanced at the bed. The knot in his belly tightened. The woman who usually ripped a strip off his ego was lying far too still. Dark purple bruises shaded the left side of her face, giving her the appearance of being masked. A couple of stitches above her eyebrow were oozing, and her lower lip was swollen.

God almighty, Caitie girl, what have you gotten yourself into?

Then Aaron was throwing his arms around him and patting him on the back.

"You're here. Thank God you're here," Aaron whispered.

"How is she?" Mac asked.

"She's fine." When Mac frowned, Aaron added, "Really, she's fine...or at least she's going to be. Nothing's broken. Her concussion is mild. She's bruised, on her face and her shoulder, and her wrists are sprained from the fall, but she's going to be okay."

"Have the cops got any leads?" Mac asked.

Aaron shook his head.

"Why isn't there a guard on her door?"

Aaron rolled his eyes and then pulled his brother out into the hallway, so they could talk without fear of waking her up.

"Because they don't see the imminent danger, that's why," Aaron said. "I called them a few hours ago, and they said that even though we have the letters and the bomb threat, they don't consider what happened as anything more than an accident. They think she was jostled at the curb and, because of everything else, imagined she was pushed."

"She's been getting letters, too?" Mac asked, and then cursed when Aaron nodded.

Aaron grinned. "That's one of the things I always

admired about you. You have such a succinct way of stating the obvious.''

Mac managed a smile, then glanced back into the room where Caitlin lay sleeping.

"Go home, Aaron. I'm here now, and you look beat.''

Aaron hesitated. "I don't know...if she wakes and I'm not here, I'm afraid she'll feel as if I've abandoned her.''

Mac shook his head. "She can look at me instead. Maybe she'll be pissed off enough to forget she's afraid.''

Aaron sighed. "I don't understand it,'' he muttered. "You are the two people I love most in this world, and you fight like cats and dogs.''

Mac shrugged. "Chemistry. Sometimes it works, sometimes it doesn't. Go home. Get some rest. There's a lot to be done tomorrow, and I'll need your help.''

"You're right,'' Aaron said, then pointed to Mac's bags. "Would you like me to take those to my apartment?''

"No. Take them to Caitlin's instead.''

Aaron's eyes widened. "But she won't—''

"Hell no, she won't like it, and frankly, neither will I. But someone's going to have to play bodyguard until this mess is straightened out, and you're afraid of guns.''

Aaron blanched. "So is she. You better not let her know you're carrying one."

"Just go home, little brother, and leave the woman-stuff to me," Mac said, cuffing Aaron's shoulder in a teasing manner.

Aaron sighed. "She's going to kill me for bringing you into this."

"Then we'll just have to remind her that if some-one hadn't tried to kill her, I wouldn't be here."

"Right.... I'm going home now."

"See you in the morning."

Aaron picked up Mac's bags. "Thank you again."

"For what?"

"For always coming to my rescue."

"That's what family is for."

Aaron looked back at Caitlin. From the doorway, she was almost invisible in the darkened room.

"It's a damn shame she doesn't have any," he said.

Mac laid his hand on Aaron's shoulder. "She has you."

"And now you," Aaron added.

From the doorway, Mac watched his brother get on the elevator, then walked into Caitlin's room, quietly closing the door behind him. The air in the room was still, broken only by the intermittent sound of her breathing. He moved toward the bed, then stopped at the foot, making himself look at the bruised and bat-tered woman beneath the covers. He wished she was awake, spitting fire and spearing him with her dark, expressive eyes. Then he wouldn't feel this horrible empathy, this need to gather her up in his arms and hold her close against the night.

He pulled off his coat and sat down in the chair that Aaron had been using, well aware that that put him at eye level with her—that when she awoke, his face would be the first thing she saw.

He sighed.

So be it.

She needed help, and he was here.

Let the games begin.

Four

Buddy slipped through the fourth-floor exit door, pausing quietly at the doorway before moving any farther. He hated the smell of a hospital. It reminded him of the days and nights spent sitting by his mother's bedside and watching her die. Money would have made such a difference in their lives and, in her latter days, in the type of care she received. But they'd had none to spare. His gut knotted. In this world, money was so unevenly distributed. The bulk of it rested in the hands of a few, while the majority of people never had enough.

He thought of the woman he'd come to kill and took a deep, calming breath. Death had no prejudices. It took rich and poor, young and old alike, and that was what he wanted—to put Caitlin Bennett on the same level as his mother. Caitlin didn't deserve what she had, because she had what should have been his.

Satisfied with the lack of activity, he glanced at his watch. It was forty-five minutes after three in the morning. Except for the sound of an old woman moaning at the far end of the hall, the floor was silent.

He ran a nervous finger over the fake mustache he was wearing, tested his wig for security and ran his hand down the front of his borrowed lab coat. The name tag signified it belonged to a Dr. Frost. He grinned. When he was ten, he'd wanted to be a doctor. Tonight he was living out his fantasy. Then his focus shifted as he stared down the hall. At best estimate, it was less than fifty yards to Caitlin's room.

Aaron Workman had gone home more than three hours ago. He knew, because he'd waited outside the hospital, watching as the man had gotten into a cab. And then he'd waited some more, making certain that the shift change at midnight had come and gone and the nurses were finished with all the bed checks and meds.

As he stood, a nurse came out of a hallway and headed toward the far end of the hall. He waited until she disappeared into a room, then made his move.

His soft-soled shoes made almost no noise on the highly polished floor as he hurried down the hall. When he reached Caitlin's door, he pushed it open, taking comfort from the dark within.

Satisfied that she was sound asleep, he slipped inside and closed the door, looking back over his shoulder as he went. It wasn't until the door was completely shut that he realized she was not alone. In the shadows, he could see the outline of a man sitting in a chair beside her bed. His head was bent, his posture slumped.

Shock coupled with a sudden need to urinate had him fumbling for the door, but before he could get out, the man suddenly lifted his head.

"Who's there?"

Buddy froze. Thinking more quickly than he'd realized he could, he said, "Dr. Frost. I'm here to check on Mr. Benton."

"You've got the wrong room," the man said and started to rise.

"Sorry," Buddy said quickly, and turned and walked out the door.

The moment he cleared the room, he bolted down the hall toward the stairwell, afraid to look back. He ran down the stairs, then continued on to the basement, dropping the lab coat into a laundry cart as he passed. The basement door he'd jimmied was still ajar. Glancing back over his shoulder one last time, he smiled. Satisfied he wasn't being followed, he slipped outside into the alley, then paused again, double-checking that no one was behind him.

To his intense relief, no one was in sight. But Buddy was a careful man, staying in the shadows as he walked away. Three blocks over, he tossed the wig and mustache into a Dumpster and headed for the nearest subway station. That had been a very close call. He thought he'd known everything there was to know about Caitlin Bennett, but he'd been wrong. He didn't like surprises.

While Buddy was making his getaway, Mac was

in the hall, looking for the nearest nurse. It had taken him a few seconds to circle Caitlin's bed, and by the time he'd reached the hallway, the doctor was nowhere in sight. At that point, his instincts had gone into overdrive. The flesh on his arms was still crawling from the shock of awakening to find a stranger in the room, even though he knew that it could have been a simple error in names. Bennett and Benton weren't all that different, but he had a gut feeling that something wasn't right. A nurse emerged from a nearby room, and he stopped her on her way back to the desk.

"Ma'am, I need to ask you a question."

The nurse recognized him. "Is Miss Bennett all right?"

"Yes, she's still sleeping. A few moments ago Dr. Frost came into her room looking for a Mr. Benton. Is there a patient by that name on this floor?"

The nurse frowned. "No."

"Are you sure?"

"Yes, and you must be mistaken about the doctor's name, too."

The skin started tightening on the back of his neck. "Why?"

"Dr. Frost is an OB/GYN. He doesn't have patients on this floor, and even if he did, they wouldn't be male."

"Shit," Mac said, and headed toward Caitlin's room.

The light was on over her bed, and she was reaching for the button to call a nurse. It was hard to say who was more surprised.

Caitlin gasped. "You!"

Mac sighed. "Yes, it's me."

Shock mingled with confusion. She'd fallen asleep listening to Aaron's voice and woken up to find herself alone. And now Mac was here. If she hadn't been in so much pain, she could almost have believed this was all a bad dream.

"What are you doing here, and where is Aaron?"

"I'm here because he asked me to come. And he's at home, where I sent him."

Caitlin's eyes flashed angrily. "He asked you? Why?"

"To help."

"I don't need *your* help."

Ignoring the emphasis she put on the word, he shoved his hands into his pockets and glared back.

"Oh, I think you do. And if I wasn't sure before, I am now."

Caitlin knew as she asked that she wasn't going to like his answer, but she asked it just the same.

"Why?"

"A few minutes ago, someone came into your room. I don't think he expected me to be here."

Her heart skipped a beat. Again she imagined the feel of that hand on her back, pushing.

"What do you mean?"

"I asked him what he wanted. He said his name was Dr. Frost and that he was looking for a Mr. Benton."

"Our names are similar...Bennett, Benton. Maybe it was an honest mistake."

"There wasn't anything honest about it, Caitie girl. There is no patient named Benton, and the real Dr. Frost is a gynecologist."

Caitlin ignored the diminutive he'd made of her name and focused on stifling a scream. She stared at Connor until her eyes filled with tears, and then she covered her face with her hands.

Mac groaned beneath his breath and crossed the floor in long strides. Struggling with an urge to hold her, he settled for an awkward pat on her shoulder instead.

"Don't worry, kid. We'll figure out what's going on, and before you know it, it will be nothing but a bad memory."

"I want to go home," Caitlin whispered.

"Yeah, I know. Maybe in the morning, okay?"

She dropped her hands and nodded while looking away, still unwilling to let him see her cry. But when he turned, she grabbed his wrist before she thought.

Mac stopped, looking down at the fingers encircling his wrist and wondered if she screamed when she came. The moment he thought it, he felt ashamed. When he looked up, he got caught in her fear and knew he was a goner.

"What?" he muttered.

"Don't leave."

A muscle jerked in his jaw as he tried to smile.

"I'm going over there to get the cell phone out of my coat, okay?"

She nodded, and then, realizing she was holding his wrist, reluctantly turned him loose.

Yeah baby, I know just how you feel, Mac thought as he took the phone out of an inner pocket.

"Who are you calling?" Caitlin asked.

"The cops. Now close your eyes and try to get some sleep. Want me to turn out the light? I can go into the hall to make my call."

"No, it's okay."

He nodded, then dialed Aaron's number, well aware that he was going to incite a small panic in the process, but he wanted the name of the person to contact regarding Caitlin's case. Aaron answered on the second ring, his voice thick with sleep.

"Hello?"

"It's me. Sorry to wake you."

"Oh, that's all right," Aaron mumbled, reaching for the lamp as he sat up in bed. The light came on at the same time he looked at the clock, and he groaned. "It's freakin' four o'clock in the morning. Couldn't this have waited until daylight?"

"Someone came into Caitlin's room, lied about who he was and why he was here, and disappeared before I could get into the hall to talk to him."

"Oh shit."

"Exactly."

"Have you called the police?"

"Not yet. I wanted the name of the person to contact before I made the call."

"I could have told you that," Caitlin muttered behind him.

Mac turned, eyeing her with trepidation. That slightly belligerent tone in her voice told him she was regaining her strength. Ignoring the frown on her face, he tried not to glare. It would seem that the honeymoon was over.

"Don't worry," Aaron said. "I'll call them. You just stay with Caitlin. Don't let her out of your sight."

"I never turn my back on people who might like to slit my throat."

Caitlin snorted softly.

"My God," Aaron said. "She looks as if she's been beaten all to hell and you're already fighting?"

"Aaron. Please. Just shut up and call the cops."

"Consider it done."

Mac hung up the phone, then strode over to the chair in which he'd been sleeping and dropped into it with a heavy sigh.

Caitlin gave him one last look and then closed her eyes, as if she couldn't bear to look at his face.

Mac sighed again. There was nothing left to do but wait for daylight or the cops, whichever came first.

* * *

It was almost daylight before Buddy got home. After finding out that his execution of Miss Bennett was going to have to wait, he'd taken out a little insurance, so to speak. It had been a simple thing, really, going across the rooftops to the Bennett Building. She occupied the penthouse, which meant he didn't have far to go. A quick lock picking job, a thorough investigation of the setup, and after that it was a matter of finding the correct ventilation shaft.

He liked old buildings, but they were hell to get into. Their walls were often crumbling, and there was little or no access from floor to floor except for stairs and creaking elevators in dark, dangerous shafts. Even with their so-called security systems, it was the new ones, with all their modern conveniences, that made breaking and entering a breeze. He found the main ventilation shaft and, with a grunt and a jump, pulled himself up and then in, crawling carefully through the slick metal tunnels until he found where he needed to go.

Gaining access to her apartment was too easy. He was through the vent above her desk and into the room within seconds. Once his feet touched the floor, he stopped, listening to the quiet until he was satisfied he was the only one there. A quick scan of the area assured him there were no security cameras in view. After that, the place was all his.

There was a light on down a hall, giving him enough illumination by which to see the understated opulence. An original Degas hung on the wall by the door, and there was am antique Chinese vase on a pedestal next to a bookshelf. Nothing more than little splashes of color, intimate touches from a female point of view.

He looked and coveted and hated her for who she was, then moved from room to room, touching her things, moving clothes in her closet, fingering the toothbrush she used. Like a male animal in new territory, he was putting his mark on everything that belonged to Caitlin Bennett.

It was exhaustion that brought his foray to an end. That and the knowledge that he had to be at work by nine. After a quick sweep of the rooms, discarding one place after another as an option to plant a listening device, he walked back into the living room, looked up at the chandelier and smiled.

Using a kitchen chair and two phone books for a ladder, he climbed up on the stack and dropped a small, translucent bug into the bowl of one of the lights. He got down, then looked up and started to grin. He knew where it was and still couldn't see it.

"Perfect," he said, then put back the chair and replaced the phone books.

It took a little longer to get out than it had to come in, but he did it without leaving a mark on the walls. With careful precision, he replaced the screen over the vent, then crawled out the same way he'd come in.

Fifteen minutes later, he was on the street.

Trudy handed J.R. a cup of coffee as he walked into the precinct.

"What's that for?"

"Just drink it," she said. "You're gonna need it."

"Why?"

"Caitlin Bennett...the woman we figured was jumping at ghosts?"

"Yeah, what about her?"

"Someone impersonating a doctor got into her room last night and was scared off by her guard."

J.R. set the coffee cup down on his desk. "You're kidding."

"The call was on my desk when I arrived. I've just been waiting for you to get here so we could go talk to her."

"Damn," J.R. said, then shifted his thoughts. "But then, there's another way of looking at this. If someone saw him, maybe this is the break we needed."

"Yeah, maybe."

"So, let's go to the hospital and see what she has to say."

"I called," Trudy said. "She's no longer there. She checked out this morning and went home. This time we talk on her territory."

"As long as we get the job done, right?"

Trudy grinned. "I'm thinking it's not going to break your heart to see her again, either."

"Just what are you getting at?"

"Oh, nothing," she said, ignoring the frown on his face. "It's just that you seemed rather taken with her before, and I thought—"

"You're a good partner and a good detective, Kowalksi, but you're also a female, which means you think too much. Save it and let's get going."

Trudy took a last drink of her coffee and set the cup on her desk. "Right behind you."

Kenny Leibowitz stalked into the lobby of Caitlin's apartment building and leaned over the desk, eyeing the security guard.

"I need to see Caitlin Bennett."

Mike Mazurka looked up. "Is she expecting you?"

"No, but she'll see me. Just ring the penthouse, please."

Mike frowned. "She just got home from the hospital, and she don't look too good."

Kenny hit the counter with his fist. "I'm her publicist. Ring the damned penthouse."

Mike frowned as he buzzed the penthouse. He knew who Leibowitz was, and he didn't like him, but he accepted the fact that it was none of his business. A few seconds later, his call was answered.

"Bennett residence."

"Mr. Workman, Mr. Leibowitz to see Miss Bennett."

Aaron mouthed the word *Kenny* to Caitlin. When she rolled her eyes, he covered the phone.

"I can get rid of him."

She shook her head. "No, let him come up. The sooner I get this over with, the better off I'll feel."

"Send him up," Aaron said.

Mike hung up the phone and then nodded to Kenny, who immediately strode toward the elevator that went directly to the penthouse. Without a key card, he had to wait for Mike to use the console at his desk to send him up. When the doors closed, he turned to the mirrored panels, admiring his reflection. Even though he was pissed that Caitlin hadn't bothered to call him, he wasn't going to give Aaron Workman the satisfaction of knowing he was mad.

The elevator stopped and opened. He strode across the hall and rang the bell. Moments later, the door opened.

"Morning, Kenny," Aaron said, and stepped aside to let him in.

"Workman," Kenny muttered, then lifted his head like a dog testing the air for the scent of prey. "Where is she?"

"In her room, lying down. Follow me, I'll show you."

"I know where her bedroom is," Kenny said, and pushed past him.

Aaron was right on his heels. He wasn't going to give Leibowitz the opportunity to hassle Caitlin. Not today. She already had more on her plate than she could say grace over.

Kenny knocked once, then strode into Caitlin's room without waiting for permission to enter. He'd practiced what he was going to say all the way across town, debating with himself as to whether he should admit to being insulted that she hadn't called him personally or be completely sympathetic to her injuries. When he saw her face, he opted for the sympathy route.

"My God!" he gasped, then crossed the room to sit down on the side of her bed. "You poor, poor darling. Are you all right? Why didn't you call me? I should have been there for you." Then he glared at Aaron, as if it was all his fault.

Aaron ignored him and looked at Caitlin. "Want me to stay?"

Kenny spun, his face twisted in anger. "What the hell do you mean? I'm not going to pounce on her the moment your back is turned. Get out, before I throw you out."

"Kenny, for God's sake, lower your voice," Caitlin murmured, clutching her hands to her head. "My head hurts, and I'm not in the mood to listen to you two fight."

"Sorry," he said. "But I won't be treated like a—"

"The next person who raises a voice in this room is going out of here on his ass."

Caitlin moaned and closed her eyes, shutting out the big man standing in the doorway. This was getting better by the moment. Aaron and Kenny barely tolerated each other, but it had never been a problem before. Now they were acting like two jealous suitors. Toss in the added distraction of dealing with Connor McKee and the sanctity of her home had pretty much been screwed.

"Really," she muttered, glaring at Mac from the bed. "I fail to see the need to resort to physical violence."

"I haven't hurt him...yet," Mac drawled.

Kenny paled. The man in the doorway was a stranger—a big stranger. And from the look on his face and the size of his hands, he looked as if he could make good on his threat. His mood shift was immediate as he laid a proprietary hand on Caitlin's leg.

"Who is he?" he asked.

"He's Aaron's brother, Connor McKee." She looked at Mac and spoke a little louder. "Mac, Kenny Leibowitz is my publicist."

Mac did little more than nod, while Kenny's eyebrows arched dramatically. His gaze slid from Aaron to Mac and back again.

"Well...it's easy to see where all the testosterone went in your family," he drawled.

The slight made the gleam in Mac's eyes a little brighter, but Aaron just laughed.

"Kenny, Kenny, Kenny, methinks you doth protest too much about your own."

Kenny stood abruptly, his fists doubled. At that moment, Mac took charge.

"You," he said, pointing at Kenny. "Get out. Now. Aaron, explain the situation to Mr. Leibowitz and then show him out the door. If he has any more communicating to do with Caitie, he can do it by phone."

Kenny's face grew red with anger. "You can't just—"

"Please, Kenny, I'm not up to this. The doctor told me to rest, not referee. Aaron, fill Kenny in on what's happening and, Kenny, I'd better not find out you're using any of it to publicize *Dead Lines.*"

Caitlin's voice was soft and shaky, but it got the desired result. Leibowitz flushed as Aaron walked out of the room. He looked at Caitlin with something close to regret. He'd made an impression on her, all right, but nothing like he'd planned.

"Forgive me, darling," he said softly. "Chalk all of this up to worry. I'll be in touch." He strode out of the room past Mac, giving him a cold, angry stare.

Other than a narrowing of his eyes, Mac's reaction to Leibowitz was mute and hard to gauge.

Once they were alone, Mac found himself locked into another staring match, this time with Caitlin. After a few moments of total silence, he took a deep breath, started to speak, then cursed beneath his breath and walked away, closing the door behind him.

Caitlin reached for the bottle of pain pills and shook one out, only realizing afterward that her water glass was empty. Groaning beneath her breath, she swung her legs off the bed and sat up, knowing it was going to hurt like hell to stand. She leaned forward, hoping to use her body weight as leverage, and knocked the empty water glass off the nightstand. It hit the hardwood floor, shattering into pieces. Seconds later, Mac burst into the room.

"What happened? Are you all right? Hellsfire, woman, why didn't you call for help?"

"I broke a glass, yes, I'm fine, and I only wanted to go to the bathroom to get some water so I could take a pain pill, because I hurt from my teeth to my toenails, and if you yell at me one more time, I am going to cry." At which point, having stated the obvious, she burst into tears.

Connor McKee felt like the lowest of the low. He bit the inside of his mouth to keep from saying anything more and simply walked across the room, scooped her out of the bed and carried her into the bathroom, gingerly stepping over the broken glass as he went. Then he set her on her feet by the commode and walked out, quietly closing the door behind him.

Caitlin used the drinking glass on the sink to take her pill and then sat on the closed commode to wait. Mac hadn't said he would be back, but she knew him well enough to know that since he'd brought her here, he would eventually come back to get her.

She sat, feeling sorry for herself for the mess she was in, and heard Aaron's cry of surprise, then offer of help as he ran to get a broom and dustpan. When she heard the occasional clink of glass, she guessed Mac was dropping the shards into the wastebasket by her bed.

She sat without moving, straining toward the sound of their voices. They were too low for her to hear what was being said, although she knew they were talking about her. About the letters. And the bomb threat. And the fact that someone wanted her dead.

From where she was sitting, the full-length mirror on the inside of her bathroom door was both a help and a hindrance. She didn't have to move to see the extent of the damage that had been done to her body. She just wasn't sure she wanted to see it all at once. Her face was bad enough. If she hadn't known it was her own reflection, she would not have recognized herself. Half her face was streaked with dark purple hues, and the eyebrow with the stitches was swollen to half again its normal size. Her lower lip was puffy, and there was a series of small abrasions on the left side of her cheek. Still curious, she unbuttoned the top three buttons of her pajama top and let it drop off her shoulder.

Her eyes widened in shock at the extent of the contusions. With shaking hands, she pulled her pajama top back in place and redid the buttons. It was difficult to accept that someone wanted her dead, but the facts were too blatant to ignore. She closed her eyes, willing herself to a calm she didn't feel, and was sitting quietly, her crying spell over, when the knock sounded on the door.

"Come in," she said.

Mac opened the door. "Are you ready to get back in bed?"

"Yes, please," she said, then held her breath as he came toward her.

He picked her up as if she weighed nothing at all and carried her back to her bed, laying her gently down on her pillows.

Caitlin winced as she reached for the covers.

"Let me," Mac said, and pulled them up to her waist, where she could adjust them to her satisfaction.

"Thank you," she said, and heard Mac sigh.

"You're welcome," he answered. He'd started to leave when he stopped and turned.

"Caitie?"

"Yes?"

"I'm sorry...really, really sorry I made you cry."

The tenderness was unexpected, especially from this man. And because it was so unexpected, she found herself unable to say much for fear of crying all over again.

"Yes...well, thank you," she said, then turned on

her side and closed her eyes, listening to the sound of his footsteps as he walked away.

A short while later, as she was drifting in a haze induced by the painkiller she had taken, the phone rang. She burrowed deeper beneath her covers, knowing that, for the time being, Connor McKee was standing between her and the world. She didn't bother to consider why that didn't seem as bizarre as it once might have, or why her opinion of him had changed. All that mattered was that he was here and, for the first time in months, she knew she was safe.

The next morning she awakened to the sound of strangers' voices and a lot of hammering and banging. Swinging her legs to the side of the bed, she grabbed her robe and house shoes and bolted from the room, to find Connor and two men in a tangle of boxes and wires.

"Connor McKee, what on earth are you doing?" she demanded, eyeing the pair of strangers and the mess on her living room floor.

Mac grinned. Her hair was tangled, the belt of her robe was dragging on the floor and the house shoes she persisted in wearing were nothing short of a joke.

"Installing your security system."

"Well, no one asked *me*," she huffed.

"Caitie, if you want to be taken seriously, you're going to have to wear another pair of shoes."

She glanced down at her puppy slippers and then up at him in disgust.

"There's nothing wrong with my shoes."

"You need the security."

She sighed. "You should have warned me."

"You're right. I'm sorry."

"Well, as long as it doesn't happen again."

"No, ma'am. It sure won't."

She twiddled with the end of her belt and then realized all three men were trying not to laugh. Disgusted with herself and with the male species in general, she pivoted sharply, and as she did, stepped on the ear of one of her puppy slippers. Staggering forward, she caught herself before falling.

"You all right?" Mac asked.

She wouldn't turn around. It sounded like he was laughing.

"I'm fine," she said, and stomped out of the room.

Seconds later she heard a choked, gurgling sound and then a soft guffaw. Damn them. Damn them all straight to hell.

She slammed the door, making sure that it echoed, and crawled back into bed.

Five

When the doorbell sounded, Mac rushed to answer it before it awakened Caitlin. He knew who it was and why they were here, but they'd taken their sweet time in coming. He'd expected them to show before he and Caitlin had left the hospital. The men from the security company had long since gone, and it was almost noon.

Aaron had reported the fake doctor incident to the police. Knowing his brother's penchant for dramatics, Mac figured he'd more than made his point that Caitlin Bennett was in danger and it was about damned time someone admitted it. With that thought in mind, he opened the door.

"Yes?"

Neil flashed his badge.

"Detective Neil," he said shortly. "This is my partner, Detective Kowalski. I understand there was another incident involving Miss Bennett?"

"I suppose you could call it that," Mac said. "Come in." Then he stepped aside to let them enter and closed the door. "This way," he said, and led the way into the living room, then paused, gesturing for them to be seated. "What took you so long?" Mac asked.

Neil took one end of the sofa, while his partner took the other. He waited until Mac had seated himself on the opposite side of the coffee table before speaking. "We had an emergency call to answer. Sorry." Then he shifted mental gears and pinned Mac with a hard look.

"I was given to understand that Miss Bennett doesn't have any family," J.R. said.

"She doesn't."

"Then who are you?"

"My name is Connor McKee. I own McKee Security, out of Atlanta. Aaron Workman, her editor, is my stepbrother. He called me. I came."

Neil made a couple of notes and then looked up. "Where is Miss Bennett?"

"Asleep. She's still in a lot of pain, and I'd rather not disturb her. Besides, if you're here about what happened at the hospital last night, there's no need to talk to her."

"Why not?" Neil asked.

"Because she slept through it. I'm the one who woke up and saw the man standing in her room, and I'm the one he spoke to."

"He spoke to you?" Trudy asked.

"Yes, but I think I surprised him. He came into the room sometime after three in the morning. When

I stood up and asked him what he was doing, he gave me some cock-and-bull story that didn't check out."

"Exactly what did he say?" J.R. asked.

"He said his name was Dr. Frost and that he was looking for a Mr. Benton's room."

"That doesn't sound out of the ordinary," Trudy said. "The last names are pretty similar...Benton...Bennett. Maybe it was just a case of mistaken identity."

"That's what I thought at first, until I asked a nurse if there was a patient by the name of Benton on the floor. She told me there wasn't, and then asked why I wanted to know. I told her a man identifying himself as Dr. Frost had been looking for his room."

"And?" Trudy prompted.

"She said Dr. Frost is an OB/GYN. He wouldn't have any male patients, no matter what floor they were on."

"Oops. Looks like your intruder didn't do his homework," she said, then eyed him carefully. "But you did, didn't you? What tipped you off?"

"Have you ever been hospitalized?" Mac asked.

Trudy nodded.

"No matter what time of night it is or how soundly you're sleeping, when a doctor or nurse comes into the room, they always turn on the lights, don't they?"

Trudy's red curls bobbed as she nodded again. "A couple of years ago I had an appendectomy. Didn't get a wink of sleep until I got to go home."

"Exactly. But this man didn't turn on the lights or make a sound. In fact, he was halfway to Caitlin's bed in the dark when I stood up."

Neil leaned forward, his elbows on his knees. "And why were you there?"

"Protecting her."

"How long have you known Miss Bennett?"

"A little more than three years."

Neil took silent note of the way McKee answered—almost as if he was uncomfortable being on the receiving end of their questions.

"Have you always been in security?" he asked.

"No, I was with Atlanta PD for fifteen years."

"Why did you quit?"

"Lost one too many partners. Watched one too many perps walk because of a legal technicality. You name it. I burned out, pure and simple."

"Boy, do I understand that," Trudy said.

But Neil wasn't comfortable with the man's presence and made it known.

"This is our investigation," he said shortly. "We don't need any vigilantes."

Mac resisted the urge to smirk. "Miss Bennett will be pleased to know that you've finally admitted there's something to investigate."

The detective's lips thinned in anger, but he kept his silence as Mac added, "I have no intention of investigating anything. I'm not a P.I. I own and operate a company that installs and upgrades security systems...period. I volunteered to stay with Caitlin until the man is caught, so the sooner you get your job done, the happier we'll all be.''

"Can you give us a description of the man?'' Trudy asked.

Mac frowned. "Not really. I only got a glimpse of him as he opened the door and slipped out. It was pretty fast, and I'd been asleep when he walked in. I do know that he was Caucasian, at least six feet tall. He had brown curly hair and a mustache, and was probably in his late thirties. However, if he was there to finish what he started, I would guess he was wearing a disguise.''

"Is there anything else?'' Trudy asked.

"No.''

"You're pretty sure of yourself,'' Neil said.

Mac shrugged. "Yeah, so I've been told.''

Neil's jaw set as he handed Mac a card. "If you think of anything else, give us a call.''

Mac dropped the card into his pocket without comment.

"By the way, where is Aaron Workman?'' Neil asked. "I expected him to be here.''

"He went to work. If you need to talk to him, he's at his office.''

Neil stood up. "Thank you for your help. We'll be in touch.''

"So will we,'' Mac said, and ushered them to the door, then locked it behind them.

The two detectives heard the distinct click of tumblers and grinned before heading to the elevator.

"I wouldn't mind being guarded by a man like that," Trudy said.

J.R. arched an eyebrow. "Well, well, Kowalski, you never fail to amaze me."

The elevator opened. They walked in, then turned to face the door as J.R. punched the button to take them down.

"Why?" Trudy asked, as the car began to descend.

"I didn't know you were into oversize thugs."

"Just because he's bigger than you doesn't make him a thug," Trudy said. "Besides, I was always a sucker for men with dark hair and blue eyes."

Neil shook his head in pretend disgust as the door opened. They exited into the lobby, their strides equally matched in spite of their difference in size.

"When we get to the hospital to check out the story, maybe I'd better have your blood pressure checked, too."

Trudy hesitated, staring at him in disbelief. "You're jealous!"

"You're full of shit," J.R. said as they crossed the lobby toward their car. "And I'm driving."

"Good. I don't like to drive in snow."

J.R. grinned. "That's because you were raised in Mobile. Your blood's too thin, Kowalksi. When I was a kid, I had a paper route and delivered papers in all kinds of weather. It was snowing the day I had my first driving lesson.''

She grinned at him as she got in on the passenger side of the car.

''Yeah, and next you'll be telling me you cut your teeth on icicles and made your first snowman before you could walk.''

J.R.'s smile widened, but he refrained from comment. He knew Trudy well enough to know that she wouldn't stop until she had the last word, even if it was wrong. He started the car and pulled away from the curb into traffic.

''Where are we going?'' she asked.

''To the hospital. Maybe a security camera caught something we can use.''

''Good idea.''

''Yeah, I know,'' J.R. said.

Trudy snorted lightly. ''You are such an egotist.''

''But I'm good.''

Trudy rolled her eyes and laughed.

Caitlin opened her eyes and then groaned at the squall of a passing siren. Instinctively she started to stretch, then winced as sore muscles reminded her not to make any drastic moves.

''Oh God,'' she muttered, pushing a hand carefully through her hair, then feeling the stitches above her eyebrow. They felt like thorns.

Her tummy growled as she rolled to the side of the

bed and sat up. Her body was at odds with her pain. It didn't seem possible that she could be hungry when everything hurt, but she was. Without making any sudden moves, she shuffled toward the bathroom, pausing to look at herself in the mirror. The bruises looked worse, but the swelling in her lower lip seemed better.

"One thing at a time," she muttered, and turned away.

A few minutes later she came out, her face carefully washed, her hair combed and caught at the back of her neck in a bright pink scrunchie. She paused at the foot of her bed for her robe, knowing she would need all her defenses to keep Connor at arm's length, including proper clothing. Even though her pajamas were sensible blue flannel, a robe seemed in order. Stepping into her slippers, she made her way to the kitchen and found Mac standing at the stove, stirring something in a pot.

"That smells good," she said. "What is it?"

Startled by the sound of her voice, he banged the spoon on the side of the pot as he turned around.

"I didn't know you were awake. Why didn't you call me?"

"I wanted to get up," Caitlin said. "Is that soup?"

"Yes, are you hungry?"

"Yes."

"I'll bring you some, just please sit back down."

Caitlin sighed. "I'm not that fragile."

Mac's eyes were dark and unreadable, but the husky tremor in his voice gave him away. "You could have fooled me," he said. "Have you looked in the mirror?"

She made a face at him and then grimaced. "Oh, that hurt," she muttered as she eased herself into a kitchen chair, refusing to admit he'd been right. Her legs were shaking.

"Then don't try to bite the hand that's going to feed you. Literally."

Caitlin rested her chin in her hands and settled for a glare at his backside as he reached into the cabinet for a plate and a bowl. As she watched, it occurred to her that the last time she'd been in this kitchen there had been little in the way of food to eat.

"Did you buy groceries?" she asked.

"Aaron did."

She nodded. "Aaron thinks I eat like a teenager."

Mac gave her a curious look. "Well, do you?"

Caitlin's gaze caught and held on the way his eyes crinkled when he smiled and forgot what he'd said.

"Caitlin?"

She blinked. "Hmm? What?"

"Do you eat like a teenager?"

She shrugged. "I don't know. How does a teenager eat?"

"Whatever is handy that's salty or sweet and full of fat, ready in a minute or less, and comes in bulk."

"I don't put Pepsi on my cereal," she said, without admitting to anything else.

Mac laughed aloud. "That's a start." Then he set the soup before her and handed her a spoon. "Eat up while it's hot."

His laughter caused a funny twinge in her stomach, which she chalked up to hunger. The idea of making friends with this man made her think of trying to tame a tiger, and she wasn't that stupid. Instead, she leaned over the bowl, inhaling the aroma as her mouth watered.

"It smells wonderful. What is it?"

"Potato soup. I seasoned it according to my taste, so if it's a bit too salty for you, I can add some more milk."

"You mean this didn't come out of a can?"

"Nope. Want a sandwich to go with it?"

"Sounds good, but I'd better stay with just soup for now...at least until my mouth isn't so sore."

Mac frowned. "Sorry. I wasn't thinking. Maybe I should run the soup through a food processor. You could drink it rather than chew."

"That's assuming I have a food processor, which I don't," she muttered, then slipped the first bite into her mouth, relishing the warmth as well as the flavor. "No need. This is perfect." She waved her spoon toward the stove. "Aren't you going to have some?"

He hesitated. Sitting at the table with Caitlin Bennett meant drawing some kind of a truce. He wasn't sure if that was such a good idea, but he was hungry, and she had offered.

"Yeah, I guess," he said, and dipped himself a hearty bowl, grabbed a handful of crackers and sat down in the chair across from hers without looking up.

For a few minutes there was nothing to be heard but the occasional clink of a spoon against a bowl. Caitlin was the first to finish.

"That was very good. Thank you."

Mac shifted in his seat, uncomfortable with her congenial mood. "You're welcome."

"Somehow I never pictured you being so domestic," Caitlin drawled.

Mac's eyes narrowed sharply. Something told him that congeniality was fading fast.

"What's that supposed to mean?"

"Oh, nothing," Caitlin said. "It's just that when I think of you, I picture underdone meat and knives with big blades."

Mac leaned across the table and grinned. "Why, Caitlin, I didn't know you thought of me at all. Just goes to show how wrong first impressions can be."

Mentally cursing herself for getting personal with a man who pushed all her warning buttons, she scooted her chair back from the table and stood up.

"Where are you going?" he asked as she headed out the door.

"To my office to check my e-mail. Were there any calls while I was asleep?"

"No, but the police came by."

She frowned. "Why didn't you wake me? Now they'll just have to come back, and I don't want this to go on for—"

"They didn't have anything new to tell you, and you had nothing new to tell them."

"But the man in the—"

"Did you see him?"

She frowned. "Well, no, but..."

"Right. You didn't even know he'd been there until I told you, so there was nothing you could have said that would add to the investigation. You needed your rest. I talked to them. Told them everything that happened." And then he added, "For all the good it did. I'm not too impressed with either one of them, especially Detective Neil."

"What do you mean?" Caitlin asked. "I thought he was nice."

Mac resisted the urge to roll his eyes. "You would."

Her chin jutted. "What's that supposed to mean?"

"It's not *supposed* to mean anything other than what I said. He's a cocky, pretty-faced cop with a badge and a gun. From the way your nostrils are flaring, I'm guessing that turns you on."

Caitlin gasped. "You are beyond belief! My *nostrils* are not flaring, and he did not turn me on! If I went for cocky, gun-toting males, then you'd be at the top of the list, wouldn't you?''

Mac stuffed his hands in his pockets to keep from putting them around her neck and glared.

Caitlin sniffed delicately. Satisfied that she'd scored the last point, she walked away.

"Your nostrils did flare," Mac said beneath his breath.

"I heard that," Caitlin yelled.

"Christ almighty," Mac muttered, then pivoted angrily, grabbed the empty soup pan from the stove and shoved it into the sink. Banging pans was the next best thing to wringing her neck.

Sweat oozed and ran from every pore on Buddy's body as he pounded the heavy punching bag in the corner of the gym.

Bam.

The blow jarred all the way to his back teeth.

Bam. Bam.

The one-two made his right ear pop.

Bam.

Bam.

Bam.

After the trio of rapid-fire blows, he tasted blood and knew he'd bitten his tongue. But he couldn't stop. The need to punish was uppermost in his mind. Damn Caitlin Bennett for not dying. Damn her rich bitch self to hell.

"Easy there, fella, you're gonna blow a gasket."

But Buddy ignored the trainer and kept on punching until he was so blinded by his own sweat that he could no longer see the bag. Exhausted, he staggered backward until he came up against the wall, then bent forward, his gloves on his knees, struggling to stay upright.

"Is he dead?"

At the question, Buddy took a deep breath and looked up. "What did you say?"

The trainer tossed him a towel and grinned. "I asked you, is he dead?"

Buddy's voice iced. "What the hell do you mean?"

"Chill, man, it's just a figure of speech," the trainer said. "You were nailing that bag so hard, I don't have to be a genius to know somebody pissed you off. Right?"

Buddy sighed. "Oh...yeah...right."

"Sit down," the trainer said. "I'll help you take off your gloves."

Buddy straddled a weight bench and held out a glove. In a few moments, he was free of them both.

"Thanks," he said, and stood up. "It's been a long day. I'm going to shower and head for home."

"Yeah, sure. See you around."

Buddy was already walking away.

Half an hour later he came out of the locker room and headed for the door, taking the stairs three flights down to the street. The stairwell was cold, and as he started down, he pulled his coat collar up around his neck, wishing he'd had the foresight to bring a sock cap to cover his wet hair. Bracing himself for the worst, he took the steps down in a hurry, exiting the building onto the street. The cold air hit his lungs like a fist to the chest. Before he'd gone half a block, his hair was stiff, the moisture frozen from the rapidly dropping temperature.

"Son of a bitch," he muttered, and hunched his shoulders up around his ears.

A light dusting of snow was falling, and from the looks of the sidewalks, it had been falling for quite a while, obliterating all but the deepest of tracks. A thin crust had formed on the surface, and as he walked, his steps made crunching noises that echoed in the air. Traffic was light but steady, and he forgot his discomfort in the monotonous motion of putting one foot in front of the other.

In the next block, he saw a taxi suddenly pull to the curb and let out a fare. The luxury of taking a cab home rather than the subway seemed like a wise investment, and he yelled for it to wait, but the driver sped away into the night. Cursing beneath his breath, he continued to walk. Only five more blocks to the subway station and he would at least be out of the snow.

Another block up, the lights of a diner spilled through the windows onto the snow. A couple emerged as he walked past the door, bringing with them the scent of warm food and hot coffee.

On impulse, Buddy did a one-eighty and went back to the diner. A hot meal seemed prudent, considering the fact that he hadn't eaten since breakfast. He slid onto a stool at the counter and picked up a menu.

"Hey, handsome, how about some coffee?"

Buddy looked up. The waitress was young and smiling. He smiled back.

"Yes, please," he said. "Black."

She set a cup in front of him and filled it to within a quarter-inch of the brim.

"Do you know what you want to eat?" she asked.

"Got any chili?"

"Oh, yeah. Gus makes good chili. Hot, though. If you don't eat your food spicy, you might not like it."

Buddy leaned forward, flashing the young waitress another heart-stopping smile.

"Oh...I like spice," he said softly. "In my food *and* my women."

She giggled and went to fill his order, leaving him with his coffee and his thoughts. A couple of minutes later she was back with a steaming bowl of chili and a side of corn bread, along with a small bowl of diced onions.

"Do you want some cheese with that?" she asked.

"No, this looks good as is," Buddy said, and scooped up a big bite, rolling his eyes as the first taste sensation hit. "Um, you tell Gus this is damned good chili, okay?"

She smiled and nodded, then moved on to tend to a couple who'd taken a seat in a booth.

Buddy ate without thought, simply savoring the warmth of food in his belly and the peace in his mind. He was both physically and mentally exhausted. Surely he would be able to sleep tonight, despite the fact that Caitlin Bennett still drew breath.

He was almost through eating when the woman came in. He saw her from the corner of his eye, watching as she took a seat at the counter, three stools down from where he sat. Her voice was low and husky, but her clothes and her demeanor screamed whore. She asked the time, then ordered a cup of coffee.

Thinking about the possibility of getting a quick fuck, he turned for a good look and then stifled a gasp. The food he'd just eaten threatened to come up. He stared in disbelief, watching her lift the coffee cup to her lips. She had dark shoulder-length hair and a mouth so like Caitlin's that it caused him true pain.

He stood abruptly, threw some money down on the counter and strode out without looking back. The subway station was only a couple of blocks ahead. He found himself running toward it like a man hurrying toward salvation. But the closer he got to it, the slower his steps became.

Then he stopped. For several moments he stared

down at the sidewalk, studying the snow on the toes of his shoes as his fingers curled and uncurled and then curled again into fists. He stood that way for what seemed like an hour, making a bet with himself that if she came this way, then she was his, but if she left the diner and walked north instead of south, then it wasn't meant to be.

Several people passed him as he waited, his back to the diner. Every time he heard approaching footsteps, he held his breath, waiting to see if it was her. Then, when his feet were so cold he couldn't feel his toes, he told himself, just one more person, and if it wasn't her, he would go home.

Within a few seconds of the promise, he heard footsteps again, this time shorter ones, moving faster than those that had come before. His breath came in short, jerky puffs, like small white clouds beneath his nose. He lifted his head, then found himself turning—turning—and watching the concentration on her face as she tried to stay upright in the snow on those three-inch heels.

"You should have worn boots," he said softly.

She pulled her coat a little closer around her slim body, then smiled. One more john before the night was over couldn't hurt.

"Not when there are good-looking men like you to keep me on my feet," she countered.

"But, honey, I don't want you on your feet, I want you on your back."

Her eyes narrowed as she raked him with a predatory gaze.

"You can have me any way you want me," she countered, "but it'll cost you."

"Not as much as it's going to cost you," he said under his breath and grabbed her by the hand.

Six

The squeal of brakes from the incoming subway train drowned out the sound of onlookers' voices as Detectives Amato and Hahn ducked under the strip of yellow crime scene tape and moved to the end of the platform. The medical examiner was already packing up, but the photographer from forensics was still taking pictures.

Sal spoke to the coroner as he waited for the photographer to finish.

"What have we got?"

The warmth of the M.E.'s breath hit the cold morning air, giving him the appearance of "blowing smoke" as he picked up his bags.

"Trouble," he said, and pointed toward the body with his chin. "She died here. The killer turned her body to the wall and covered her from the waist down with that newspaper. Probably so any passersby might think she was just drunk or sleeping. Best guess is she died around midnight, maybe a little later, and if I was a betting man, I'd say the same killer as before, but I'll know more after I get her into the lab."

Sal's eyes widened. "What do you mean, the same killer?"

"They didn't tell you?" the M.E. asked.

Amato shook his head.

"Look for yourself," the M.E. said, and headed for the stairs as Sal moved toward the body. He cursed softly beneath his breath as he took his first look.

"Hell," he muttered, then stood abruptly as his partner, Paulie Hahn, looked over his shoulder. "Christ almighty, just what we need."

"This is only the second body. We can't jump to conclusions with only two victims," Paulie said.

Amato pointed to the woman's neatly quartered face. "We can when they look like that. Call the lieutenant and tell him he'd better get down here fast. Someone is bound to leak this to the press, and when they do, the media will have a field day."

Paulie took out his radio just as the doors of the train began to open. The noise level, borne of curiosity over an ongoing police investigation, made a call momentarily impossible.

"Can't hear thunder here," Paulie said. "I'm going to the far end of the platform to make the call."

As Paulie moved away, Sal began taking notes from the patrolmen who'd been first on the scene, gathering any available information that might aid in their investigation.

"Hey, Sal, anything we can do to help?" Trudy asked.

Amato turned; he'd been unaware that Kowalski and Neil had arrived. He frowned as he pointed to the victim.

"Take a look," he said.

Trudy gasped, her gaze immediately shifting to her partner's face to see if he was drawing the same conclusion. When she saw his lips firm and his nostrils flare, she knew he had. She looked over at Sal.

"Was she killed here?" she asked, her gaze raking the far corner of the subway platform on which they were standing.

"The M.E. says yes."

"Time of death?"

"Sometime around midnight."

"Who found her?"

"Don't know. The first officer on the scene responded to an anonymous call around 6:00 a.m. It's anyone's guess, other than that."

"Got an ID on her?" J.R. asked.

Sal checked his notes. "Yeah. Sylvia Polanski, age 33. Got an address in Queens, although we haven't checked it out yet."

J.R. moved toward her body, silently observing the condition of her clothes.

"It will be hard to tell if this one got raped," he stated.

Sal frowned. "Why's that?"

"Looks like a hooker to me," J.R. said. "Depending on the number of johns she had last night, she could be carrying multiple DNA.''

"How can you tell she's a hooker?" Sal asked.

"More than half her clothes are missing."

J.R. pointed to her right foot. "I could be wrong," he said. "But the only women I've seen walking around these snow-packed streets in three-inch heels are hookers."

Sal nodded. "You might be right, and then again, she could have been coming from a Christmas party somewhere."

"Maybe so," J.R. said. "What do you want us to do?"

Amato sighed. "Hell if I know," he muttered, then shook off the feeling of helplessness. "Well, it's damned cold. You know where the homeless go when the shelters are full and it starts to snow."

"Inside or underground," Trudy said, well aware that there was an entire community of homeless people who lived beneath the city.

But the thought of prowling through the cavernous recesses gave her the shudders. Instinctively she felt beneath her coat for her gun, relaxing only slightly as she felt the bulge beneath her fingers.

Amato pointed toward the crowd. "You and Neil check around. See if you can come up with any witnesses, however reluctant they might be. It's a long shot, but right now it's all we've got."

J.R. paused, glancing down as two men from the

coroner's office began putting Sylvia Polanski's body into a bag. The photographer had finished and was nowhere in sight.

"Got any leads on the first victim?" he asked.

Amato shook his head. "Hell no. That would be too easy. Now go find me a witness. We need to get this sicko off the streets."

"Come on, Red, let's shake the mattress of Mother Earth and see what crawls out of the cracks."

Trudy popped a piece of gum into her mouth and winked at Amato. "My partner is cuter than yours...and poetic, too."

Amato chuckled at the delicate ribbing between Neil and Kowalksi, accepting it as the stuff that only partners could say to each other and get away with, and then watched the coroner's men carrying away the body of Sylvia Polanski. As he turned, he saw Paulie heading his way.

"Did you tell the lieutenant?" he asked.

Paulie nodded. "He's not a happy camper."

Amato shuddered. "Hell, neither am I. We've got to go all the way to Queens to check out the vic's address."

Paulie pulled the collar of his coat up around his ears as they started up the stairs.

"Look at it this way," he said. "Maybe there will be something in Sylvia Polanski's apartment that will break this thing wide-open."

Sal snorted beneath his breath. "Yeah, and maybe

there will be a one-way ticket in my Christmas stocking to a place where it never snows.''

''I like the snow,'' Paulie said as they exited onto the street.

Sal wrinkled his eyes in protest of the cold blast of air, then looked up at the gray morning sky with a shudder.

''Then you're gonna be a bundle full of joy today,'' he said. ''It's starting to snow again.''

Mac woke abruptly and sat straight up in bed, his heart pounding, his face covered in sweat. When he realized he'd been dreaming, he sagged with relief. He didn't know where the hell that nightmare had come from, but he didn't want to go back there again. He'd been dreaming of Caitlin, and as dreams went, it had been a doozy. Only she kept turning into a woman from his past, and that was where the nightmare had come in. Only once in his life had he considered marriage. Her name had been Sarah, and she'd died in his arms. He'd watched the cancer ravage her body until there had been nothing left but a shell. He'd sworn to himself never to care for another woman in that way again. Then he'd met Caitlin, and she'd haunted his dreams ever since. Most of the time he told himself he didn't even like her. But then there were the times when he wondered if he would ever get enough of her. Staying in her home—under these conditions—was getting to him. He didn't want to fall in love. It was easier and safer being in hate. As he sat, debating with himself about the wisdom of lying back down and trying for more sleep or making coffee instead, his focus began to shift.

Click, click, click.

The sound was faint and slightly familiar as he reached for a pair of sweats. After a quick trip to the bathroom, he finished dressing, then left his bedroom, following the faint, repetitive clicks into the hallway of Caitlin's apartment. He paused outside a partially open door, then looked inside.

Slowly he relaxed.

It was Caitlin at the computer, and the sound he'd been hearing was nothing more sinister than the click of her keyboard as she typed.

He grinned at the way she was sitting. Perched on the edge of the chair, as if readying herself to bolt. Her knees were bent, her legs locked around the legs like a bareback rider on a pissed-off horse. An old chenille bathrobe hung over the back of the chair, as if discarded in a fit of disregard, while the blue flannel pajamas she was wearing bore a scattered array of white fluffy clouds. Her hair was piled up on top of her head, secured by a piece of brown plastic that slightly resembled the rib cage of a small dinosaur. Her bruises were turning green, and one of the stitches over her eyebrow poked out from her forehead like grass in need of cutting. If all his senses had been in good working order, he would have been bordering on a good laugh over her lack of fashion. Instead his thoughts were wavering between admiration and pure attraction.

He had to give it to her. She was tenacious. Aggravating, but tenacious. He liked that in a woman. And then, the moment he thought it, he flinched. He wasn't supposed to like Caitlin Bennett. She damn sure didn't like him.

Having settled that in his mind, he quietly backed out. But instead of walking away, he hesitated, listening to the steady click of the keys and wondering how a mind like hers worked, developing the intricacies of her bestselling stories without mixing up or losing track of all the facts. Even if they didn't like each other, it didn't hurt to admit that she had skill. That wasn't giving her any slack. He was only acknowledging her place on earth, just as he would expect her to acknowledge his.

He had been a cop—a protector and purveyor of justice. She was a writer—a creator of worlds and magician of words. It was fair to say that they both had their place.

He frowned and walked away. It was just unfortunate that, for the time being, they were forced to carry out their roles beneath the same roof.

He turned up the thermostat as he entered the kitchen, then walked to the window and pulled the curtains aside.

Well, hell. It was snowing again.

His bones had gotten too used to Georgia winters to tolerate this much cold for long. As he ran water into the coffeepot and then spooned coffee into the filter, he kept reminding himself that he wouldn't be here forever. But he knew that when he left, things would never be the same.

A short while later he was taking strips of bacon out of a skillet and laying them to drain on paper towels when Caitlin wandered into the room.

"You're cooking," she said, her eyes wide with interest.

Before Mac could answer, she had ducked under his arm and snagged a strip of bacon.

"Um," she said as she took a bite, taking care to chew only on the right side of her mouth. "I love breakfast food," she added, blessing him with an unusually friendly smile.

"Yeah?" he said, staring at a tiny bacon crumb at the corner of her mouth.

"That one's burning," Caitlin offered, pointing to the last strip still in the pan.

Mac cursed softly as he quickly retrieved the bacon from the burning grease.

"I'll eat it," he said, and laid it on his plate as he took the skillet off the heat. "Want some eggs?"

"Scrambled?"

He reached over her head to the cabinet above and took out a small glass bowl.

"Sure. How many?" he asked as he started breaking eggs into the bowl.

Caitlin's eyes widened. When she ate eggs, which was rare, she only cooked one at a time. And if she hadn't lost count, he'd already broken six into the bowl.

"Oh...just one," she said, pointing to the thick, yellow mixture he was beating into a fluff.

He paused and looked up. "One?"

She nodded.

His gaze slid from her face down the front of her body all the way to her sock-clad feet and then up, moving more slowly as he traced the faint outline of curves hidden beneath the baggy flannel pajamas.

"You need to eat more than that," he announced, then poured the bacon grease into a bowl, dumped the eggs into the skillet and began to stir.

"Are you saying I'm skinny?" Caitlin asked.

The tone of her voice made the hair crawl on the back of his neck, but he held his ground.

"Did I say you were skinny?" he drawled as he dumped a good-sized portion of the cooked eggs on her plate and then emptied the rest onto his.

"No, but you—"

"Do you think you could eat toast, or is your mouth too sore?" he asked, completely ignoring the fact that she was pushing herself toward pissed.

"Um, I, uh..."

"Your eggs are getting cold," he said.

Caitlin frowned. He made her so mad. He'd all but called her skinny, and now he was completely ignoring the fact that she wanted an apology. With a frustrated sigh, she snatched the plate from the counter, filched a couple of extra slices of bacon and headed for the table. It was hard to demonstrate an effective stomp when her body was this sore, but she did the best she could.

"You weren't hired to be my cook," she said and, the moment she said it, could have kicked herself all over the room.

He stiffened, then turned, his face a study in disbelief; he picked up his plate, his face red with anger.

"Actually I wasn't hired to be anything," he said, pointing a fork in her direction. "If you will remember, Aaron asked me to help. I did not come because I was being paid, nor do I want any money from you. Now, if you don't mind, I wish you would take a deep breath and eat your breakfast without saying another goddamned thing to me."

He strode out of the kitchen, carrying his food with him.

Caitlin's eyes filled with tears as she watched him leave. She tried to take a breath but choked on a sob as she looked at her plate. A second passed, then another and another, while huge, silent tears rolled down her face.

Why do I feel this constant need to hurt his feel-

*ings? Why am I such a rampant bitch when he's
around? This isn't me. This isn't who I am.*

To her dismay, she heard him coming back into the
kitchen and scrambled for a napkin to blot her tears,
but it was too late.

Mac had come back for his coffee but got a kick
in the stomach instead. He took one look at the tears
on her face and groaned. They'd done it again. His
shoulders slumped, his hands twitching at his sides as
he dropped his head.

"Goddamn it, Caitie, I didn't mean to make you
cry."

She looked up, her face still streaked with tears.

"I was rude. I had it coming," she whispered. "I
was raised with better manners. I don't know why I
behave this way around you."

Mac sighed, then crossed the room and pulled her
out of the chair and into his arms, taking care not to
hold her too tight.

"I'm sorry."

Stunned by the thunder of his heartbeat against her
ear, she couldn't find breath to answer. And then his
hands slid across her back and she felt as if she were
being cradled.

"I'm sorry, too," she mumbled.

Mac leaned back, wanting to see her face, but she
wouldn't look up. Sighing, he tilted her chin with the
tip of his finger until they were eye to eye.

"Truce?" he asked.

Another set of tears pooled and rolled as she nodded.

Mac's gaze slid downward. He found himself staring at her mouth—at the slightly swollen bottom lip as well as the tremble in her chin. His resistance crumbled. Well, hell. He was already in trouble, but what he was about to do was going to make it worse. He exhaled softly, then lowered his head. The last thing he remembered before the floor tilted beneath his feet was thinking how unbelievably soft her mouth was and how well she fit in his arms.

Time ceased.

It wasn't until he heard Caitlin moan that he realized what he'd done. He tore his mouth from her lips and held up his hands in surrender. She looked as stunned as he felt. His voice softened, even though his words were still taunting.

"Don't hit me, Caitie. You're in no shape for me to hit back."

Caitlin shuddered, then took a deep breath, as if coming out of a trance.

"You wouldn't hit me," she stated. "You don't like me, but you wouldn't hit me."

Mac frowned. He didn't want her to be forgiving.

"I don't kiss women I don't like. At least, I didn't used to," he muttered, then grabbed his coffee from the counter and stalked out of the kitchen.

Still reeling from the feel of Mac's mouth on her lips, Caitlin sat down at the table, picked up her fork and started to take a bite of her eggs when Mac's parting shot finally sank in.

"Oh," she said, and then laid down her fork. "Oh my," she mumbled, and looked up in disbelief. "Oh my Lord," she moaned, and cast a frantic look toward the door where he'd disappeared.

When had animosity turned into attraction? Better yet, what in the name of God was she going to do about it? She was on the verge of panic when Mac yelled at her from the other room.

"Are you eating your breakfast?"

The bubble burst.

Attraction? That wasn't attraction she'd felt. It was insanity. Chalk it up to the truck bumper colliding with her forehead.

"Are you minding your own business?" she muttered.

"I heard that."

"Just proving your chest isn't the only big body part you have," Caitlin yelled, then rolled her eyes.

She'd been referring to his ears, but knowing Connor McKee, he was going to assume she was referring to what lay south of his belt buckle. If her lower lip hadn't been so sore, she would have bitten it.

To her relief, he said nothing, although she was certain she heard him laughing. Completely furious that she'd let herself be baited, she stabbed a fork into her eggs and ate, not stopping until her plate was empty and her stomach was full. She felt better for having eaten the meal, even if she'd made a fool of herself in the process. Shoving her chair back from the table, she carried her plate and cutlery to the sink, then poured herself a cup of coffee with the full intention of going back to her office when her phone rang.

"Yes?"

"Miss Bennett, Mr. Workman is here to see you."

"Good morning, Mike. Send him up."

"Good morning to you, too, miss. I trust you're feeling better?"

She smiled. "I'm fine. How's that new grandson?" She was picturing the security guard's smile as she asked.

"He's just great, and thanks for asking."

Mac walked into the room behind her as she was hanging up the phone.

"Who was that?"

Caitlin turned, gauged the distance between them and decided it was safe.

"Aaron is on his way up. I'm going to get dressed. Please let him in."

An eyebrow arched. "You're dressing for him?"

Caitlin grinned before she thought. "He thinks I'm a heathen because I don't get out of my nightclothes unless I'm going out."

His other eyebrow arched. "You really stay in your pajamas all day?"

She shrugged. "Sometimes...well, most of the

time, yes. So what? Just because I'm Devlin Bennett's daughter doesn't make me some social butterfly.''

He eyed the belligerent thrust to her chin and resisted the urge to grin. Damned if he wasn't starting to understand her need to assert herself. It couldn't have been easy being Bennett's daughter. The man had been on the cover of every important national magazine, had been written up constantly in the newspapers, as well as serving as a constant source of news for the television network.

"Easy, Caitie. That wasn't a dig. Actually, that could be considered quite sexy."

Her eyes widened and her heart skipped a beat.

"What do you mean, sexy?"

"A woman in her nightclothes is a woman one step away from bed. Some men might take that as an invitation.''

"Yes, I suppose," Caitlin said, praying that her shock didn't show. "But some men also eat with their fingers and burp for their own entertainment, and it doesn't endear them to me, so I'm thinking that the playing field is even. Just let your brother in when he rings and stop baiting me. My head hurts too much to argue with you."

The devilment in his eyes faded immediately. "Did you take your pain medicine this morning? How long were you working before you stopped? Sitting at that computer can't be good for you, with your side so bruised.''

Taken aback by his concern, Caitlin sputtered, then was saved from having to answer by a knock on the door.

"That's Aaron," she said, bolting out of the kitchen and down the hall.

Mac shook his head as he answered the door.

"Good morning, little brother," he said, as Aaron sailed into the room.

"Good morning to you, too," Aaron said. "Where's Caitlin? Did she get any rest? Are you behaving yourself?"

"She's getting dressed, and I suppose she slept...some, at least. I woke up to hear her typing in her office." Then he frowned. "And just for the record, I resent the implication that I would behave inappropriately."

Aaron sighed. "You know what I mean, so don't be so huffy. I just want you to be nice."

"If I was any nicer, I could be looking at getting sued for child support," he muttered. "Want some coffee?"

Aaron nodded, too stunned to speak. He stared at the set of Mac's shoulders as he strode from the room, then listened to the sound of slamming doors and banging crockery before he started to smile. He was still absorbing the child support crack when Caitlin entered the room.

"Aaron, how good of you to stop by."

He blinked. Caitlin was coming toward him with a

forced smile on her face. For once he didn't even notice what she was wearing. He loved her as much as it was possible for him to love any woman. He couldn't marry her, but Connor could. Of course, that all hinged upon mutual desire. But from the way Mac was acting and the fake smile on Caitlin's face, something was up. He just didn't know whether it was good or bad.

Seven

Sylvia Polanski's apartment was a total surprise. It was chic, understated and obviously very expensive. Whatever Sylvia's profession, she had been successful at it.

Paulie Hahn picked up a small porcelain statuette of a shepherdess and turned it over, looking at the stamp on the bottom.

"Dresden," he said, and set it back on the table where he'd found it. "Sylvia Polanski might have been a hooker, but she had good taste."

"We don't know she was a hooker," Sal said, as he poked through a desk drawer for something that might give them a clue as to who Sylvia's killer could be. "Just because Neil said it, that doesn't make it so."

"You don't like him much, do you?" Paulie asked.

Sal shrugged. "He's all right. Just got too much hair."

Paulie grinned. "We aren't gonna find anything here to link the two women."

Sal straightened and turned. "Why do you say that? Have you gone psychic on me?"

"Because the two women don't connect," Paulie said. "Donna Dorian was a twenty-year-old university student still living with her mother. Coroner said she was a virgin before the rape. Sylvia Polanski is in her thirties, right?"

"Yeah, but—"

"I think Neil was right. I think she was a hooker. You heard what the super said when he let us in. She slept all day and was out all night. She didn't bring anyone here. This was home. So she's either got a place somewhere in Manhattan where she takes her johns, or she uses their places."

"We don't know that," Sal said, pushing a drawer shut and opening another.

Paulie shrugged. "Well, if she *is* a hooker, she's a high-class one. Lofts like these rent for a pretty penny. She was either independently wealthy or damn good at her job."

"Hey, look at this," Sal said, as he pulled a small leather-bound book from beneath a pile of receipts.

"What is it?"

Sal whistled between his teeth. "It's what my old man used to call a 'little black book.'"

"Let me see," Paulie said.

Sal handed it over.

"Man, look at all these names and numbers."

Sal studied it a moment and then handed it back to

his partner. "Okay, so it looks like Neil might have been right after all."

"Unless she's their stockbroker or something, I'd agree."

Sal turned, scanning the room for a new place to search when he saw a photo on the wall near the windows. He walked over for a closer look.

"This must be her," he said, pointing toward the picture. "She was a fine-looking woman before that crazy son of a bitch got a hold of her."

Paulie looked. "Yeah. Let's take it with us. It's a damned sight better than the one the coroner will send."

Sal laid it beside his coat and kept on digging. A few minutes later, he turned up a small address book with what appeared to be personal phone numbers.

"I think I just found her next of kin," Sal said. "What looks like her mother's phone number is in here."

Paulie frowned. "That's the worst thing I hate about working homicide. It's your turn to break the news."

Sal sat down on the sofa and picked up the picture, staring intently at the woman's face. Dark, shoulder-length hair and dark eyes—and a real pretty mouth. He laid the picture aside.

"You know, you have kids. Raise them the best way you know how, then they turn to shit like this.

No woman I ever heard of made plans to give birth to a hooker.''

Paulie shrugged. ''You think too much, Sal. Come on, this place is giving me the creeps. We've got her book. We can run the names and phone numbers from the office. Let's get out of here.''

Two days later

Awakened by the sound of the wind, Caitlin quickly became aware of a distinct drop in the room temperature. She opened her eyes to darkness and then glanced at the clock. Almost 3:00 a.m. If she didn't turn up the heat, it would be freezing in the apartment by morning. Reluctantly she turned on the light and then crawled out of bed, moving quietly through the house in her sock feet until she reached the living room. With instinct born of familiarity, she felt along the wall for the thermostat, upped it a couple of notches until she heard it kick on and then headed back to bed. But when she got to the hall, she stopped abruptly. Connor was standing in her doorway wearing nothing but a pair of sweat pants.

''What's wrong?''

''It's getting colder. I just turned the thermostat up a bit,'' she said. ''Sorry I woke you.''

''You didn't wake me. I wasn't asleep.''

When he took a step forward, the light spilling out of her bedroom wrapped around his body, bathing it in a warm, soft-white glow. Breath caught in the back of her throat. His chest rippled with muscles the weight lifters called six-packs, and his sweats rode too low on his hips for her comfort. Instinctively she crossed her arms beneath her breasts and took a slow breath, trying to remember what they'd been saying. Sleep. It was something about not being able to sleep.

"You said you couldn't sleep, are you ill?"

"No."

"It's almost three."

Mac watched the panic on her face and wondered if his was as obvious. This attraction to her was scary as hell.

"I know," he said, and took another step toward her.

Caitlin shrunk within herself, too scattered to move.

"Do you suffer from insomnia?" She thought she heard him sigh.

I'm suffering all right, but it's not insomnia, you little witch, it's you.

He eyed her tousled hair and fading bruises, as well as those ridiculous flannel pajamas, and wondered why in hell he kept dreaming about making love to her.

"I guess it's something like that."

"There are some sleeping pills in the bathroom," she offered. "But don't take more than one or you'll sleep through tomorrow."

"I don't do drugs," he muttered.

Caitlin felt herself bristling. "Are you insinuating that I do? Because if you are, I can assure you that—"

The next thing she knew, he had her pinned against the wall, his hands still gentle on her shoulders.

"I wasn't insinuating anything, you ungrateful little wretch, but if you're about to light into me again, then I may as well give you something real to be pissed about."

Before she could answer, he lowered his head. She felt the warmth of his breath and then his hands sliding from her shoulders to her back, urging her toward him.

She put her hands between them in reflex.

It was a mistake.

Instead of pushing him back, she found herself stroking his chest, pausing as the ricochet of his heartbeat seared into her palms.

Then she made her second mistake.

She looked up.

"I warned you," he whispered.

His lips were warm, the pressure gentle yet persistent. Caitlin lost all sense of self. The danger to her life, the blizzard outside—all of it was gone. Everything that had come and gone before seemed frivolous and shallow. Right now—at this moment—she felt reborn. She was starting over with just one kiss.

It wasn't until she moaned that Mac came to his

senses. He immediately turned her loose, certain he was hurting her.

"Oh hell, I'm sorry. I didn't mean to hurt you." Then he shoved his hands through his hair and looked away, unwilling to face any more of her accusations. "The only thing I seem to get right around you is an apology."

Caitlin stared at him in confusion. Her head was spinning, her heartbeat out of control, as she tried to come to terms with what he was saying. The imprint of his mouth was so real she had to touch her own lips to assure herself he was gone. At that point, she drew a shuddering breath.

"I don't know where you got your information, but I wasn't the one complaining."

Then she lifted her chin and walked into her room, quickly closing the door behind her before she followed her own impulse to invite him in.

Staggered by what he'd done, Mac stood in the hall, seriously considering the option of going in after her. Fortunately sanity returned. Cursing himself for a fool, he turned abruptly and strode into his bedroom, dropping to the side of the bed in quiet dismay.

He'd learned long ago that, between midnight and morning, caution had a tendency to go to hell. He'd come to protect her, not complicate her life even more. And, he reminded himself, *he* didn't want any complications, either. He wasn't a settling down kind of man, and Caitlin Bennett wasn't anyone's one-night stand. The fact that their mutual attraction left her angry and confused and him hard and hurting was too damned bad.

But as the wind continued to shriek outside the building, his worries became true fears. How long could they hold out against this growing attraction when there was a blizzard snowing them in?

Buddy paced the floor of his apartment, wishing he'd gone in to work. It was just after daybreak, and even though he'd taken a personal day off, he thought about reconsidering. He paused at the window and frowned.

The wind was fierce, the snow blinding, slowing vehicles to a crawl. Pedestrian traffic was sparse, and those who dared to venture out spent more time holding on to their coats and trying to stay on their feet than getting to any particular destination. He shuddered as he turned away, revamping his previous thoughts. Work be damned. There were other ways to occupy his time besides freezing his ass off.

The euphoria of killing the hooker had passed, leaving him with the unpalatable fact that no matter how many substitutes he killed, his target still lived.

He moved from the living room to his bedroom, taking comfort in the newspaper clippings, as well as the pictures he had plastered all over the walls. A poster-size photo of her hung above his bed. The beauty of her face had been marred many times over, but the act had done nothing to assuage his rage. The fact that there was now a bodyguard between him and justice was a thorn in his side, but not a pertinent issue. There were plenty of ways to get to her, and he was a patient man.

As he stood, he became aware of the silence. Except for the occasional rattle of the windows from the storm, everything was muted, buried beneath the wind and the snow. He closed his eyes and took a slow, deep breath, concentrating on the sound of his heartbeat. After a while, he crawled into bed and pulled up the covers, letting his mind go free. And as he listened, the race of thoughts with which he usually lived stilled and peace settled within.

He was on the verge of sleep when the silence in the room was broken by a series of scratching sounds, followed by one very distinct squeak. His eyes opened, his nostrils flaring in anger. A large part of his paycheck went toward the rent on this apartment. It was a nice place in a decent part of the city, and yet there was no mistaking what he'd heard. There was a rat in the walls. That was something that belonged with his childhood. He wasn't going to live in that kind of poverty again.

He climbed out of bed, yanking on clothes as he went, then stalked out of his apartment. Just as he reached the elevator, the power flickered. Unwilling to chance getting trapped in the elevator he took the five flights of stairs down to the super's apartment.

By the time he arrived, he was furious. It showed in the fervor with which he knocked.

"Who is it?" the superintendent called.

"It's me!" Buddy yelled. "The tenant in 505."

Buddy heard locks turning and then the door opened on the chain. When the superintendent recognized Buddy's face, he came out into the hall.

"What seems to be the problem?" he asked.

Buddy's voice was soft, a deceptive indicator of his state of mind.

"There are rats in the walls of my apartment."

The superintendent's eyes widened nervously. "Can't be," he denied.

Buddy inhaled slowly, maintaining his composure. "Oh, but there are. I heard them."

The superintendent shrugged. "I ain't sayin' you're right and I ain't sayin' you're wrong, but it ain't my problem. I just work and live here, like you."

"And part of your job is to see that the complaints of the tenants are dealt with. I expect traps to be set in the basement and the owner to be notified. You tell him to get an exterminator into this building before he finds himself sued."

The superintendent frowned. "You ain't gonna win no lawsuit because of rats. The city is full of 'em."

Buddy's fingers curled into fists. The urge to punch that smug expression off the superintendent's face was overwhelming, but he held his ground, maintaining the hold on his emotions.

"Not at the rent I'm paying," Buddy said. "You know what I do for a living. I know important people. I could make big trouble for you and for the owner. You think about that. You think long and hard. You hear me?"

The man nodded nervously, unsure of the tenant's true power, but unwilling to push the issue.

"Yeah, I hear you," he muttered.

"I'm going back to my apartment now," Buddy said, then poked his finger into the soft flesh of the man's chest. "And you'd better pray I don't hear any more scratches or squeaks."

Without waiting for the man to answer, he pivoted angrily and stalked back up the stairs and into his apartment, slamming and locking the door behind him as he went.

Mac stood at the window of Caitlin's living room, his hands stuffed in the pockets of his jeans. The stress of being snowed in with her was driving him nuts. Half the time he wanted to throttle her, the rest of the time he was dying to take off her clothes.

"It's still snowing."

"I know," Caitlin said, without looking up from the pages she was editing.

She thought she heard a muffled curse but ignored it. She understood Mac's frustration but she couldn't change it. The snow of the past few days had turned into a full-fledged blizzard sometime after midnight, but its power was nothing to the kiss they'd shared in the hall. Afterward, she'd run like the coward she was and, by daybreak, convinced herself it meant nothing. But now Mac's predatory prowl was starting to bother her. And when he turned around, she realized she'd been right to worry.

"Caitlin, we need to talk."

She marked her place on the manuscript with a small red check and then looked up.

"Yes?"

"Something's happening between us—something I didn't expect."

Taken aback by his openness, she didn't quite know what to say.

"I don't know...maybe it's the close quarters we're in," he said. "And maybe it's nothing more than compassion for what's happening to you, but I'm not in the habit of wantonly kissing my clients."

Her mouth snapped shut, her eyes narrowing. "I'm not a client. I didn't hire you, remember? You are free to leave any time you feel the need."

He sighed and shoved his hands through his hair in frustration.

"See? We don't get along at all. You don't like me and truthfully, I didn't think I liked you all that much, either. But I don't want to mislead you about what's been happening."

"I'm not misled," Caitlin said. "You kissed me

twice, both times in anger. I think you need counseling to rechannel your emotions.''

He stared at her for a moment and then burst out laughing. It was the last thing Caitlin had expected him to do.

"What?'' she muttered.

He was still chuckling when he walked over to where she was sitting and absently ruffled the top of her hair, as if he was petting a dog.

"You know something, kiddo? You just might be right. It's after two. Aren't you hungry?''

She shrugged. "I don't know. I hadn't thought about it.''

"Well, think,'' he said, and grabbed her by the hand, pulling her off the couch and toward the kitchen. "I'm starving, and I'm bored. So feed me or take me to bed.''

She grinned and punched him on the arm, not realizing it was their first friendly exchange.

"It will be a cold day in hell before I go anywhere near a bed with you.''

Mac grinned back and pointed out the window. "Wrong choice of words, girl. Have you looked outside lately?''

She looked startled, then laughed as she moved toward the refrigerator, unaware that Mac hadn't followed.

For Mac, movement at that moment would have been impossible. He'd been intrigued by her smile, but her laughter had struck him dumb. He caught himself watching the sway of her hips and the lithe motion of her body as she leaned forward to peer into the refrigerator.

Oh man...this isn't happening. I won't let this happen.

And then she turned around, a jar of peanut butter in one hand, a jar of dill pickles in the other.

"Mac?"

"Huh?

"Do you like peanut butter sandwiches?"

He looked at the jar of oversize green dills with dismay. "With pickles?"

"I have jelly."

"Sold."

She eyed him curiously. "Somehow I pictured you as a more adventurous sort of man."

"Adventure is one thing, gastronomic disaster is another."

She set the jars on the counter and reached back into the refrigerator for the bread and jelly.

Mac set his jaw and strode toward the sink to wash his hands. He wasn't going to let this thing happen, and that was that. They would eat peanut butter. They would fuss. They might even have the occasional amiable conversation. But there would not be any more kisses, that was for damned sure.

The phone rang as he was drying his hands. Caitlin answered, balancing the phone against her ear and shoulder as she spread a dollop of peanut butter across a slice of bread.

"Hello?"

"Miss Bennett, Detective Neil here. How are you feeling?"

Caitlin smiled, still holding the peanut butter as she leaned against the wall.

"Detective Neil, how kind of you to call. I'm doing quite well, actually. Of course, I won't win any beauty contests, but then, I don't think that would have been possible before the accident, either, so I can't say all that much has changed."

"I disagree completely," J.R. said.

Caitlin smiled.

"Thank you, but I think you're just being kind."

From across the room, Mac watched the play of emotions coming and going on her face. The way she was cuddling that phone was disgusting, and that stupid smile she was wearing was a total disgrace. He yanked the jar of peanut butter out of her hands, slammed two pieces of bread on his plate, slathered one side with peanut butter, the other with grape jelly, and slapping them together just as Caitlin giggled. He didn't care what she did. It didn't matter to him who turned her on or off. All he wanted was some food and a plane ticket back to Georgia. Chewing angrily, he poured himself a cup of coffee and then stalked to the window, realizing as he did so that he'd done little else since he'd been here but get hard for Caitlin and stare out windows.

Damned snow. Stupid, eternally miserable damned snow.

She laughed again. His nostrils flared as he tore a bite from the sandwich, his eyes narrowing angrily as he dug a hunk of peanut butter from the roof of his mouth with his tongue, then began to chew.

Damned stupid peanut butter. Then he realized the phone call was coming to an end and turned just as Caitlin said her goodbyes.

"That would be lovely," Caitlin said. "Yes, and thank you for calling."

She hung up the phone, the smile still on her face, and looked around for the peanut butter to finish making her sandwich. Mac swallowed his bite as he watched her, listening to the clink of the knife against the plate, the soft, almost nonexistent sound of her breathing, and then inhaling the tangy scent of dill as she opened the jar of pickles. Finally he couldn't stand it anymore.

"Well?"

Caitlin looked up, surprised by the tone of his voice.

"Well what?"

"It was the cop, wasn't it?"

"Oh...well, yes, it was, actually."

"Did he have anything new on your case?"

She frowned as she licked a smear of peanut butter from the end of her finger.

"I don't think so. Actually he called just to check on me. Wasn't that nice of him?"

Mac slammed his half-eaten sandwich back on the plate and set his coffee cup down on the cabinet, a sarcastic smirk on his face.

"Yes, Caitlin, it was nice...so nice. In fact, I don't think I can remember a time when anyone was nicer."

Taken aback by his sarcasm, Caitlin was at a momentary loss for words.

"Well," she muttered, and then got her second wind, "I think you're behaving rather childishly. What's wrong with someone asking after my health?"

"Nothing."

"Then stop acting so weird," she said, as she resumed making her sandwich. "If I didn't know better, I'd think you were jealous."

"Not in this lifetime," he said, managing a weak chuckle while his legs went weak. *Oh God, oh God. I am.*

He looked around frantically for something to do and, in a panic, picked up his sandwich and took another big bite. But the more he chewed, the more certain he became that his life was out of control. He'd come to help his brother, not fall for some straitlaced bookworm who treated him as if he was only one rung above a snake.

Caitlin cut her sandwich into four pieces, then carried her plate to the table.

"Mmm," she said, rolling her eyes in satisfaction as she took her first bite.

Mac felt himself gulp. If he could figure out how to become as attractive to her as that damned peanut butter and pickle sandwich, he would be in like Flynn.

"I need to make a few calls," he said. "Check on the business...that sort of thing."

"Feel free," Caitlin said as she took another bite.

"Nothing's free in this life," he murmured, and walked out of the room.

Eight

Mac tossed aside the letters and then stood, a deep frown etched upon his forehead. He'd just reread the entire file of threatening letters that Caitlin had received, and the acceleration of anger in each one seemed so obvious, he still couldn't believe the police had ever hesitated. Even from the start, the letters had crossed the line.

Yesterday he'd faxed them to a friend who was a profiler for the Federal Bureau of Investigation. Now all he could do was wait to see if his personal analysis was right. His gut feeling was that Caitlin Bennett's life was in imminent danger. But how to track a faceless enemy? He'd been a good cop, and he was an even better businessman than he'd believed he would be, but unless they got a really big break in this case, Caitlin was going to be just what she was right now—a sitting duck, waiting for the hunter to pull the trigger.

"What do you think?"

He turned. Caitlin was in the doorway, her hands

on her hips, her head cocked to one side in a questioning manner.

I think you look good enough to eat. "I think you were right to be concerned. I think whoever is writing these is past crazy."

Her face paled.

Though he hated the fear on her face, it was still only fair to tell her the truth as he knew it.

"I'm waiting for a call from a friend in the Bureau. Maybe she'll be able to help us."

"What kind of a friend?" Caitlin asked, her interest piqued.

"A profiler."

"Oh!" Interest replaced her fear as she thought about her book in progress. "Do you think when she calls I might talk to her?"

Mac sighed. "Caitie, I don't know if—"

"It's this book I'm working on," she said. "I'm stuck on this scene and I thought if—"

He started to laugh. "God, but you're something, you know that?"

"What's so funny?"

"You've got a crazed fan writing you death threats. You got mowed down by a truck. And all you're interested in is getting research for a book."

She grinned, a bit self-conscious. "Okay, so you've found us out."

"Us, who?" Mac asked.

"Us writers. I'm afraid it's a common failing we

have, to take life experiences and store them like a squirrel stores nuts. It's in our genes. Never know when we might need to use something in a book.''

He frowned. ''Hell. I better not show up in one of those stories.''

She smiled primly. ''Of course not...unless, of course, I ever need a male chauvinist character with tunnel vision toward women.''

''I don't have tunnel vision toward women.''

She chose not to remind him that he hadn't denied being a male chauvinist.

''I'm willing to bet you do,'' she countered.

Interested in spite of himself, the words came out of his mouth before he could stop them. ''What kind of bet?''

She thought a moment and then started to smile. ''If I win, I want to go to the park and make a snow-man.''

''Hell's bells, Caitie, it's freezing out there.''

''But it quit snowing.''

He sighed. ''And if you lose, what's in it for me?''

She hesitated, unsure how far to push the tentative truce under which they were living.

''I don't know what sort of things you like.''

A slow grin spread across his face. ''I like women.''

Her mouth pursed primly. ''That's not news. Aaron speaks often of your prowess with the opposite sex.''

This time he frowned. ''I wouldn't call it prowess.

I'm just unattached. You know how it is when you're single.''

''If by 'unattached' you mean promiscuous, then no, I can't say that I do. I don't sleep around, Connor McKee.''

''I know,'' he said softly. ''That's part of my problem.''

Her eyes widened nervously. ''What do you mean?''

''I don't think I've ever been in this situation before.''

''What kind of situation?''

''You want the truth?'' he asked.

Suddenly she wasn't so sure. ''Oh...never mind the bet. I'm going out. You're welcome to come along.''

''I don't have tunnel vision when it comes to women.''

Her eyes narrowed as she looked him over.

''You like women with big boobs and round hips and little bitty waists, and if they giggle when they talk, so much the better. You're partial to redheads but won't turn down an invitation from a blue-eyed blonde.'' Then she crossed her arms over her chest and grinned. ''How am I doing?''

She had so nailed the redhead from the ski lodge that it shamed him. God, when had he become so shallow?

''I'll get my coat.''

"So you're admitting I won the bet?" Caitlin asked.

"Don't push your luck, woman. I thought you wanted to go outside."

"What about your feet? You'll need protection."

"Now that you've bullied me into having your way, you're worrying about my anatomy?"

"Connor, so help me—"

He grinned. "I packed an old pair of boots. They'll do."

"I'm going to change clothes," she announced. "I'd advise you to do the same. Wear layers of clothing. It's warmer than one really heavy coat, okay?"

"Yes, Mother."

"I am not your mother, God rest her soul," Caitlin muttered, and stomped out of the room.

And I thank the Lord for small favors. The way he was feeling, he didn't want to be any relation to Caitlin Bennett at all.

"Where are you going? You just got here."

Buddy turned, his coat draped across his arm.

"I've got some personal business to tend to. I'll be back in a couple of hours," he said.

He left before further explanations were requested, shrugging into his coat and pulling on his gloves as he took the stairs down two at a time.

As he stepped outside, he patted the bulky packet

inside the pocket of his coat to make sure it was still there. It was.

As he looked up, he saw the drivers of a trio of cabs on a collision course with disaster, blasting their horns at each other as they came together at an intersection, each refusing to yield. He winced, expecting to see them collide and then laughed when they slid past each other in a flurry of snow and curses. He could only imagine what their passengers were thinking.

The city was digging out from beneath the blizzard and doing a remarkable job, but it was going to take at least another twenty-four, maybe even forty-eight, hours before things would be back to normal. In the meantime, he had a mission of his own to accomplish that had nothing to do with snow.

As he started up the street, the cold hit him like a slap in the face. He paused at the corner, the breath from his mouth forming small, perfect clouds. They refused to dissipate, as if reluctant to leave the warmth from which they had been birthed. Debating with himself as to whether to risk his life and take a cab or use the subway, which would take longer, the decision was taken out of his hands. A cab pulled up to the curb in front of him and let out a passenger. Taking it as a sign, he jumped in the back seat as the passenger paid off the driver.

"Where to?" the driver asked.

"Manhattan...Riverside Drive. I'll tell you when to stop."

Then he settled in for the ride, taking care to buckle up as the driver pulled away from the curb.

As the driver sped over the snow-packed streets, Buddy got an unexpected view of a strange anomaly. The distinction of the buildings had been so blurred by the snowfall that they all looked the same. If it wasn't for the street signs on the blocks they were passing, he might have believed they were going in circles. Snowplows were out in full force, but it would be nightfall before all the main avenues had been plowed and probably another thirty-six hours before the side streets were finished.

Shop owners were out on the sidewalks, trying to shovel pathways to their stores, and so much snow was drifted everywhere that delivery trucks had to park halfway into the street in order to unload their goods.

"Hey, buddy, it's a real mess, ain't it?"

Startled to hear a stranger call him by name, it took a moment for him to realize the driver was using it as a gesture of friendliness, rather than recognition.

"I'm sorry. What did you say?"

"The snow. It's a mess."

He shrugged. "A reflection of life," he said, and then suddenly leaned close to the bullet-proof partition. "Let me out on the next corner."

The driver eased in toward the curb. Buddy paid

and got out, cursing as the snow went over his boots. The cab pulled away as he stumbled toward the curb. Once on the sidewalk, he looked around, judging his location against his final destination.

When he got his bearings, he smiled. A block north, then a half a block east, and he would be in the alley behind the Bennett Building. Feeling his coat pocket to make sure the package he'd come to deliver was still in its place, he lowered his head and started walking.

There were more people out than he had expected, and the closer he got to the building, the more he wished he'd worn a disguise. Thanks to a friend at City Hall, he had a copy of the blueprint for the building, and he reminded himself that he had been inside before. All he had to do was follow the plan and he would be fine.

He glanced down at his watch, judging how long he'd been gone against the time it would take to deliver his little treat. When he looked up, his heart nearly stopped. Caitlin Bennett and her bodyguard were coming toward him from less than half a block away. Without thinking, he ducked into the nearest business, which turned out to be a stationery store.

"May I help you, sir?"

"Just looking," he said, and stepped away from the door as Caitlin and her escort passed in front of the building.

He stood without moving, watching the animation

on her face and resenting the way her smile curved
upward in delight at something the man must have
said. Her behavior puzzled him. He would have sworn
she was more intelligent than this. How dare she be
happy when her life was in danger?

By the time they were gone, he was shaking with
anger. It was time to get serious. What he had in his
pocket was just a taste of what he had in store for
her. Oh, if he could only be a fly on the wall when
she opened his little surprise. But since he couldn't,
he would have to be satisfied with the fact that it
would surely wipe that smile off her face.

All he had to do was jimmy the maintenance door
in the rear of the building, follow the map in his head
to the elevator shaft leading to the penthouse, leave
his little ''gift'' and be on his way.

Mac didn't know whether to be glad that Caitlin
was happy or pick a fight with her just to regain some
emotional distance. Every time he thought about saying something rude, she would look up at him and
smile, and he would forget what he'd been going to
say. Finally he decided to just let the day be. They'd
been snowed in too long for him to bring the outing
to a premature halt.

''I'm starving,'' Caitlin said, pointing toward an
entrepreneurial vendor who'd dared the cold to sell
his wares. ''Let's get a pretzel.''

"You eat from those things?" he asked, unable to keep shock out of his voice.

Caitlin rolled her eyes as she dug into her pocket for some money.

"You are such a wuss. How do you think you're going to protect me from bad guys when you're too chicken to eat a simple pretzel? Besides that, I forgot my money. You'll have to pay."

"I'm not chicken," he muttered as they stopped at the push cart, standing behind a man with two kids. He eyed the vendor suspiciously, watching him handling the pretzels, then taking money and making change with the same hands. "I just like my food handlers to wash their hands once in a while."

Caitlin grinned and leaned toward him, whispering in a conspiratorial tone, "Oh, I'm sure he washes now and then, don't you think?"

Mac glared. "You're making fun of me."

Caitlin laughed. "You're an easy mark, McKee. It's hard not to bait you."

He started to argue, then saw his own reflection in the mirrored surface of her sunglasses and felt his stomach drop. He looked like a lovesick calf.

"Damn it," he mumbled, and looked away.

Caitlin frowned. "Don't be mad," she said softly. "I didn't mean to hurt your feelings."

"My feelings are not up for discussion," he said shortly. "Tell the man what you want."

Caitlin turned, only then realizing that they were next in line.

"We'll have two pretzels, please."

"Four bucks," the vendor said.

"For pretzels?" Mac asked.

"Do you see a better deal?" the vendor quipped, well aware that he had a corner on the market today.

Considering the fact that Caitlin was already chewing the first bite of her pretzel, he handed the man the money, took his food and moved on.

"Another reason why I left New York City," he said.

Caitlin frowned. "Street vendors?"

"No. The high cost of living."

"You can't put a price on the place you call home," Caitlin said.

The profundity of her words brought him to a halt.

"What's wrong?" Caitlin asked.

He looked at her then, with the weak sunlight highlighting the fading bruises on her face. He sighed.

"Nothing is wrong," he said softly. "The pretzel is tasty and hot, and you, my dear Caitie, have a fine way with words. Did anyone ever tell you that you had the makings of a writer?"

His tenderness was as unexpected as the compliment, and she could only stare at him in mute disbelief.

"Are you cold?" he asked.

She shook her head no.

"Tell me when you want to start back," he said.

She nodded, still too dumbstruck to speak. And so they walked and ate, occasionally talking of things they saw until the food was gone and Caitlin's cheeks were a bright, rosy red.

"We've been out over an hour," Mac said. "Time to start back."

Mac took her hand to help her over a slick spot and didn't bother to let go. The farther they walked, the larger the lump in Caitlin's throat became. If she wasn't careful, she might begin to think he really liked her. And if she ever deluded herself about that fact, she would be setting herself up for such a fall. Connor McKee wasn't the kind of man women like her fell for—not unless they wanted their hearts broken. He'd said it himself. He wasn't into lasting relationships, and she was not the kind of woman who could live with one-night stands. She wanted a forever kind of love, with a home and family. She dreamed of being a mother, sharing things with her children that she'd never had. Oh, she'd had everything money could buy, but little else.

If only Connor liked her, she could let herself believe something more than antagonism might grow between them.

By the time they got to the apartment building, her toes were numb and her cheeks were burning from the cold. Mike, the security guard, looked up as they entered.

"Have yourself a good walk, did you, Miss Bennett?"

"Yes, although I think I froze my nose."

He smiled while eyeing the man beside her. "And how are you liking our fair city, Mr. McKee?"

Mac grinned. "Ask me that after the snow melts and I'll have a better opinion."

"It's been a bugger, all right," Mike said. "You staying long?"

"As long as it takes," he said, then eyed Caitlin. "I want to talk to Mike about...stuff. Don't you agree?"

Caitlin hesitated, then nodded. It would be foolish not to alert the security guard in her own building that her life was being threatened.

"Yes, but if you don't mind, I'm going to go on up. The hems of my jeans are wet, and I want a hot shower and dry clothes, in that order."

Mac started to argue, then stopped. She was going straight up to the penthouse. He would be right behind her. What could it hurt?

"Okay. I won't be long."

She waved goodbye to Mike and headed for the elevator, taking off her scarf and gloves as she went. Behind her, Mac began explaining the reason for Caitlin's injuries and the danger she faced.

The almost silent upward motion of the elevator was expected, as was the elegant bouquet of flowers on the hall table beside the elevator doors. Pausing a moment to admire the arrangement and sniff a favorite flower, she took her mail from the mail basket and let herself in, disarming the alarm as she went.

The warmth of the rooms enveloped her as she shut the door. Absently dropping her wet gloves on the entryway's black-and-white tiles, she shrugged out of her coat and hung it on the hall tree, tossing her red scarf over it. Her feet were so cold they felt numb, but her shoes were still wet, so she sat down on a bench and pulled them off, too, before taking her mail to the living room. The thought of a warm shower was enticing, but she wanted to check for threatening letters.

A quick look at the envelopes assured her she was safe. The dark block letters the writer favored were on none of them. Relieved, she tossed the envelopes aside and picked up the packet that had been with her mail. Curious, she turned it over to see who it was from and then froze.

There on the front, written in bold, black letters, was her name and a holiday greeting. She picked it up, testing the contents by squeezing, then turned it over, staring at the flap as if it might burst into flames.

Finally she took a deep breath and opened, then turned it upside down over the coffee table and gave it a shake.

The contents fell out in hairy, blood-soaked chunks. When the head fell out, she started to scream.

*   *   *

Mac felt good about the day. Their truce was working, at least most of the time, and getting outside had
done both of them good. Also, warning Mike
Mazurka was like adding one more soldier to the bat-
tle, which Mac knew was far from over. He entered
the elevator with a spring in his step. As it began to
rise, he started reminiscing about their outing, remembering the way the sunlight had highlighted the silky
texture of Caitie's hair and thinking to himself that
he'd always been a sucker for a woman in silk, when
he heard her screams above him.

For a few endless seconds it was like watching
helplessly as someone you love dies, and then the
elevator stopped and the doors slid open. He came
out shouting her name and ran through the unlocked
door, following the sounds of her screams.

It took him several heart-stopping seconds to see
her crouched in a corner of the living room, her head
bent to her knees, her hands clutching her head as if
she were being beaten. Once, when he had still been
a cop, he'd seen a man burning to death in a car, and
his screams were not unlike what he was hearing now.
The sheer terror of the sounds cut all the way to his
soul.

Readying himself for an attack, he gave the living
room a quick, frantic glance, only to see she was
alone. In three strides he had her on her feet and in
his arms. Frantically he searched her body for signs

of injury, but he saw nothing but the terror on her face.

"Caitie! Honey...what happened?"

The moment she heard Mac's voice, her eyes rolled back in her head.

"No you don't! I need you to talk to me!" he yelled, shaking her quickly to bring her back to her senses. If there was imminent danger, he needed to be aware of the direction from which it might come.

Caitie moaned as consciousness hovered. She was trembling so hard Mac had to hold her upright, and her screams had turned to huge, gulping sobs.

He was scared to death. Something had threatened her, and he didn't know where to look.

"Caitie, talk to me. I can't help you if you don't talk."

She pointed and then covered her face, unable to look again.

Mac turned, looking without success for answers. His gaze raked the room, skipping twice across the furniture before he focused on the coffee table. And then he stared for a moment longer before he realized what he was seeing.

"Son of a holy bitch," he said, then led her to a chair by the window. "Sit here, honey. I'll be right back."

He moved across the room, coming to a stop beside the table but not touching what lay on top.

"Did it come in the mail?"

"There's no postmark," she said.

Mac's gut knotted. That meant he'd been here—at the least inside the building, at the worst outside her door.

He squatted down, looking inside the envelope without touching it and saw something white inside. He stood abruptly, took off his coat and gloves and laid them on a chair, and then opened his knife and squatted back down. Careful not to disturb anything more, he worked the small piece of paper out of the envelope and rocked back on his heels.

The message was brief.

You're next.

He stared at the rat. It had been hacked to pieces. The meaning was clear.

He flipped the note over with the tip of his knife, only to see it wasn't a piece of paper after all, but the back of a photograph—a photograph of her.

It was the head shot used on the jackets of her books, only this one had been horribly defaced.

Mac's stomach turned as he looked at the cuts on the picture, symbolically slashing her face into quarters. He'd seen enough of this during his years on the force in Atlanta to know they were dealing with a very dangerous individual.

He closed his knife as he stood, dropping it carefully into his pocket as he studied the gory message before him. Then he turned to look at Caitlin. The fear in his gut was turning to rage.

She looked at him then, her gaze on his face, searching for signs of hope, and he grunted as if he'd been punched. This wasn't personal, it was worse. Those occasional twinges of jealously he'd been having, coupled with moments of unadulterated lust, had turned into something to which he'd sworn never to succumb.

He went to her and quietly took her in his arms. Somewhere between the sound of her screams and the moment she'd almost passed out, he'd fallen in love. He hadn't meant for it to happen to him—not ever. But it had, just the same.

She curled into his embrace as if she'd been born to fit. He closed his eyes, resting his chin on the top of her head, and pulled her a little bit closer. Her voice was shaking, her words thick with unshed sobs.

"Oh, Connor."

"I know," he said, rubbing her back as he would have a child's.

"I don't want to die."

He felt cold from the inside out. Right or wrong, whether she liked it or not, she was his.

"You're not going to die. I won't let you," he muttered. "I promise you, Caitie, I will make it all right."

Nine

Kenny Leibowitz's cell phone rang just as he entered the lobby of Caitlin's apartment building. Pausing, he juggled the gift he was carrying to dig the phone out of his coat pocket.

"Leibowitz."

"It's Susan, Mr. Leibowitz. Your two o'clock appointment wants to reschedule for earlier today. You have an opening at one. Is that convenient for you?"

Kenny thought quickly, running down the places he was going after he left Caitlin and then answered.

"It's cutting it too close," he said. "See if tomorrow is okay. I won't be back in the office today, so let me know."

"Yes, sir," she said, and disconnected.

Kenny waved at Mike as he dropped the cell phone back into his pocket.

"She's expecting me," he lied, as he strode to the elevators.

"Yes, sir. I'm not surprised," the security guard said.

Kenny frowned as he entered the elevator and

pressed the button. Mazurka's comment seemed odd, and then he shrugged it off, choosing instead to admire his reflection in the mirrored walls. Smoothing his hair, he smiled cockily at himself as the car rose quietly to the top of the building. It pleased him to have clients who occupied the entire floor of a building. It pleased him even more when the clients owned the building, which Caitlin did. What would please him even more was if she would see him as more than a publicist. But he was going to have to mend fences before that happened, which was why he'd come.

The gaily wrapped package under his arm was a combination Christmas and get-well present for Caitlin. He hadn't talked to her since the day she'd been released from the hospital. The fact that they had parted under less than congenial circumstances still rankled. She wasn't his only client. She wasn't even his most lucrative client, although she was by far the wealthiest in her own right. But he'd invested too many years in getting close to the woman to give up now. Just because Connor McKee had stepped between them—even if only figuratively—there was no reason to stop his pursuit.

So when the car stopped, he shifted the present to his other arm, strode off the elevator and across the hall, then rang the bell. As he waited, he began practicing his smile and opening lines, but it was Aaron

Workman who let him in, and he never got to put them to use.

Distracted by the latest development in Caitlin's case and the police who were now in the living room, Aaron was less than congenial when he saw the publicist.

"Oh. It's you. Did Caitlin know you were coming?"

Kenny frowned as he took off his coat, handing it to Aaron to hang up as if he were hired help.

"No. I just wanted to stop by and see how she's doing. Is she in the living room?"

"Wait!" Aaron said, and grabbed him by the arm as he started to walk past him. "Don't go in there."

"Why? What's going on?"

Aaron lowered his voice. "The police are here. If you want to wait, you'll have to wait in the kitchen."

Kenny frowned. "Police? I thought they'd already taken Caitlin's statement at the hospital. Why are they here now?" When Aaron wouldn't meet his gaze, his heart skipped a beat. "Workman...has something else happened?"

Aaron shrugged.

Kenny's anger surged. It had, he knew it. And once again, it would seem he was the last to know what was happening to his own client. He grabbed his coat from Aaron's arms and then thrust the present at him instead.

"Here," he muttered. "Give this to Caitlin with my compliments, although I don't know why I bother. It's obvious that I'm continually the last person to know what the hell is happening to her, when I should be one of the first. How can I do my job when everyone keeps secrets?" He cursed beneath his breath as he thrust his arms into his coat. "Just tell Miss Bennett I was here. She has my number."

He strode out of the apartment without looking back. Once in the elevator, he called his secretary.

"Susan, have you rescheduled my two o'clock yet?"

"No, sir. His line is busy."

"Well, when you get him, tell him that one o'clock is fine after all. I assume it was to be at the same place?"

"Yes, sir. He was going to change the reservation if you could accommodate him."

"Tell him I'll be there," he said and disconnected.

His face was a study in controlled fury as he rode the elevator down in silence. He was tired of being yanked around and tired of being figuratively gutted every time he was around her. A few moments later, the car stopped and he exited, still full of righteous indignation.

Mike looked up from reading the morning paper and smiled.

"That was quick."

"Rejection usually is," he muttered, and kept on walking.

Aaron frowned as he carried the present into the living room and set it down. There was something strange about Leibowitz's behavior. It was too damned proprietorial, and as far as he knew, there was no basis for it. He reminded himself that he didn't know *everything* there was to know about Caitlin. Maybe she and Kenny once had a thing going and Caitlin had called it off. Or maybe Kenny wanted more from Caitlin than she was willing to give. Then he shrugged. He didn't know, and he didn't care. All he knew was that Kenny didn't like him. Maybe it was jealousy because he and Caitlin had more than a working relationship, or maybe Leibowitz was just homophobic. At any rate, it wasn't worth a worry, because he didn't like Leibowitz, either.

He slipped quietly into a nearby chair, noting that the detectives were still taking copious notes, especially the female, Kowalski. Neil seemed determined to connect with Caitlin on a personal level, but Aaron had seen the look on his brother's face when Neil had taken the seat closest to her. If it happened, Mac wasn't going down without a fight. Even more suspect, Aaron had seen Neil place a hand on Caitlin's shoulder in a manner meant to be comforting. Personally Aaron thought he was stepping over the line. Then he looked at Caitlin. She sat huddled in a corner of the sofa beneath her favorite afghan, her expression shell-shocked, her eyes brimming with tears. His stomach knotted. He loved Caitlin like a sister, and the threats to her life were escalating at a frightening rate. And they had no suspect—not even a glimmer of a clue as to who was behind them.

His frown deepened as he studied Caitlin's hesitant, almost breathless answers to the questions the detectives were asking. Her fragility was evident. One harsh word, an unexpected noise, and she appeared as if she would come unglued.

He glanced at the large padded envelope on the floor near the female detective's bag and shuddered. They were taking the rat to the lab, but he couldn't imagine what they expected to find. It was a dead rat. Period. Granted, it had been hacked to pieces, but still... He shuddered again. What kind of a mind would come up with something like that?

His gaze moved from Caitlin to Mac, and as he watched, he saw something he'd never seen before. Always before, the antagonism between them had been palpable. But there was a difference now. He just couldn't put his finger on what it was.

Then suddenly she looked at Mac. Whatever passed between them brought Mac rushing to her side. He sat down on the sofa beside her, and when he did, Caitlin grabbed his arm as if the simple contact would keep her afloat. Tears came to Aaron's eyes as he watched Mac smile, then carefully straighten the afghan back over her feet so they wouldn't get cold. It seemed to Aaron that Mac had, both mentally and physically, put himself between Caitlin and the rest of the world, and God help whoever tried to move him. He scooted a little closer, curious as to what was being said.

Neil leaned closer to Caitlin, briefly touching her knee to draw her wavering attention.

At his touch, Caitlin turned, her focus shifting to the detective.

"Were you talking to me?"

Neil nodded.

"I'm sorry. What did you say?"

Satisfied that, once again, he had her undivided attention, he continued. "I know this is difficult, but did you happen to see anyone lingering around the lobby when you and Mr. McKee came back from your walk?"

"Mike was the only person in the lobby."

Neil's focus shifted to Connor.

"Mr. McKee, during your outing with Miss Bennett, did you happen to notice anything out of the ordinary...like seeing the same person several times or—"

"No."

"Are you certain? Think back. Was there anyone who—"

"Detective...I used to be a cop," Mac said shortly.
"I would have known if we were being followed."
Neil's expression didn't change.

"Out of curiosity, what precinct did you work in?"
Kowalksi asked.

"Not here. I live in Atlanta. I worked for the Atlanta PD for almost fifteen years before I started my own business."

"Why did you leave the force?" Neil asked.

Mac glanced back at the detective and frowned.

"I wasn't kicked off, if that's what you're getting at," he said shortly. "Besides, what possible difference could it make what my career changes have been? You're supposed to be investigating Caitlin's background, not me."

"Just covering all the angles," Neil countered.

But Mac wasn't through making his point. He resented the familiarity in the detective's manner toward Caitlin and the condescension in his behavior toward him.

"I was at my ski lodge in Vail when I got the call that Caitlin had been hurt. Where the hell were you?"

Neil flinched, reeling from the unexpected attack as Kowalski stepped in.

"It's not personal, Mr. McKee, and with your background, you should understand that."

Mac turned a cool glance on the woman. "Detective Kowalski, isn't it?"

She nodded.

"Ever been on the receiving end of an interrogation?"

"No, but—"

"Neither had I until now, and I'll tell you flat out, it's an insult."

"I'm sorry?" Kowalski said.

"The questions you're asking...the way in which they're asked...they're insulting. Four times in four different ways, you and your partner have questioned Miss Bennett's memory and sanity. If she said she didn't see anyone, she didn't see anyone. If she doesn't remember, she doesn't remember. If someone had been following us...trust me, I would have noticed."

Then he stood and pointed to the padded envelope at Kowalski's feet.

"Some son of a bitch wasted hours of his life catching and butchering a stupid rodent just to scare an innocent woman. Personally I think he's watched too damned many horror movies. I also think he's trying to take her down, both mentally and physically, because he knows he'll never be able to rise to her level. Now, if there are no new questions, I'll show you to the door. You'll be wanting to interview the security guard, as well as check out the building. Oh...you might want to make a note of this. The security system inside Miss Bennett's apartment is impenetrable. I know, because I designed it and had it installed. So...the nut can mail all the crap he wants, but he's never going to touch her. Understand?''

"Bombs have been mailed," Neil countered.

"People who hack up rats don't have the intelligence to make a bomb. Besides, then the game would be over, wouldn't it? And the game is what it's all about."

Caitlin had been silent throughout the conversation until Mac's last statement. But she couldn't let this pass.

"Mac?"

He turned. "What, honey?"

"What do you mean, the game is what it's all about?"

He threw his hands up in frustration.

"Think about it, Caitie. I'm betting that since those letters began, he could have killed you a hundred times over, but he hasn't. He's getting off on your fear."

Caitlin's eyes widened as Mac's words sank in.

"You're right," she said softly. "You're absolutely right. I've been out on the streets alone countless times. The opportunity has been there at every turn. And still, what does he do? He writes letters. Maybe the police were right all along!" She jumped to her feet. "Maybe I was imagining things. Maybe it was an accident when I fell into the street. Maybe my only contact with this nut has been the letters after all."

Now everyone, including Aaron, was staring at Caitlin as if she'd just lost what was left of her mind.

"What are you talking about?" Mac asked.

"You said it. He writes. I write. But he only writes letters. I write books. It isn't the subject matter of my books that sets him off. It's the fact that I can create something more than fear." Then she shook her head, trying to make herself understood. "It's like this," she said, as she began to pace. "When a writer begins a new book, he or she is creating a whole world, populated with characters with a varying set of conflicts and problems. And during the story, we the writers are in control of everything. Oh...sometimes the characters take over, but that's beside the point. What I mean is...from a skewed point of view, we give life...though only to our stories. This man, whoever he is, has no power. No control. The only thing he can create is fear, and although the letters can't hurt me, I've given him control by giving into the fear." She slapped the table with the flat of her hand. "But no more! I will not be frightened anymore."

Neil stood, following Caitlin across the room. "Please, Miss Bennett, I urge you to reconsider your attitude. Complacency is dangerous. Don't bet your life on such a far-fetched theory. You don't know what a man like this might do."

"My partner is right," Kowalski said.

Mac frowned. Both detectives were pushing Caitlin pretty hard. The look on her face was somewhere between frustrated and cornered. Without thinking, he stepped between them, breaking their focus and giving Caitlin some breathing room.

"Look," he said, "right now, it's a toss-up as to what will happen next. The only sure thing is if the little bastard tries to get to Caitlin, he's going to have to come through me first."

Caitlin's gasp was soft, but Aaron heard it just the same. He started to tease his brother about his unexpected show of chivalry, then saw the look on her face. It occurred to him that there were far too many people in the room. Now it was time for the other brother to come to her aid.

"I'll see you to the door," Aaron announced, then waved to the detectives and sailed out of the room, giving them no option but to follow, and leaving Mac and Caitlin alone.

Caitlin was still in shock. She'd heard what he'd said, but the enormity of the vow was just starting to sink in. When she saw his expression and the cold anger in his eyes, her heart started to pound.

"Mac?"

The grim lines softened slightly around his mouth as he answered. "What, honey?"

"Just now, when you said he would have to come through you to get to me? You were serious, weren't you?"

His nostrils flared. "Damn right."

"But why? I've been nothing but rude to you since

you came. Until a day or two ago, I wasn't even sure that you liked me."

He took a deep breath, as if considering his answer, and then he smiled ruefully. "Until a day or two ago, I wasn't sure if I liked you, either."

"What changed?" she asked.

"Us."

"But how—"

"It's like this," he said. "I'm not too crazy about your choice of foods, but I like your honesty. I think you have more guts than any woman I've ever met, you're beautiful and sexy, and I like to kiss you." His voice softened. "I like it a whole damn lot."

Now her hands were trembling so hard she clasped them together in hopes he wouldn't notice.

"I don't see how you could think I'm sexy. My face is black-and-blue."

"And a little bit green," he said, pointing toward her eyebrow. "Especially around the stitches."

She rolled her eyes. "Such a sweet-talking man. No wonder the women flock to you."

"I'm not interested in *women,* just you."

"I don't want you to be interested," she said quietly.

Mac took a step toward her, then cupped her face with both hands.

"Why, Caitie? Why don't you want me to care?"

She looked up at him then, her heart in her eyes.

"Because it won't last. It can't. We're too different. Besides, I don't want to be hurt."

"I would never hurt you," he said softly, rubbing his thumbs across the edge of her lower lip.

A longing hit Caitlin in the pit of her stomach as his fingers grazed her lips, then her cheeks, and she shuddered, wondering, if she let this happen, how long it would take her to go up in smoke.

"You wouldn't mean to, but you would. It couldn't be any other way," she said.

"I would *never* hurt you," he repeated, and then lowered his head.

His mouth was warm, bathing her lips in tenderness; then the pressure intensified. Caitlin reached for him then, wrapping her arms around his neck and leaning into his strength. He felt the trembling in her body and the hesitance in her kiss, and ached for so much more.

Suddenly aware of footsteps, they broke apart. When Aaron came back into the room, Caitlin was on her way into the kitchen and Mac was standing at the window with his hands in his pockets.

"What did I miss?" Aaron asked.

Mac turned, his expression blank. "What did you say?"

"Don't play innocent with me," Aaron said. "I saw the look that passed between you two. I may not be straight, but I know lust when I see it."

"It's not lust," Mac said before he thought, and

then cursed beneath his breath. "Oh God, Aaron, I'm in over my head."

"What do you mean?"

"Caitlin. I do not want this to be happening."

Aaron resisted the urge to clap his hands and continued to play dumb. "I'm not following you," he said. "What don't you want to happen?"

Mac turned then, glaring pointedly at his brother's smirk.

"If I didn't know better, I would think you set this whole thing up just to get us together. You've talked about it incessantly for years."

Aaron's smirk blossomed. "Is it working?"

Mac's glare darkened. "If by working, you mean am I going out of my mind worrying about her, then yes. This needs to be over—and soon. We've got to find out who's threatening her and stop it before I do something I might regret."

The smirk faded, leaving Aaron with a worried frown.

"Stop speaking in riddles, damn it. For once, can't you just say what you mean?"

Mac sighed. "I'm attracted to Caitlin."

Aaron's eyes widened. "I fail to see the problem there," he said. "She's a wonderful woman. Why is that bad?"

"Because I don't do commitments, and you know it."

"Well...I've heard you say that for years now, but

frankly, I think that's been your safety net. Sarah has been gone for years and now you date airheads who can't even spell commitment. That precludes you having to invest anything of yourself in them." He punched Mac playfully on the arm. "Hot damn, big brother, I think it's finally happened."

"What?" Mac muttered.

"You're falling in love. Now I'm going to tell Caitlin goodbye and leave you two alone."

Mac's stomach knotted. "Come on, Aaron. Don't leave now. Stay and have dinner with us tonight."

Aaron hesitated, then shook his head. "I've got an appointment in less than an hour. As for dinner, I can't do that, either. I have a date."

Mac shoved his hands into his pockets and hunched his shoulders. "Have fun," he muttered.

"You, too," Aaron said. "And be nice, while you're at it."

"That's just it," he said. "Being nice and having fun have never been synonymous."

Aaron laughed. "It's a shame you're so damned tall."

Mac frowned. "What the hell does my height have to do with anything?"

"It's just that much farther for you to fall."

Mac sighed in defeat. "Weren't you leaving?"

"On my way," Aaron said. "Oh...just in case you want to do something to impress her, she likes—"

Mac interrupted. "It doesn't matter what she

likes,'' he said. "This isn't going to happen, no matter what you think. I'll call you if anything breaks on the case. See yourself out. I'm going to make some calls. God only knows what's happening to my business.''

"If you were so reluctant to have anything to do with Caitlin, then how come you dropped everything the moment I said she was in trouble?'' Aaron held up his hands. "Never mind. You don't have to answer. But think about it, will you? You know what they say about the fine line between love and hate. Personally I think there's been something between you two all along, but you were both too afraid to acknowledge it.''

Aaron left with a flourish. Mac heard him calling out a goodbye to Caitlin and then heard the front door slam. Seconds later, the phone rang. He waited, knowing Caitlin would answer. A few moments later, he heard footsteps coming down the hall from her office. Holding his breath, he waited. She came into the room carrying the phone.

"It's Atlanta...for you.''

"Caitlin, I—''

"I'll be working in my office for the next few hours. Order up if you get hungry.''

He'd been dismissed without fanfare. Glaring at her backside, he shoved the phone to his ear.

Ten

"How do I look?" Caitlin asked as she exited the doctor's office. The stitches were gone, and two tiny butterfly bandages had been left in their place.

Mac glanced at her eyebrow and then into her eyes. "You've been crying."

She grimaced. "It hurt when he took the stitches out. I'm fine. How does it look?"

"Fine."

"Right answer, wrong tone of voice," Caitlin said. "Just for that, you have to take me shopping."

"Shopping? I thought we were—"

"It's almost Christmas. I still don't have Aaron's gift, and I want to buy something for Uncle John and Mike."

Mac frowned. "I didn't think your father had any living relatives."

"He didn't."

"Then who's Uncle John?"

Caitlin smiled. "John Steiner. He was Daddy's chauffeur for years. After Daddy's death, he refused retirement to work for me. He isn't really a relative, but he feels like it in my heart.''

Envious of the tender way in which she spoke of the man, Mac popped off before he thought.

"So you inspire loyalty," Mac said. "I am surprised."

Caitlin waggled her finger in his face. "Strike two, mister. Now you have to buy me dinner, as well."

"Don't push your luck, honey, or you'll be the one furnishing dessert," he said, taking some measure of satisfaction in the blush on her face as he helped her into her coat. "So...where to first?"

"FAO Schwartz."

"For Aaron?"

"Are you going to argue with me the whole evening? Because if you are, you can just take yourself back to my apartment. I'll do my shopping and eat dinner by myself. It's not like it will be the first time a man has let me down."

Mac glared. She'd been perverse all day. He suspected it had something to do with the kiss. Well, he had news for her. He felt like picking a fight with someone, too. She might not know it, but she wasn't the only one floundering for footing in the turn their relationship had taken.

They reached the elevator in silence. Mac pushed the button and then, as they waited, noticed that the top two buttons of her coat were undone.

"You missed a couple," he said, and gently turned

her to face him, then did up the buttons. "It's cold out. You don't want to get sick on top of everything else now, do you?"

Suddenly the antagonism between them was gone.

"No," she said, quietly watching the concentration on his face as he fastened her coat and noticing that there were tiny gold flecks in the blue of his eyes.

"There, that's better," he said, and then the elevator opened and he ushered her on.

As they exited the office building onto the street, Mac felt Caitlin slip her hand beneath his elbow.

"Do we take a cab?" he asked.

"No. FAO Schwartz is only a few blocks away."

They started walking, sometimes moving with, sometimes against, the crowds on the street. Mac soon noticed Caitlin's unusual silence, but when he glanced down at her, he knew something was wrong. Her face was chalk-white, her eyes wide and fixed upon the face of everyone they met. It hit him then that this was Caitlin's first venture out in public since the rat had been delivered.

"Are you all right?" he asked.

She nodded without answering.

A block passed, and then a second, before they hit a red light. They reached the curb and stood within the gathering crowd, waiting for the light to change. As they did, Mac could feel her trembling. Without comment, he lifted his arm and slipped it around her shoulder in a sheltering manner, pulling her close against his side.

It was his gentleness that was her undoing. Caitlin started to cry. Softly, without sound, she turned in his arms and buried her face against his chest, her shoulders shaking with suppressed sobs.

The light changed, but they didn't move. Foot traffic parted and spilled around them like breaking waves, but he was too engrossed to notice. His first instinct was to protect her. Carefully searching the passing crowds for a sign of danger, he saw nothing that caused him alarm. When the crowd of people thinned, he pulled her back from the curb against a building, his arms tightening around her as her tears continued to flow.

"Caitie? Sweetheart?"

"I can't do this," she said. "I tried, but I can't make this work."

"Make what work?"

She lifted her head, her face streaked with tears.

"Pretend it didn't happen. I know what I told the detectives...that maybe it was an accident when I was pushed. But I don't believe it. I felt the hand in the middle of my back. Someone wants me dead, and I don't know why. I'm afraid. I'm so terribly, terribly afraid."

Mac wanted to shout; he needed to rage against the injustice of what was happening to her. But all he could do was stay close.

"Come with me," he said, grabbing her arm and bolting toward the curb just as a phalanx of taxis came speeding down the street. "I'm taking you home."

The nearest cab wheeled toward the curb as Mac hailed it. Moments later, she was inside and he was beside her, pulling her close. Still shuddering, she laid her head against his chest and closed her eyes. All the way home she kept thanking God for the man beside her, because she couldn't do this by herself.

A short while later they entered the penthouse. Mac punched in the security code, disarming the alarm before it was activated, then helped her out of her coat.

"Do you want to lie down? Are you hungry? I can make you something to eat."

She turned, her eyes still glimmering with unshed tears, and put her arms around his neck. She saw the shock on his face and knew what she was about to do would make it worse.

"You asked me what I want. I want you to make love to me. I'm so tired of being afraid. I need to remember what it's like to know joy."

"Caitie...sweetheart...that won't—"

"Mac, for God's sake, I know you've made love with women for less reason. Am I so awful that you can't even sum up enough—"

He groaned. Seconds later, he lifted her off her feet and into his arms.

"That's just the problem. I have been summoning up

passion for you for some time now. What I want and what we should do are two entirely different things. I don't just want to make love to you. It would be my pleasure. But it will change everything between us."

"It doesn't have to," she mumbled.

"But it will," he said softly, then lowered his head and kissed her tearstained cheeks.

Caitie shuddered on a sob. "I just need to feel something besides despair."

Mac looked at her then, at the windblown tangles in her hair and her slightly swollen lips. At the tiny adhesive strips over her eyebrow and the very faint bruising still evident on one cheek. Never had a woman been as desirable to him, and never had it seemed so wrong. But he didn't have it in him to deny her—not now. Not after he'd seen her cry.

"Then come to bed with me, love. It would be my pleasure to give you joy."

He carried her down the hall and into her bedroom, then set her on her feet. Without speaking, he undressed himself first, instinctively giving her time to change her mind. But by the time he was down to his slacks, she was already minus her shoes and sweater.

"Wait, baby...let me," he said, and gently removed the rest of her clothes, then pulled back the covers and laid her on the bed.

Caitlin's heart was pounding, her skin tingling and flushed. His body was lean and muscular, his erection impossible to ignore. She reached for him, encircling him as he came down to her. She heard him groan, then felt the warmth of his breath on her face. After that, everything became a blur: Mac's hands, his mouth, the weight of his body pressing her deep into the mattress, then the joining, filling not only her body, but fulfilling his promise.

The joy...the joy.

Caitlin dozed in the shelter of Mac's embrace, her dark hair in tangles on his shoulder, her ear against his chest while he lay wide-eyed and stunned, staring up at the ceiling. He'd never considered himself prophetic, but he was about to change his mind. This *had* more than changed everything. It had changed *him*. He'd never wanted just one woman before—at least, never for long. But the thought of ever making love to anyone else felt like a betrayal, and the idea of giving her up to another man was obscene.

She jerked in her sleep, and he tightened his hold. There was a slight frown between her eyebrows and a tremble in her lower lip. He knew she was dreaming, and God only knew what horror was playing out in her head.

"Shh," he said softly. "I'm here."

At the sound of his voice, the tension in her muscles began to lessen.

"You're safe," he said softly. "You're safe."

She sighed as she rolled, curving her backside

against him as one arm dangled off the side of the bed.

He turned then, spooning himself against her body and pulling the covers up over them both. She was warm and pliant, and his heart ached for her vulnerability. He slid his arm across her body and held her close, letting his hand rest just beneath the weight of her breasts. He closed his eyes. He felt privileged that she'd asked him to make love to her and guilty that he'd given in to her plea. She'd trusted him enough to let him into her home. Then she'd let him into her bed. Now there was something else—something she didn't know—and he wasn't sure when, or even if, he would ever tell her. But while he was playing the gallant bodyguard, he'd let down his guard and let her into his heart.

Buddy had been watching the clock for almost an hour. The moment it ticked over to six o'clock, he got up from his desk and headed for the door. Every leash he had on his emotions was coming undone, and he needed to be away from his colleagues before it showed.

On his more rational days, he accepted that learned experiences naturally became a part of the human psyche. But now there were far more days when rationality was not a part of Buddy's world. The more he fixated on Caitlin Bennett, the more scattered his mind became. At work, he was the man in charge.

People came to him to fix their problems. And most of the time he did. No one knew how much he struggled to remain calm and organized. He was beyond suspicion in every way, yet when he left the job, he left sanity behind.

Out on the street, sounds were magnified, colors bled and ran one into the other like a kaleidoscope. He saw people's mouths moving and knew they were talking, but the words echoed in his head, blurring consonants and vowels until he couldn't distinguish one from the other.

In a panic, his stride lengthened until he was running for the subway. Once on board, he slid into a seat and closed his eyes, letting his head loll back against the window. Someone slid into the seat beside him, roughly jostling his arm as the car lurched into motion. He couldn't bring himself to look for fear he would come undone. When he heard his stop being called, he came upright as if he'd been catapulted from the seat, pushing and shoving his way out of the car. He moved with the crowd as it flowed upward toward the streets. Moments later he emerged from the belly of the city, taking short, jerky breaths, like a newborn baby testing the world into which he'd been thrust.

"Hey, mister, step aside please," someone said.

"Sorry," Buddy mumbled. He shoved his hands into his pockets, lowered his head against the wind and started walking.

By the time he reached his apartment, he was on the verge of screaming. Thrusting his key into the lock with shaking hands, he was inside within seconds. Slamming and locking the door behind him, he moved through the rooms; ignoring dust and dirty dishes, he aimed for the bedroom. As he entered, he hit the light switch with the flat of his hand, illuminating the true insanity. Caitlin was everywhere in here. On walls, on the ceiling, bits and pieces of her had even been strewn on the floor. Only his bed remained unsullied by her presence. He shed his coat and gloves, letting them drop to the floor where he stood. Next came his shoes, then his clothes, and finally he stood naked. Without a care for the pile of garments he'd just shed, he crawled into bed and pulled the covers up over his head. Sleep. He just needed to sleep. After that, everything would be okay.

"Buddy... Buddy... I can't see you."
"I'm here, Mother...right beside your bed."
"Make it stop, Buddy. You have to make it stop."
Buddy covered his ears, unable to hear her ask it again. Every day for the last month she had begged him to take away her pain. The cancer she'd been battling had finally gotten the upper hand. The tumors were huge knots beneath her flesh, their poison infiltrating vital organs—sucking the strength from her body with every breath she took. Short of putting a gun to her head, there was nothing left to do but wait

*for her to die. And oh God...as much as he loved her,
he prayed for it to happen.*

*The guilt of thinking that was killing him, too, only
by degrees. She was the only person who'd ever loved
him—had sacrificed many times during her life so that
he might have the superficial luxuries that his school-
mates had—and now he didn't have the guts to grant
her dying wish? How could this be? How could he
be so weak?*

She coughed and then moaned.

*He stared at her face, holding his breath and pray-
ing she didn't take another. But, like everything else
in his life, his prayer wasn't answered.*

*She gasped, her fingers curling into clawlike fists
upon the sheets.*

*He laid his head down on the side of the bed and
closed his eyes.*

*"Please," he begged. "Please, God, no more. She
can't take any more...and neither can I."*

"Sir...is there anything I can get you?"

*He looked up to see a nurse standing by his
mother's bed. He hadn't heard her come in.*

"No...no...there's nothing I need."

*The nurse smiled gently and then patted his
mother's arm.*

"This isn't one of her better days, is it?"

*Better days? He looked at her, wondering why peo-
ple didn't just come out and say it. For God's sake,*

she was dying. Why couldn't they just say, "Your mother is dying"?

"She's in pain," he said.

"Doctor is giving her the maximum dosage."

"I know."

The nurse sighed and then lowered her voice.

"She doesn't have long, you know."

Another minute is too long, he thought, but he didn't say it aloud.

"Ring if you need me," she said, and left the room.

His mother moaned. He stood abruptly and strode to the window, unable to look upon the colorless, wasting flesh.

"Buddy is Momma's good boy."

Her words hit him like a knife in the back. He looked past the windows into the night beyond the hospital walls. It was starting to snow. He hated the cold. When spring came he would—

His thoughts stopped. When spring came, she would be locked in some casket and six feet under. His mother's springs had come and gone. This was the winter of her life—her last winter—and it would be over none too soon for him.

"I hurt, Buddy. Kiss away the hurts."

He turned then, his face wreathed in torment, and walked to the side of her bed. The scent of death was all around her. He leaned down, ashamed to be holding his breath as he placed a quick, gentle kiss on her cheek.

Even though she'd been out of her head for more than a week, he would have sworn at that moment she knew it was him. At the touch of his lips, her thrashing stopped, her breathing slowed, as the muscles in her body relaxed.

He sighed. "I love you, Mother."

Her eyes opened suddenly, startling him to the point that he took a step back.

"The pain...take away the pain."

"I can't," he whispered. "You can't ask that of me."

She blinked, and as she did, tears rolled from the corners of her eyes.

"My son."

"Yes, I'm your son."

"Mind your momma," she mumbled.

It came to him then, not in a blinding flash of clarity, but as a slow and final acceptance that this was the last thing he could do for her. Everything inside him began to shut down as he took a tissue from the packet at her bedside and made a small wad of it in his hands.

"Close your eyes," he said softly, and as she did, he put the tissue against her nostrils, taking great care not to put pressure on anything that might later show a bruise. Then he covered her mouth with his hand and waited for it all to stop.

She bucked once beneath his hand, which surprised him. He'd expected her to lie still and die. But as he watched her struggling to breathe, he supposed it was just the body's instinct for survival that made it happen, because he was only doing what she'd asked.

Her tiny little fingers curled around his wrist, the brittle nails digging deep into the flesh, and still he stood his ground, stifling her intake of oxygen.

Suddenly it was over. Her fingers slid off his arm and onto the bed. He stuffed the tissue into his pocket, took one quick look at the heart monitor that had flatlined, and made a run for the door.

"Nurse! Nurse!" he called, as he dashed into the hall. "Come quick. Mother isn't breathing."

Buddy woke abruptly, gasping for breath, only to stare around the room in disbelief. It took several seconds for him to realize he was not in his mother's hospital room and that she'd been dead for several years. He swung his legs out of bed and strode to the window. Feathery white flakes drifted past the glass on their way to the ground.

Hell and damnation, it was still snowing. God, but he hated the cold. And the snow. He hated the snow. There had been snow everywhere on the day of his mother's funeral.

His stomach growled as he began to dress; then he went to the kitchen for something to eat.

The refrigerator was quite literally bare. After a quick search of the cabinets, he realized that if he wanted to eat, it was either order in or go out. Suddenly the thought of spending another night alone in this place seemed too much to bear. Hurrying back into the bedroom, he began to dress to go out. Out of curiosity, he turned on the surveillance device and listened to a bit of the tape that was recording, but he heard nothing and supposed they were asleep. He turned off the speakers and bent down to pull on his boots. When he had time, he would listen to all the tapes. Right now, he wanted to eat.

Once he paused and cocked his head, thinking he heard something scratching in the wall, and then he smiled, remembering. It wasn't the rat, that was for damn sure. He'd sent that to dear Caitlin—in pieces, of course, but he'd sent it just the same. It seemed only fitting, since he considered her the rat in the woodpile of his life.

Only after he exited the building did he think to look at the time. It was almost midnight. Maybe, if he hurried, he could make Dubai's Market before it closed. He started to jog.

Ten blocks later, he turned the corner and breathed a sigh of relief. The lights were still on. He could already taste the pastrami on rye. But to his dismay, when he was still about half a block from the deli, he saw the lights go out. A woman was coming out of the door, her back to the street as he started to run.

"Wait!" he yelled. "Wait!"

Angela Dubai spun, a look of fear flashing across

her face as she saw a man running toward her in the dark.

Fumbling for her keys, she turned in a panic toward the door she'd just locked, seeking safety inside the store. Her heart was hammering against her eardrums as his footsteps came closer and closer. Suddenly the lock turned and she dashed inside, but before she could shut the door behind her, she felt his hand upon her shoulder. She screamed as she spun, flailing out at him with her fists.

He hit her without thinking, and when she slid to the floor, the keys loose in her hand, he felt surprise at seeing her lying there.

"Stupid bitch. All I wanted was some food."

He picked up the keys and locked the door behind him.

She lay limp at his feet, her neck turned at a crazy angle, and he knew that she was dead.

"It's your own fault," he muttered, and began dragging her down the center aisle away from sight.

As he did, the glow from a night-light fell on her face. He'd been to the market countless times before. He knew who she was. The owner's daughter. Her name was Angie or Agnes, something like that. Dark shoulder-length hair fell out from beneath the kerchief she'd tied around her head. But as he looked at her, fresh from his nightmare, he saw Caitlin instead.

"Caitlin? Caitlin? Why are you here? I keep killing you. Why won't you stay dead?"

In a sudden fit of rage, he pulled out his knife and slashed the woman's face. Without a heart to pump it, blood simply oozed.

"All I wanted was something to eat," he said, then wiped his knife on her coat and put it back into his pocket as if nothing had happened.

Well aware of the layout of the store, he helped himself to some bread and meat and a six-pack of beer. With her keys in his hand, he locked the door behind him as he left. Several blocks over, he tossed them down a storm drain and kept on walking.

Caitlin woke with a gasp, her eyes wide with fright, only to find herself wrapped in Mac's embrace. In that moment, everything that had transpired before came flooding back—from her wanton request to the abandon with which she'd taken him to her bed. Not wanting to wake him and face what she'd done, she stilled, her mind still in a whirl.

She didn't regret what had happened. Regret for something that wonderful would have been a lie. But she'd used it—and him—in an effort to distract herself from the truth. That wasn't fair—to him or to her. What had happened between them tonight meant nothing to him, of that she was sure. But it had opened her eyes to a whole new aspect of herself. All these years she'd been lying to herself. She didn't disapprove of Aaron's brother. On the contrary. She was smitten. Lord only knew how long the feelings had been there. Probably from the start.

Subconsciously she'd substituted disapproval for desire. She wasn't his type. She would have to get over it. But how, when he had set himself up as her bodyguard?

Darn Aaron's interfering hide. It was all his fault Mac was here. She could just as easily have hired a professional. Lord knows she had the money. And, unless something drastic happened, this stalker situation could go on indefinitely. Torn between the memories of their passion and her predicament, her thoughts raced, discarding scenario after scenario.

She glanced at the clock. It was just after two in the morning. She would think about it some more after she'd gotten some rest, so she turned in Mac's arms, snuggling herself close against his chest and taking comfort in his presence—even though she knew it couldn't last. And she dreamed.

"But, Daddy, Charlie is a nice boy. Why can't I go out with him?"

Caitlin held her breath, waiting for her father's response and praying it would be different this time.

Devlin Bennett looked up from his desk, distracted by his daughter's interruption. He had to get these papers ready before the hour was over or he wouldn't be ready for his conference call.

"Look, Caitlin, I told you why last week, and my

answer is still the same. He's just not our sort. Surely
you understand?''

Caitlin's eyes filled with tears, but she wouldn't cry.
Devlin hated it when she cried, and she needed his
good favor to win her case. If he didn't let her go to
the prom with Charlie, she was just going to die.

''His father owns his own insurance company.''

Devlin's chin jutted angrily. ''And it's going into
bankruptcy.''

Caitlin's cheeks suddenly blazed with color.

''How do you know that?''

Devlin shrugged. ''I made a few calls. I will not
have my daughter associated with failure.''

Caitlin's fingers curled into fists. ''It isn't Charlie
who's failing, Daddy. He's at the top of his class.''

Devlin glared. ''Don't mince words with me, Cait-
lin. I've given you my decision.''

Caitlin stood without moving, staring blindly at the
man who was her father. She loved him, but at the
same time, she often resented him. His obsession with
social status and perfection was impossible to live up
to.

''I'm busy,'' Devlin said shortly.

Caitlin flinched as if she's been struck, then lifted
her chin.

''Then I'll leave you to the important things in your
life,'' she said, and hurried out of the room.

The moment she was gone, Devlin knew he'd done
the wrong thing, but before he could call her back,

the phone began to ring. Torn between fatherly duties and the desire to close another big deal, his choice was easily made as he picked up the receiver.

Caitlin ran through the rooms of her father's house, blind to the opulence of the decor. By the time she'd reached her bedroom, she was numb. Throwing herself onto her bed, she began to sob. Nothing was ever good enough for her father—not even her. The only thing he really loved was money—and power. Always the power.

She cried until her head was throbbing and her eyes were almost swollen shut. Twice the housekeeper knocked on her door, and both times she called out for her to go away. There was nothing to be said that would take away the pain in Caitlin's heart now, but she knew that someday things would be different. One day she would be grown, and then no one would tall her what to do. She would find someone who loved her for herself and not for Devlin Bennett's money. They would get married and have babies, and she would never be alone again.

Caitlin woke with a start to find her cheeks wet with tears. She rolled over on her back and covered her face with her hands. It had been years since she'd thought of that incident. So why the heartache? Why the tears?

As she lay there, she became aware of the sound

of running water in her bathroom and suddenly re-membered.

Mac!

They'd made love. And oh, what love they'd made! Tenderness coupled with a heat that had seared her very soul. She felt cleansed and, at the same time, filled with a joy she'd never known.

Was this the way it happened? Falling in love? Being blindsided by a man she thought she hated? But what did she feel for him—apart from an overwhelming gratefulness that he hadn't turned her away? Was she falling in love with Connor McKee, or was what they'd shared last night simply a byproduct of the tension between them?

She rolled over onto her side and closed her eyes, savoring the memories of last night. She didn't know what was truth, but she knew how she felt. Connor had made her feel things she'd never felt before. He'd made her feel safe, and he's given her joy. Oh God, if only he was the staying kind.

Eleven

The answer to her problems came in the middle of her morning shower. And it was so simple, she didn't know why she hadn't thought of it sooner. Of course it was going to pose a risk to her personally, but she was already at risk. If she was right and it flushed the stalker out of the shadows, it would be worth a few more anxious hours.

Anxious now to put her plan into motion, she got out of the shower and quickly dried and dressed. With no more fussing than running a comb through her wet hair, she slipped into her robe and a pair of warm socks and shoes, and headed for a phone.

"Breakfast is almost ready," Mac called.

"I'm going to make a call and then I'll be right there," Caitlin answered, as she entered her office.

It was only after the phone began to ring that she looked at the time and realized Kenny wouldn't be in his office for at least another hour. Unwilling to wait to set things in motion, she hung up before the answering machine came on and dialed his home phone instead. He answered on the third ring, and she knew she'd interrupted his breakfast from the chewing sounds in her ear.

"Kenny, it's me, Caitlin."

Instead of his usual welcoming hello, there was a moment of silence. She sighed. He was pissed at her, and with good reason.

"Thank you for the chocolates you brought the other day."

She heard him grunt.

"You know they're my favorite," she said.

"You're welcome," he muttered. "Is there something you need?"

"Yes, but you have to swear to keep it a secret."

Kenny swallowed quickly, almost choking as he did. A secret? Just between them? He liked that. He liked that a lot.

"What kind of a secret?"

Caitlin glanced over her shoulder, making sure she was still alone, and then lowered her voice.

"You know about the letters I've been receiving and the police and everything?"

"Barely," he drawled.

"Okay, I deserve that," she said. "But don't quit on me now, Kenny. It's not like there was anything you could have done, and at first I didn't want everyone to know."

"I'm not everyone," he muttered.

"I know. I know. It was cowardly of me, but I think I didn't tell anyone because, if no one else knew, then I could pretend it wasn't happening. Only things have gotten worse. The day you came...when the police were here..."

"Yes?"

"He had sent something else in the mail... something awful."

Now Kenny was getting interested.

"What?" he asked.

"A rat...chopped into pieces, along with a picture of me and a note that said I was next."

"Caitlin! I had no idea it was this bad. I'm sorry...so sorry."

"And that's not all. Hudson House has been receiving threats from him, too, including a bomb threat. I was scared, Kenny. Can you understand that?"

She heard him sigh and knew he had relented.

"Yes, oddly enough, that makes a strange sort of sense. So how can I help?"

"I want it leaked to the papers that I'm being stalked by a crazed fan. I want the media to know that I was hospitalized due to a bungled attempt at murder."

Kenny's voice rose an octave in shock. "Why?"

"Because then they will call for interviews and—"

"But you don't like giving interviews. You're always on me for scheduling too many. Surely you aren't going to use this to sell more books? That doesn't sound like the Caitlin I know." Then he chuckled. "It sounds more like me."

Caitlin smiled. "I'm not responding to that," she said. "Anyway, the reason I want them to know, is that when they ask me for a statement, I'm going to humiliate that psycho."

"What if it sets him off? What if he comes after you big time?"

"Then I'll have succeeded, won't I? I'm sick and tired of hiding. I want this over."

"Good God, Caitlin, I will not be a part of this. What if he kills you? I couldn't live with myself."

"But, Kenny, he's already tried. Frankly I don't think I can live with myself unless I start to fight back."

There was another, longer, moment of silence, and then a sigh. Caitlin chewed her lower lip, awaiting his decision.

"Kenny?"

"All right, all right. But we've got to be careful. Leave it to me. I'll make a couple of calls. It will be all over the news before night, so get ready."

"Thanks, Kenny. I owe you."

"Just make sure you stay alive to pay up," he muttered. "Are you going to tell the Hulk what you're doing?"

"Hulk? Who's the Hulk?"

"That gladiator clone who seems to have attached

himself to your side like the wart that he is. Are you
going to tell him?''

"No, but he'll find out eventually. Now I've got to
go. Just do your thing for me, please. I'll be in
touch.''

"Your wish is my command,'' he drawled and disconnected with a click.

Caitlin sighed. It was going to take more than a
thank-you before he got over being miffed, but she
couldn't let it bother her. She'd done what she set out
to do.

Her steps were light as she headed for the kitchen.
She was scared, but, in a way, she was also exhila-
rated at being back in control. She wasn't Devlin Bennett's daughter for nothing. She should be able to
flush one sick bastard from the wormwood that he'd
made of her life.

Mac turned as she came into the kitchen.

"You look pleased with yourself," he said.

She flashed him a smile. "Thanks to you," she said
shyly, then gave him a kiss on the cheek before she
noticed what he was cooking. "Yum, pancakes."

Mac grinned, relieved that she wasn't embarrassed
by what she'd initiated last night.

"Yes, pancakes. As for last night, believe me, it
was all my pleasure."

"Not all," she said, then arched an eyebrow and
gave him a serious once-over.

A pleased grin replaced the frown. "Well, in that case, here, take all the pancakes you want."

She laughed.

They ate in leisure, a little uncomfortable with the change in their relationship, but willing to look for common ground. Caitlin savored the momentary peace, knowing that by nightfall, everything would change. And in a way, that made her sad. Connor McKee wasn't the settling down kind, but if he was...and if he were so inclined, she might let herself fall in love with him.

"Fourteen days until Christmas and we've got this on our plate," Sal Amato said as he ducked under the crime scene tape and headed for the small store where the latest victim had been found.

"Yeah, and nothing much to go with it," Paulie countered.

"Don't remind me," Sal said, looking beyond the uniformed officers to the woman coming out of the building. "Hey, Booker, wait up a second."

The young forensic pathologist paused on her way to her car.

"You boys aren't doing your part," she said. "By my count, this is the third vic by the same perp."

"Another voice heard," Sal muttered. "And you just answered my question."

"As to what?" Angela Booker asked.

"If this was the same perp. I take it she was cut the same way?"

"Oh, yes, and dead before he cut her. Only this one wasn't raped."

Sal's eyes widened in surprise. "You're sure?"

"Her clothes hadn't been removed, and I don't think she'd been raped and dressed again. At least, that's not been the M.O. I'll know more after I get her back to the lab."

"Do you think it's a copycat?"

Angela shrugged. "You're the detectives, but how could it be? To my knowledge, the papers haven't picked up on the fact that you've got yourself a serial killer, so who would know to do this except the man himself?"

"Yeah, right," Sal said, stomping his feet to keep them warm. "Send me a copy of your report as soon as it's finished, okay?"

"You got it," she said, and headed toward her car.

Sal glanced at Paulie. "Let's go get this over with," he said.

They entered the building, eyeing the set-up of the store as well as the old man who was crying at the back of the room.

"Who's he?" Sal asked the uniformed officer at the door.

"The owner. His name is Ari Dubai. He found the body this morning when he came to open up. She's his daughter."

"What's her name?" Sal asked.

"Angela Dubai."

Sal nodded. "Where's the body?"

"Aisle three," the officer said.

Bracing themselves for what they knew would be another grisly scene, the two detectives rounded the corner of the aisle just as two men from the coroner's office were bagging the body.

"Hey, wait a minute, guys. Let me have a look."

"It ain't pretty," one of them muttered.

"Death never is," Sal said, and unzipped the top of the body bag just enough to see the woman's face. Like the others, it had been slashed and quartered. "Son of a bitch," he mumbled and unzipped the bag further, checking Angela Booker's read on the rape aspect. The woman's clothing was rumpled and blood-soaked, but it didn't appear to have been removed.

"Paulie?"

Sal's partner nodded. "Yeah, it looks the same to me."

Sal zipped the bag and nodded to the men.

"She's all yours," he said. "Take good care of her."

"Let's go talk to her father," Paulie said. "Maybe we'll get lucky."

The old man was sitting in a chair, his shoulders bent, his hands covering his face.

Sal touched the man on the back. "Mr. Dubai?"

The old man looked up.

"I'm Detective Amato, and this is my partner, Detective Hahn. We'd like to ask you some questions."

Ari Dubai's eyes welled, his chin quivering as he spoke. "I would like to ask some questions, too. I heard an officer say that other women have died like my Angela."

Sal frowned. Damned mouthy street cops. Why couldn't they have kept their comments to themselves?

"Well, not exactly. Until we know more from the lab, we can't be sure if—"

"There were other women who were cut like my daughter?"

Sal sighed. He couldn't lie—not to this man.

"Yes."

"How many?"

"Two, sir, but—"

The old man stood. "We saw nothing in the papers."

"We didn't want to alarm the citizens until we were—"

"Had we known this danger existed, I would never have allowed my daughter to close the store alone." He straightened, his dark eyes flashing with anger and pain. "I am old, but I am still a man." Then his voice broke. "A parent should not outlive a child. It isn't right. It just isn't right."

"No, sir," Sal said. "And I'm sorry, but I need to ask you some questions."

The old man shuddered, then dropped back into the chair.

"When did you last talk to your daughter?"

"Last night, as she was closing the store. It would have been around midnight. We've been staying open later because of the holidays, you know."

"Yes, sir. So you spoke to her then?"

"Yes. She said she was locking up. That she'd put the daily deposit in the safe and that she would see me in the morning."

"She doesn't live with you?"

"No. She has...had...her own place about five blocks from here."

"Have you had time to check and see if anything is missing? Has the safe been tampered with?"

"The safe is fine. The meat case was open, but that was all." His voice cracked again. "Except for my baby...my poor baby."

Sal glanced at Paulie and then back at the old man. "The meat case?"

The old man drew a shuddering breath.

"Yes, it has sliding doors.... One of them was open. I can't believe that Angela forgot to shut it. All the meat has spoiled. She wouldn't do a thing like that." And then he started to cry. "Why do I care? Spoiled meat is nothing. My daughter is no more."

Paulie looked at Sal and then pointed upward with

his chin. Sal's gaze followed, his eyes widening in sudden understanding.

"Sir? You have a security camera on the premises?"

"Yes, but just the one in front is working. I've been meaning to call and get this one fixed, but what with the holidays and all, I haven't had time."

"But you do have one in operation?"

The old man nodded. "The one near the front door."

"May we have the tape? Maybe there's something on it that will help us catch your daughter's killer."

"Yes, yes," he said. "Anything that would catch this terrible fiend." He headed for the back room, returning moments later carrying a video cassette. "This is the one. The time and date show up at the bottom of the picture when you view it."

"Thank you, Mr. Dubai. You've been most helpful."

The old man grabbed Sal by the wrist as they started to leave.

"You catch this man. You catch him fast...before he does this to another woman."

"Yes, sir. We're trying."

Sal Amato left the old man in the back of the store and wished he could leave his guilt there with him.

"This shouldn't have happened," he muttered.

"None of it should have," Paulie said. "But it's not our fault they died."

"No, but it becomes our fault when he keeps killing and we don't stop him."

"Maybe the tape will give us our first break."

"Yeah, maybe," Sal said. "God knows we need one."

"Here come Neil and Kowalski," Paulie said, pointing toward the street.

"Good. Lieutenant said to utilize all our help in stopping this psycho. They can check out the neighborhood."

"Heard you got another one?" J.R. said as he and Trudy met up with Amato and Hahn.

"Yeah, we think so," Sal said.

"Think? Is this one different?" Trudy Kowalski asked.

"She was cut up like the other two victims, but Booker doesn't think she was raped."

Trudy shrugged. "So the bastard wasn't in the mood. Half the time, neither is my old man."

They grinned. It was common knowledge that Trudy's husband, Mick, was too fond of his liquor.

"So, you two here to gawk or help?" Sal asked.

"Name it," J.R. said.

"Check the adjacent buildings. See if anyone saw or heard anything suspicious around midnight."

"That's the time of death?"

"Maybe," Sal said. "Just see what you can come up with."

"Will do," Neil said, and then pointed to the video Sal was holding. "What do you have there?"

Sal grinned. "They had one functioning security camera," he said. "Maybe we got lucky."

J.R. stared at the video and then back up at Sal.

"That would be a nice change, wouldn't it? The woman ran out of luck last night, but maybe this is your lucky day."

Sal grimaced. "One can only hope. See you back at headquarters."

Neil and Kowalksi nodded as they walked off, spoke a few moments to each other and then split up to canvass the neighborhood.

"He's not so bad," Paulie said as they started toward their car.

"Who?" Sal asked.

"Neil."

"Oh hell, I never said he was bad. I just don't like his hair."

Paulie grinned. "And the fact that you have none? Good thing I'm only five foot four or I'd be on your shit list, too."

Sal grinned back. "Naw. You're too ugly to be jealous of."

Paulie laughed as he got in the car.

Moments later they were on their way back to headquarters, anxious to view the tape. Traffic was heavy, delaying their return. They arrived to find headquarters in an uproar. The power had failed just long enough for all the computers to go down. Booking had come to a standstill, and two panel trucks from the power company were parked out in front of the building.

"I wonder what the hell's going on here?" Sal said as he parked and got out.

"Who knows," Paulie said, then waved down another detective who was just getting into his car. "Hey, Murphy, what's going on?"

"Power went out," he said. "It's back on now, but it's a mess in there. The computers got screwed, and about half a dozen perps in booking tried to escape when the lights went out."

"I thought we had a backup generator to prevent this kind of thing from happening?"

The detective grinned. "Yeah, well, you and the lieutenant thought the same thing. He's pissed all to hell, and someone's ass is gonna be grass for this. If you're going in to see him, you'd better be wearing a smile. He is not a happy man."

Sal looked at Paulie and patted the video in his pocket.

"Maybe we got something to put the smile back on his face."

"And maybe we don't," Paulie said. "Wait'll we see what we got before we start crowing."

"Yeah. Good idea."

They hurried inside, anxious to get out of the cold. True to Murphy's word, headquarters was in chaos.

Between the repairmen and the regular day-to-day traffic between criminals, cops and victims, it was a mess.

Outside the lieutenant's office, they paused; then, at Amato's nod, Paulie knocked.

"What?"

The bellow came from within. They rolled their eyes at each other and then walked in.

"Lieutenant, we just came from the crime scene. The M.E.'s office is pretty sure the victim down at that market was slashed by the same person who killed the Dorian woman and the Polanski woman."

Del Franconi's morning had been too hectic for him to spare time on manners. "What the hell does 'pretty sure' mean?"

"They don't think this victim had been raped."

Franconi slapped the flat of his hand on his desk as he got out of his chair.

"I don't want guesses, damn it. I want answers. If the M.E.'s right, this is the killer's third victim. That means serial killer, and we all know what kind of crap that's going to bring. Copycats. Goddamn it, I hate copycat killers. And I hate all the sickos who come out of the woodwork afterward so they can confess to someone else's crimes because they haven't got the guts to confess, even to themselves, as to the guilt of their own lives!" Franconi yelled. Then, bracing his hands on the top of his desk, he leaned forward, his voice just below a shout. "I'm going to have to go to the papers on this, and I don't have a goddamned thing to tell them except that women are dying on our watch and we don't know why.''

Amato pulled the video out of his coat pocket and handed it across the desk to his lieutenant.

"Maybe this will help," he said.

"What is that?" Franconi asked.

"The security tape from the market where the last victim was found.''

Franconi snatched it from Amato. "Why didn't you say something sooner?'' he said, and abruptly strode across the room to his television set.

Amato and Hahn watched, metaphorically crossing their fingers, as Franconi turned on his television and VCR, then inserted the tape.

"Pull up a chair and let's see what we've got,'' Franconi ordered.

They stared at the blank screen, all but holding their breaths as the lieutenant pressed Play. All three of them leaned forward, their elbows on their knees, their gazes fixed.

An hour and a half later, they were still watching when Neil and Kowalski knocked on the door and then entered.

"Is that the tape from the market?" Neil asked.

"Yeah, come in and shut the door,'' Franconi said.

J.R. and Trudy entered.

"Anything we can use?'' Trudy asked.

"Not so far,'' Sal said, then pointed to the bottom

of the screen. "But it's almost closing time. See...
11:45 p.m."

Neil took a seat on the corner of the lieutenant's
desk while his partner took the only other chair.

"M.E. said the incident happened sometime around
midnight or soon after, right?" he asked.

"Right," Sal said. "See, she's starting to lock up.
She took the money out of the till and bagged it. Now
she disappears out of camera range."

"Was any money missing?" Kowalski asked.

Sal shook his head. "No. It was in the safe when
her father came to open up this morning."

"Look," Paulie said. "She's wiping off the glass
on the meat counter. The door is closed there, but
didn't her father say someone left it open?"

Sal frowned. "Yeah, you're right. He did say that.
But it's closed. And see...she's walking away." His
frown deepened. "That doesn't make sense."

"Now she's getting her coat and gloves. She's putting a wallet into her coat pocket and...what's she
doing there, can you tell? Oh...she's going for the
phone."

Again Paulie filled in the blanks. "Her old man
said she called him right before she left, remember?
That must be what she's doing now."

Sal pointed. "Now she's going toward the front
door. Can't see her face, just the back of her head.
They need to reposition that damned camera toward
the door instead of the cash register."

"Not necessarily," Franconi said. "If you want to catch a thief, you catch him in the act, and that's usually where the money is kept, which would be the cash register."

"I know," Sal muttered. "But it's not going to help our case if we can't see the door."

"It's not over yet," Franconi said.

They watched as she turned out the main lights, leaving only the strategically placed night-lights burning. Moments later, there was nothing to see but aisles and canned goods and the quick glare from the lights of a passing car.

Suddenly the woman reappeared, her mouth open in a scream they couldn't hear. Trudy gasped as a man's hand suddenly appeared on camera, grabbing and pulling her by the back of the coat collar. Her face was in full view as he yanked her around. Then she started to hit him, flailing her arms and fists.

"Jesus," she muttered. "She must have been scared out of her wits."

"Look," Paulie said. "There he is. There he is!"

They all stared, praying that the man in the picture would turn around.

"Turn around, you sick bastard," Sal muttered. "Come on...turn your sorry self around."

But he didn't. All they could see was the back of his head and then his shoulders. Nothing unusual about him. Nothing that would separate him from the millions of men who lived in the city.

They saw the blow that he struck. Saw the woman they knew to be Angela Dubai fall lifelessly to the floor, then witnessed him dragging her around the corner between aisles and out of view of the camera.

"No," Sal said. "That can't be it!"

They watched in horror, knowing what must be happening on the other side of the aisle of canned goods.

A minute passed, then a second and a third. Just when they thought it was over, he passed between the camera and an aisle.

"We still can't see his face," Sal moaned. "Son of a bitch, we still can't see his face."

"Wait!" Trudy cried. "Back up the tape. He's carrying something."

Franconi hit Rewind and then Play again. They watched as the man reappeared.

"There." She pointed.

The lieutenant hit Pause.

They stared.

Paulie jumped to his feet, startling them all.

"The meat counter," he said. "It was him. The son-of-a-bitch got himself something to eat. That's a loaf of bread in one hand, and see that little bit of white under his arm? I'll lay odds he wrapped himself up some meat."

The lieutenant hit Play.

"You're right, Hahn, and look, in the other hand. Isn't that a six-pack?"

Neil stood up from the desk, his expression blank and fixed.

"He killed her and got something to eat...or did he go to get something to eat and then kill her as an afterthought?"

They all looked at him as if he'd gone mad.

"What are you getting at?" Lieutenant Franconi asked.

"Sal said she wasn't raped, right?"

Amato nodded. "We don't think she was."

"So...that makes this one a little different, doesn't it?" Neil said.

"Yes, but—"

"No buts, just think," Neil said. "Why would he do it differently? All the other times it's been about power and control. He's the strong one, so he kills. And there's got to be something about the victims that he hates, so he rapes as a final act of disrespect."

Franconi was on his feet. "Keep talking," he said.

Neil rubbed his chin with the ball of his thumb as he thought through his theory.

"So...this time he doesn't rape her. Why? Maybe his initial intent was food. Maybe the idea to kill was secondary. Who knows? We don't know what sets him off. We don't know why he's doing it, only that it's happening. But he took the food. We saw that. That makes it different. And the other two were in isolated places, right? This was in public. In a place of business. Granted, it was closing time, but it was

still in plain sight, and there are lights. I don't think
he planned on this. I think it just happened."

Franconi looked at J.R. and then nodded. "You
might be on to something," he said. "You been
here...what...a little over a year? Who knows. We
just might make a good detective out of you yet."

Neil looked pleased with the lieutenant's praise but
refrained from comment. He knew the score. If he
wanted respect, he would have to earn it.

"So where do we go from here?" Sal asked.

"Treat this like the others," Franconi answered. "I
want all of you on this. Work up an extensive background check on the Dubai woman. There's got to be
a connection between the three victims that we're just
not seeing."

"Yes, sir," Sal said. "I don't want to have to see
another woman carved up like that, or have to tell
another parent that their daughter has been butchered
like a piece of fresh meat."

"Amato is the primary on this case," Franconi
said. "You report to him. He reports to me."

The other detectives nodded, and then, together,
they filed out of the lieutenant's office.

"Where do you want us?" Neil asked as they
paused by Amato's desk.

"Angela Dubai. Find out everything you can about
her, from where she takes her laundry to who she's
been seeing. Was she married? Engaged? You know
the drill. Paulie and I are going to go back over the

files on the other two women. See if there's something we missed."

J.R. looked at his partner. "We'll cover more territory if we split up. You talk to her father. See if she has a best friend. Most likely the best friend will know more about any lovers than Daddy will."

"What are you going to do?" Trudy asked.

J.R. glanced at Sal. "They're Catholic. So for starters, I thought I'd talk to her priest. I know he won't tell us anything specific, but maybe I can find out if she dumped a big load on him in the confessional."

"Good thinking," Sal said. "While you're at it, check out her finances. It's a long shot, but it's an angle we haven't covered."

Trudy frowned. "You mean, you think this is some loan shark's way of collecting on bad debts?"

Sal shrugged. "It's doubtful, but we've got to rule everything out, right? Like the lieutenant said, we've got to cover all the bases."

They split up—Neil and Kowalksi heading out on their separate investigations, while Amato and Hahn retreated to their desks to start making calls and shuffling paper. The sooner they corroborated their earlier facts, the closer they would be to finding their killer.

Twelve

It was fifteen minutes after four in the afternoon when Caitlin's phone began to ring. Deep into the scene she was writing, she didn't bother to answer, knowing the answering machine would pick it up. But she'd forgotten about Mac being in the apartment and that she'd had Kenny leak the story about the letters. Her thoughts were fixed upon the female protagonist in her book. Now how, she wondered, would a woman no taller than five foot two be able to—

"Caitlin!"

The roar startled her, causing her to lose her train of thought. Sighing, she hit the Save key on her computer, got up from the desk and stomped out of her office, intent on reminding Connor McKee that when a writer was deep in the throes of creation, she was not to be disturbed. About halfway down the hall, it dawned on her that her outfit was such that she wouldn't be taken as seriously as she would have liked. Her dark hair was in a frazzled topknot, and her sweats didn't match. The top was gray, the bottoms were orange, and the ears on her brown puppy

house shoes—a Christmas gift from Aaron last year—
were flopping as she walked.

"You shouted?" she drawled as she entered the
living room.

Mac's face was pale, his eyes blazing.

"Do you know who that was on the phone?"

Memory returned in a flash. *Uh-oh...the story was
out.* She shook her head and hoped he couldn't see
past the lie.

"It was a reporter from the *Times.*"

"I get interviewed every time a book comes out,
although they usually go through Kenny. What seems
to be the problem?"

Mac tossed the portable phone onto the sofa and
cursed beneath his breath.

"Problem? I'd call it more than a problem, Caitlin.
The reporter wanted to talk to you about the letters
you've been receiving and to verify the fact that
you'd been hospitalized because of an attack from an
irate fan."

"Oh dear."

Mac glared. "Is that all you have to say?"

She shrugged. "They were bound to find out
sooner or later."

"Why? I wasn't going to tell. Aaron damn sure
won't talk. There's no one left but—"

Suddenly his eyes narrowed thoughtfully. Caitlin
bit her lower lip and tugged on the tail of her sweat-
shirt.

"What did you tell him?" she asked.

"That you were unavailable for comment at the moment."

"Thank you. I guess that's best for now."

"You guess?"

"Well, eventually I'll have to respond to—"

"No...eventually you won't."

"But—"

Mac took her by both arms, resisting the urge to shake her. "Caitlin!"

"You're hurting me," she muttered.

"No, I'm not, and you know it. Look at me."

She lifted her chin and tried not to look guilty as she met his gaze.

"Just so you know...I resent your attitude," she said.

He cursed beneath his breath. "And just so you know, I don't believe you're as innocent as you're pretending."

"I don't play games," she said.

His voice softened as he pulled her to him, wrapping her close within his embrace.

"That's good, Caitie, because this isn't a game, it's serious business."

She snuggled close, feeling guilty that the source of his concern had come at her own hands and hoped that she'd done the right thing.

"I need to call the detectives on your case. They have to know about this latest turn of events."

"But—"

"No buts, lady. Maybe now they'll give you some protection."

"I don't need protection. I have you," Caitlin said.

Mac's heart soared and then took a dive south.

Lord. This was getting scarier. Not only had he gone and fallen in love with the maddening woman he'd promised to guard, but now her life was, quite literally, in his hands. He wanted backup. Big backup with big guns. With a sigh, he gave her a swift hug and kissed the top of her head.

"I'm still calling Detective Neil."

Caitlin dropped into a nearby chair. Everything was happening as she'd planned, only she hadn't expected to feel guilty. She sat back, her hands in her lap, and watched as Mac picked up the phone.

He turned and looked at her, stifling a grin as the phone on the other end began to ring. It was difficult to imagine how truly rich she was, because at the moment, she looked like a tag sale reject. Only a man in love could think she was sexy.

"Where in hell did you get those slippers?" he asked as he waited for his call to be answered.

"Last year's Christmas present from Aaron."

Mac rolled his eyes and then turned abruptly as his call was finally answered.

"I need to speak to Detective Neil," he said.

"He's out on assignment," a woman said. "Can anyone else help you?"

Mac frowned. "How about his partner, Detective Kowalski?"

"She's out on assignment, too."

"Look," Mac said, "this is important. Isn't there any way you can get a message to them?"

"Yes, but I can't guarantee when they can—"

"Never mind," Mac said. "We'll come to the precinct."

"But, sir, I—"

Mac hung up the phone and then pointed at Caitlin. "Change your clothes. We're going downtown."

Caitlin's eyes widened. "But—"

"I've got to go, and you're not staying here by yourself, so please get dressed. And hurry. I don't want to get caught in rush hour traffic."

"It's always rush hour in New York City," Caitlin said as she got up from the sofa.

"Caitlin…"

The tone of his voice was warning enough.

"I'm going, I'm going," she muttered, and then realized this might work to her benefit after all.

Maybe there would be a couple of reporters hanging around the building, waiting for her to come out. If so, it would be the opportunity she'd been waiting for. Anxious to get this over with, she dressed quickly, choosing a bulky blue sweater and black woolen pants, then added knee-high Cossack boots as further protection against the snow-packed streets.

She left her hair down, liking the weight and

warmth of it brushing against her shoulders. With a little moisturizer on her face as protection against the cold and a bright slash of color on her lips, she was good to go.

"I'm ready," she announced as she walked into the living room.

Mac turned and then exhaled softly.

"You are so beautiful."

"Why, thank you," Caitlin said. "You don't look so bad yourself."

He frowned. "Here's your coat," he said gruffly. "There's a cab waiting downstairs."

"Good call," she said, putting on the coat as they walked across the hall to the elevator. The frown on Mac's face kept growing deeper. "What's wrong?" Caitlin said.

"Nothing," he said, but he was lying.

It had just occurred to him how outlandish it was to expect someone of Caitlin Bennett's caliber to fall for a man like him. Granted they'd had sex, but that did not make for a commitment—not in this day and age. And he was so far below her financial status that it didn't bear consideration. He needed to face the fact that he was out of her league, yet the idea of parting from her was not only saddening, but painful.

They exited the elevator in silence, but the calm didn't last. They were met on the street by three people simultaneously calling her name.

Startled, Mac stepped between her and them as he

tried to push Caitlin back into the lobby, out of danger.

"Wait!" one woman cried. "Please, Miss Bennett. May we get a statement from you regarding your stalker?"

"Mac, they're reporters. I need to talk to them," Caitlin said. "The sooner they get their stories, the sooner they'll leave me alone."

"Stay!" he yelled, pointing toward the trio, then turned her around, pinning her between his body and the building.

"I don't like this," he said.

"And I don't like being the target for some nut case. You don't know what it's like, to be afraid every time the doorbell rings. I'm not even comfortable opening my mail, for God's sake. This has got to end, and if talking to them will help, I'm willing to give it a try."

His voice was low, his expression grim. "You leaked the story yourself, didn't you?"

She wouldn't answer. Instead she ducked under his arm to face the trio. "Before I say anything, may I see some credentials?"

All three produced proof that they worked for the three major papers in the city. She nodded.

"You may ask your questions," she said.

The woman was first.

"Miss Bennett, is it true that you've been receiving threatening letters?"

"Yes."

"Do you have any information regarding the person sending them?"

"No. Only that his behavior is juvenile and cowardly."

"How so?"

"The letters are theatrically threatening and written in red pen, complete with little droplets of blood, like something from a Hollywood horror film. Recently he's progressed to dismembering rodents and mailing them to me. In my opinion, he's acting like some disturbed teenager who needs his head examined. It isn't frightening, just disgusting."

She heard Mac's swift intake of breath and clenched her jaw.

One of the men chimed in.

"We understand that you were recently hospitalized after an attack from this fan. Is that true? Is that scar above your eyebrow from the attack?"

"Yes, and yes."

"But weren't you scared then?"

"Of the truck, yes. Of him, certainly not. Again, he was too cowardly to face me and resorted to a childish push in the middle of my back."

The last reporter threw a question at her, anxious to get his own spin on the story.

"Did you get a good look at him? Have the police made an ID?"

"No, I didn't see him. It happened at a very

crowded intersection. I was deliberately pushed from behind into the path of an oncoming truck. Only the driver's quick thinking saved me. As for the police, they are working on the case. That's all I can tell you. Now, if you'll excuse us, we have an appointment.''

"Thank you, Miss Bennett.''

"You're welcome,'' she said, and strode toward the waiting cab, leaving Mac to follow behind, which he did.

As they got in the cab, his silence was not encouraging, nor was the glare he gave her before barking out their destination to the driver.

"Mac?''

He wouldn't even look at her.

She sighed. "I had to do it.''

Again, silence.

"Damn it, Connor, it's my life. Shouldn't I be allowed to make the decisions as to how I live it?''

"Why ask me?'' he muttered. "You're the one in charge, remember?''

"But I—''

"It's done, Caitlin. Now we're just going to have to deal with it. All I'm saying is, you'd better pray to God that the lunatic who's stalking you doesn't have a hair-trigger temper, or you'll be getting a lot more than dead rats in the mail.''

His warning sent goose bumps up the back of her neck, and then she dismissed her nervousness. Devlin

Bennett would have faced this trouble head-on. As his daughter, she could do no less.

A short while later, they arrived at police head-quarters. Mac paid the cabdriver and then helped her out, steadying her steps as they made their way across the icy patches on the sidewalk. Although the sky was gray and bleak, there were no more predictions for snow—at least for a while.

Entering the police station, they were met by a mixture of warmth and confusion. A homeless woman had claimed a corner just inside the door, and the desk sergeant was compassionately ignoring her presence. Caitlin saw Mac glance at her, then stop and look at her again as they paused to gain their bearings. Central Booking was trying to process a purse snatcher, while the victim, an elderly woman, was screeching at the officer as well as the perp, demanding the return of her purse and money.

"Where do we go?" Caitlin asked.

"I don't know, but I'm going to find out," Mac said, then took her by the hand and started toward the desk.

The harried desk sergeant barely looked up. "Can I help you?" he asked.

"We need to talk to Detective Neil or Kowalksi."

"They're not here," he said. "Leave your name and number, and I'll have them call you."

"No."

It was the abruptness of the answer that finally got the sergeant's attention.

"No? No, you don't want to leave your name and number, or no you don't want them to call you?"

"No to both," Mac said. "Look, Sergeant. I was with the Atlanta PD for more than fifteen years, so I know the routine. But Neil and Kowalksi have been investigating some incidents regarding this lady, Caitlin Bennett, and it's imperative that they get some new info regarding her case."

Now the sergeant was interested. "C. D. Bennett the mystery writer?"

Caitlin slipped in front of Mac and smiled.

"I read all your stuff," the sergeant said. "In fact, I've got your latest book right here, see?"

Caitlin smiled as he reached beneath the desk and pulled up a copy of *Dead Lines.*

"Would you sign it for me?" he asked, and handed it to her without waiting for an answer.

"I'd be delighted, Sergeant. What's your first name?"

He almost blushed. "Walter," he said, watching with intent interest as she autographed his book. As soon as she handed it back, he opened it up and read it aloud. "To Sergeant Walter Blum. Thanks for all your help."

Caitlin leaned across the desk, her expression nothing but innocent.

"Is there anyone...anyone at all, who could help us in Detective Neil's absence? It's very important."

"Yes, ma'am. I imagine there is. If you'll give me a minute, I'll find out who's in."

Caitlin flashed him a smile, then turned around and patted the front of Mac's coat.

"He's checking to see who's in," she said sweetly.

"I heard," Mac muttered, accepting the fact that another man had just fallen victim to her charms, then consoling himself with the fact that at least this one was old enough to be her father. As he waited, he turned again, staring intently at the old woman by the door. There was something about her that—

"Miss Bennett?" the sergeant said.

She turned. "Yes?"

"Go upstairs, second door on your left. See Detective Amato."

"Thank you, Sergeant Blum, you've been a big help."

"My pleasure, Miss Bennett. You keep writing those stories."

"Yes, I certainly will."

She turned away from the desk and started toward the stairs then stopped, aware that Mac was not behind her.

"Mac, are you—"

At first she couldn't find him, and then she saw him by the door, speaking to the old woman they'd seen upon entering. His head was bent, his hand on her shoulder. The urgency with which Mac was speaking was as obvious as the distrust on the old woman's face. And then Caitlin saw Mac reach into his pocket and take out what appeared to be a wad of money. When he placed it in the woman's hands, she started to cry.

In that moment, Caitlin saw Mac anew, and she wasn't prepared for the surge of tenderness she felt on his behalf. Ashamed that she had so much and yet had walked right past the woman without a single thought of sharing, she looked away. When she looked again, the woman was gone and Mac was coming toward her.

He stopped at the foot of the stairs. His eyes were a little too bright, and there was a slight flush on his cheeks.

"Sorry to keep you waiting."

Caitlin didn't speak; she just took his face in her hands and kissed him square on the mouth.

"Hey, lady, can I be next?"

Reluctantly Caitlin broke the kiss, glancing toward the brash young cop who'd asked.

"No," she said, and then started up the steps. This time Mac was right beside her.

"Not that I'm complaining," he asked as they reached the first landing. "But what was that for?"

Caitlin looked up at him.

"For being a hero."

"I'm no hero."

"I think that old woman would disagree with you," she said quietly.

Mac looked away. "She used to be a teacher."

"I'm amazed that she told you that in the short time you were talking. Usually the homeless are quite protective of their privacy."

"She didn't have to tell me," Mac said. "The first year I came to live with Aaron...she was *my* teacher."

"Oh, Mac...oh my." Caitlin sighed. "Isn't life sad? I wonder how she came to be on the streets? Maybe we should try to find her. I could—"

"No," Mac said. "I tried. Pride is all she has left, Caitie. I didn't want to take that away from her, too. She said she had a sister in Erie, Pennsylvania. Maybe she'll use the money for a bus ticket home."

"How much did you give her?" she asked.

He shrugged. "All I had on me. Probably close to four hundred dollars, so the cab ride home is going to be on you."

"It will be an honor," she said softly. "And I think you deserve more than a kiss."

He looked at her then, wishing for things he had no right to want.

"Hold that thought," he said. "When we get back to your apartment, maybe we could figure out how to—"

She thumped him on the arm.

"Don't ruin the moment, McKee. Let's go find this

Amato guy and then get home. I have a book to finish.''

Sal liked to call this room the ''war room.'' It was where they assembled facts and leads in pertinent cases, and planned strategies against the criminals they had sworn to fight. It had been set aside for task force use and was, at the moment, the gathering place for information regarding the three dead women who were victims of the serial slasher. As he was in the act of pinning the last victim's photo on the wall next to the others, there was a knock on the door.

He turned.

''Hey, Amato. Blum sent some people up here to see you.''

''What about?'' Sal asked.

The detective shrugged. ''Ask them,'' he said, and left the door ajar as he went back to his desk, leaving Mac and Caitlin in the doorway on their own.

Frowning at the interruption, Sal tossed a handful of pushpins back on the table and pasted on a smile.

Caitlin's first attention had been directed at the balding, middle-aged man sauntering toward them, but then her gaze slid from his face to the wall and the pictures behind him. The gore depicted in the photos was horrifying, but she'd done worse to some of her victims in the books that she'd written. What startled her was the familiarity. It was almost as if she knew those women. But how? Her gaze slid from the crime scene photos to the pictures of what they had looked like before. What was it about them...?

Realization came slowly, like an emerging photo in a tray of developing solution. The shapes of their faces. The length and color of their hair. Even some of their features.

It was like looking at a blurry image of her own face. Then she focused on the photos from the crime scene, particularly on the close-ups of their faces, and saw another similarity that nearly sent her to her knees.

It can't be. Please, God, don't let it be true.

But the truth was impossible to ignore. Her stomach rolled as the room began to spin. In panic, she grabbed for the stability of Mac's arm, but something was wrong with her legs. The last thing she saw was the shock on Mac's face as she slipped to the floor.

"She's coming around," Amato said.

Caitlin moaned. Something cold was being wiped across her forehead, and she could hear muted conversation in the background as she struggled to come to.

"Caitie...sweetheart...can you hear me?"

Her tongue felt thick, and her ears were ringing. When she spoke, her words sounded as if they were coming from the bottom of a barrel. Her eyelids fluttered and then opened.

"Mac? What—"

"Thank God," he said, and tossed aside the wet handkerchief someone had handed him. "You fainted."

"I don't faint."

Mac looked up at the detective and grinned. "She's going to be fine."

"How can you tell?" Amato said.

"She's arguing with me."

Now fully aware of what had happened and mortified by the fact that she was flat on her back on the floor and being stared at by at least a dozen people, Caitlin grabbed Mac's arm.

"Help me up," she muttered.

He did, then led her to a nearby chair.

"What happened, honey? One minute you were fine, and the next thing I knew, you were going down."

"I don't—" Her face paled as memory returned. She stood abruptly, pushing past the men and hurrying toward the wall where she'd seen the photos.

Mac followed, as Amato called out, "Lady, wait! You don't—"

No one was listening. Cursing loudly, Amato went after them.

"Lady, this is off limits. You need to—"

But Caitlin wasn't listening. She was looking at the pictures, and the longer she looked, the more certain she was that her first impression had been correct. She spun, her gaze fixed on Mac, her voice trembling in disbelief.

"Don't you see it?" she asked.

Mac took her by the arm. "Honey, you shouldn't be in here. This is obviously a very serious investigation in progress, and research is out of place."

Caitlin felt like screaming as she shook off his grasp and turned back to the pictures. "It's not research! Don't you see it?"

She pointed to the pictures of the victims before they'd been murdered. One of them was an enlarged snapshot, the other two were obviously studio poses, but their resemblance to each other was startling.

"See what, lady?" Amato asked.

She turned, frustration evident as she waved her arm at the pictures.

"The resemblance. Dear God...look!"

And then she moved to the wall, standing just to the side of the third victim's photo, and turned and faced the two men, just as if she were standing in a lineup.

Mac was the first to understand. He stared at their faces—Caitlin and the three dead women. And while they were definitely not identical, they were all, including Caitlin, of the same type—slim, attractive young women with dark, shoulder-length hair. Taken separately, the similarities would not have been noticeable, but adding Caitlin's face to the mix had made everything click.

The first woman's eyes and nose were almost identical to Caitlin's, although her mouth and chin were different. The second woman's smile could have been a clone of Caitlin Bennett's, and the last woman's chin had the same small indentation as hers. And they all had the identical hairstyle.

Immediately his gaze moved from their smiling faces to the crime scene photos and the obscenity of what had happened to them. In two cases their half-naked bodies lay sprawled in the snow, their faces horribly slashed. Slashes that...

He thought of the picture that had been sent with the rat.

"Oh God. Oh, no."

"You see it, don't you?" Caitlin asked.

Mac swallowed suddenly, fighting a need to vomit. He turned to Detective Amato, grabbing him roughly by the arm.

"We need Detective Neil."

"He's not here," Amato said. "And I want to know what the hell is going on. I don't know who you are, but you people need to get the—"

"She's Caitlin Bennett, the mystery writer. Neil and Kowalski have been working on her case for almost a week now. For the past six months or so, Miss Bennett has been receiving threatening letters. Her publisher even received a bomb threat from the same source. Last week, while she was out, she was deliberately pushed in front of an oncoming truck, and it's only by the grace of God that she isn't dead. Two days after she came home from the hospital, the same lunatic mailed her another letter, along with a dis-membered rat and one of her pictures that he'd slashed across the face. He told her she was next. Neil has it. You need to get that picture now.''

"Look, I can see how disturbing all of this might be, but it has nothing to—"

Mac turned Amato toward Caitlin. "Look at her, man. They all look like her. And see the way their faces have been slashed? Her picture—the one that came with the dismembered rat—it was slashed the very same way.''

Amato's mouth dropped. Could it be? Was this the break they'd been waiting for? For the first time he looked past their intrusion to the woman before him. The longer he looked, the more he began to see what they meant.

"Wait here," he muttered, and bolted out of the room.

Mac went to Caitlin. Her expression was still blank with shock.

"Caitie...darlin', are you—"

"Oh, Mac. What have I done?"

"What do you mean?"

"The reporters...the newspapers. I've just dared a madman to come and get me, haven't I?"

He'd forgotten about the reporters. But he couldn't let her see his fear. One of them in panic was enough.

"It will be all right," he said. "It has to be. You may not want to hear this right now, but I can't lose you, girl."

"Then don't," she whispered, and buried her face against his chest.

Moments later Amato was back, accompanied by another man Mac assumed was their lieutenant. He was right.

"This is Lieutenant Franconi," Amato said. "I told him your theory. Thought he should see this and judge for himself."

Caitlin watched as Amato sifted through J. R. Neil's file, pulled out a bloodstained photo and then pinned it on the wall next to the other three.

Then he looked at Caitlin. "Miss Bennett, if you would stand as you were a few moments ago?"

Caitlin did as he asked, her gaze fixed on the three men's expressions.

Mac looked sick. She knew he understood.

But it was the police who had to be convinced.

"Christ almighty," Amato said. "She's right."

Del Franconi frowned. "I want to know why someone didn't see this earlier. Who the hell is working on this woman's case?"

"Neil and Kowalski, sir. But in all fairness, if you'll remember, we've pulled almost everyone off their normal work and put them on this slasher case, and I'm sure their other work has suffered accordingly."

"Find them," Franconi said. "Get them in here now, and the four of you start putting two and two together for a change. Miss Bennett, on behalf of my staff, you have my apologies. Rest assured that you will be taken seriously, very seriously, from now on. And if you don't mind, would you please stick around? I'm sure there are some questions my detectives will be wanting to ask."

"We'll be here," Mac said.

"Who are you?" Franconi asked.

Before Mac could answer, Caitlin slipped under his arm and laid her head against his chest.

"He's with me," she said softly.

Franconi shrugged. "Fine." Then he pointed at Amato. "Looks like this is the break you've been looking for. Use it."

Thirteen

Caitlin leaned forward, her head resting in her hands, and stared down at the table. Her head was throbbing, her stomach growling from hunger. The interrogation had been going on for what felt like hours, and she was ready to cry.

"Detective Neil, for the last time, to my knowledge, I have not made any enemies. This person...whoever he is...has fixated on me without reason."

"There is always a reason," he said.

She looked up at him then, her gaze like a wounded doe.

"Then explain it to me," she said, her chin trembling. "Because I damn sure don't know what it could be."

Until now, Mac had purposefully kept silent, but when he saw her on the verge of tears, he'd had enough.

"Look, guys, she just got out of the hospital less than a week ago. She hasn't eaten in hours, and from the look in her eyes, she's got one hell of a headache.

She's told you all she knows. Maybe we could go at
this from another angle. You tell us what you know
and see if any of it clicks with her.''

J.R. frowned. He didn't like Caitlin's bodyguard,
and it showed.

''I don't think that's—''

Amato interrupted Neil. ''That's a damn good
idea,'' he said. ''Did anybody tell you that you would
have made a good cop?''

Mac grinned. By now, everyone here knew his past
and his reason for associating with Caitlin. What they
didn't know, and neither did Caitlin, was that his loyalty to his brother had been superseded by his love
for her.

Amato pointed at his partner, Paulie.

''Hey, Paulie. Go get the Dubai tape. There's not
much to see that will help us, but we should have
shown it to them before on the off chance something
about the perp rings a bell in Miss Bennett's memory.''

''It's in the lieutenant's office. Be right back,''
Paulie said.

Trudy Kowalksi leaned forward, momentarily laying her hand over Caitlin's.

''I know this is tough, Miss Bennett. Bear with us,
okay?''

Caitlin nodded.

''Have you people checked into her father's background?'' Mac asked, looking pointedly at Neil.

Sensing McKee's disapproval, Neil stood defen-sively.

"We had no reason to assume that her father is connected to any of this. The letters are obviously from a deranged fan, and Miss Bennett is a writer, not Devlin Bennett."

"According to the profiler I contacted, the letters don't mention her work at all, only that she has to pay."

Neil flushed angrily. "Your profiler? And what rock did he crawl out from under?"

"She," Mac corrected. "And I believe that would be the rocks around Quantico, Virginia. My profiler is a Fed, Detective. What are your qualifications?"

Neil's flush grew darker.

"You contacted the FBI? Without our knowl-edge?"

"You weren't doing anything to further her case, and crimes aren't private property, Detective. Besides, if they belong to anyone, they belong to the victim."

Amato stepped between them. "Gentlemen—and I use the term loosely—I'm only going to say this once. Back off!"

Both men took several steps back.

"Thank you," Sal said. "I trust this won't happen again."

"I don't work for you, sir," Mac said shortly. "My interests are entirely focused on Caitlin's safety."

"Noted," Amato said. "However, we'll get a lot

more done without animosity. Now, tell me exactly what your profiler told you. Please.''

Mac nodded. ''She seems to think that the person sending the letters has a personal grudge. She says he's probably in his early to mid-thirties, never married.''

J.R. snorted softly and threw up his hands in disgust. ''Oh...and how does *she* know that?'' he asked.

''I don't know. Maybe the takeout pizza sauce on the letters...who the hell knows?'' Mac said. ''I'm not the expert, she is.''

Amato glared at Neil, who reluctantly took a seat.

Caitlin was so numb from all the questioning, she was past caring what came next. All she wanted to do was go home.

''Anything else?'' Amato asked.

''She suggested that Caitlin might be nothing more than a Judas goat for someone else's crimes. She says his letters are very nonspecific toward Caitlin. In other words...he's never blamed her or named her as the villain. He simply keeps repeating the phrase that she has to pay. I'll give you the agent's name and phone number. She'll be more than happy to help. Just mention my name.''

Amato nodded.

''Miss Bennett, did your father have enemies?''

Caitlin resisted the urge to laugh. ''A man like my father would probably have made hundreds, even thousands, of enemies in his lifetime. He was rich and powerful and a hard man to know.''

Amato frowned. ''Think, please. Are there any who come to mind?''

''Detective, I knew little about the business side of my father's life. He kept that separate from us.''

''Meaning you and your mother?''

''Yes.''

''Would she know?''

''She died years before my father, and he's been gone a little over five years. I have no siblings, no aunts, no uncles, no cousins.'' She glanced up at Mac and then added, ''Only a few very dear friends.''

Mac wanted to argue. He didn't want to be her friend. He wanted… Then he frowned. What exactly did he want? He wanted to be her lover. That was a given. And he wanted her to love him back. But did it go further? He looked at her sitting there in all her casual elegance and remembered how she'd looked earlier, in mismatched sweats and those damned puppy slippers, and felt his stomach beginning to knot. That was what he wanted. Her. Forever. In whatever getup she chose—railing at him for whatever his latest sin was and then sleeping in his arms every night.

The breath caught in the back of his throat. Here he'd spent the better part of his adult life convincing himself that he wasn't the marrying kind, and now that was exactly what he wanted. His ring on her finger, and her bearing his name and his children. In that order.

"Yeah, friends," he echoed.

"What about associates?" Amato asked. "Is there anyone who was connected to your father who might know more than you?"

"His lawyers are Bernstein and Stella. They might know something about the business of which I was unaware."

"Anyone else?"

Caitlin started to say no, and then immediately a face popped into her mind. "Juanita Delarosa!"

"Who's she?" Amato asked.

"She was my father's private secretary for over thirty-five years. When Daddy died, she retired. She lives in New Jersey."

"Do you have an address for her?" Amato asked.

"I think so," Caitlin said. "Mac, would you hand me my purse?"

He did, watching as she dug through the contents and then pulled out a small address book. A few moments later, Caitlin looked up.

"Yes, here it is." She handed him the book, watching as Amato made note of the woman's name and address, then dropped it back into her purse. "If there's anything to tell, she'll be the one to know."

"Thank you," Amato said. "We'll contact her immediately."

Moments later, Paulie was back.

"Got the tape," he said, and turned on the TV, then slipped the cassette into the VCR.

Mac glanced at Caitlin. "Honey...are you up to this?"

Caitlin shrugged. "I'm sick to my stomach and my head's going to explode. Other than that, I feel fine."

"Make this quick," Mac said. "I need to get her home."

Neil frowned at Mac, and then his glance slid to Caitlin. Even he could see how pale she was, could see the pain etched on her face. He leaned over, briefly cupping her hands with his own.

"I'm very sorry, Miss Bennett, but sometimes ugly things can't be avoided." Then he looked back at Mac, his face expressionless. "All we need from you is another couple of minutes, and then you'll both be free to go. Fortunately for you, it didn't take Miss Dubai long to die."

The shock on Caitlin's face was evident.

"You mean you have a tape of her being murdered and you still don't know who did it?"

"Just watch and you'll understand," Paulie said, fiddling with the controls.

Caitlin stood abruptly, only to find Mac at her back.

"I'm here," he said softly, and wrapped his arms around her.

Caitlin leaned against him, taking comfort in his presence and his strength.

And then the tape began to play. By the time it was over, Caitlin was sobbing.

"Play that last bit again," Mac asked.

Caitlin covered her face. "Oh God, Mac, I can't bear to—"

"Please," he said, looking at Detective Hahn. "I thought I saw something. Play it again."

Paulie shrugged and rewound it a few seconds, then hit Play. Immediately the tape picked up at the place where the killer was walking out with the food and beer.

Suddenly Mac was across the room, his finger on the television screen.

"There," he said. "Play it again."

Kowalski frowned. "I don't see—"

"You will," Mac said. "Detective Hahn?"

Again Paulie rewound and then played the last few seconds.

"Stop there!" Mac shouted.

The image from the camera high above the counter was frozen on the screen, showing only the first two aisles of the small family market, a glare of lights against the front window from a passing car highlighting the back of the killer's head and shoulders as he made his exit.

"You can't see anything except the back of his head," Amato said.

Mac pointed past the man to the window and the glare.

"Look there," he said. "In the reflection. What do you see?"

Neil leaned closer, his focus shifting to the place where Mac was pointing, and then he took a deep breath. When he looked up, he was wearing an odd, almost apologetic grin.

"Well, it looks a bit like a reflection of the killer's face, doesn't it?"

"Where? Where?" Amato asked. "I don't see it."

"Put on your glasses," Trudy said. "It's there."

Amato grabbed his glasses from the desk and slid them up his nose.

"Son of a bitch," he muttered. "How did we miss that?"

"I see it, too," Caitlin said.

"Can you tell who it is?" Amato asked.

Caitlin leaned closer, then shook her head. "No. It's too vague."

"We'll send it to the lab," Amato said.

"If they can't make anything out of it, send it to the agent at Quantico," Mac suggested. "They can pick out a fly on a horse's butt taken from satellite imaging. If there's anything there, they'll find it."

Amato pointed to Paulie. "Go make a couple of copies of that tape. Send one to our lab and the other to the Feds, compliments of Mr. McKee here."

Paulie popped the tape from the VCR and headed out of the room as Amato drained the last of a cup of cold coffee.

"Well, people, I think you can go home now," he said. "If you think of anything else, call us immediately. Mr. McKee has my card."

Weak with relief, Caitlin turned to get her coat, only to find Detective Neil holding it for her.

"Allow me," he said.

"Thank you," Caitlin said, taking comfort in the familiarity of her own things. After all that she'd been through and seen this afternoon, she felt as if she'd been attacked all over again.

Before she could move, Neil took her hand.

"You have my card. As I told you before, if you need anything...anything at all, feel free to call me, day or night."

Too exhausted to appreciate the special attention, she smiled vaguely and nodded, but all she needed was Mac, and he was deep in conversation with Amato and Kowalksi.

"Mac?"

He turned, immediately solicitous.

"Ready?"

She nodded.

"Still hungry?"

Her gaze strayed to the wall and the pictures of the slain women. Tears filled her eyes. "I may never be hungry again."

Mac pulled her into his arms. "It's not your fault, Caitie. You have to know that."

Trudy Kowalski patted Caitlin's shoulder in sympathy.

"He's right, Miss Bennett. You can't take on the guilt for these women's deaths. It's the killer who's to blame, not you."

"Theoretically, I know that," Caitlin said. "But it doesn't make their deaths any easier to bear."

Mac gave her a swift hug, then handed her his handkerchief. "Wipe your eyes. I'm taking you out for pasta. It's a good, stick-to-your-ribs meal, and you'll feel better once you've eaten."

Caitlin nodded, then shook Sal Amato's hand.

"Detective, we appreciate your help." Then she looked at Trudy and J.R. "All of you. Thank you in advance for helping me. I'm so tired of being afraid."

Trudy smiled and winked. "It's our job to help. And now, thanks to you, we have a whole new direction in which to take the case."

Mac took Caitlin by the arm. Even as they were leaving, Sal Amato was barking orders, sending Kowalksi in one direction and Neil in another.

Satisfied that, for now, the worries were out of their hands, Mac and Caitlin left quickly, anxious to leave the premises and all they represented. Yet even when they were out on the street and hailing another cab to go to the restaurant, Caitlin knew that, no matter how far they went, she could not escape what was happening. Until the killer was caught, she was living on borrowed time.

* * *

Kenny smiled in satisfaction as he hung up the phone. His source at the paper had assured him that they'd gotten the story they needed from Caitlin Bennett. It would be all over the news by evening for sure. He kicked back in his chair. Caitlin would be pleased. She owed him big time on this, and he would make sure to collect. To hell with the muscle-man who was stuck to her side. She was bound to come to her senses soon. Then she would see who really mattered in her life.

The rest of the day passed in its usual busy way. And every time the phone rang, he kept thinking it would be her, calling to tell him what a genius he was. But it wasn't, and by the time quitting time rolled around, she still had not called. Not once. Not even to say thanks.

The slight to his ego was small compared to having to come to terms with the possibility that he was nothing more to her than an employee. She paid him to do things for her, and as long as he did them to her satisfaction, their relationship, such as it was, would continue. Beyond that, there was nothing. He didn't want to accept it, but as his mother used to say, "Truth is a hard egg to swallow."

His steps were slow, his heart heavy, as he left the office for the day. And the sharp bite of winter cold was like adding insult to injury as he tried, without success, to hail a cab. With his head down, his shoulders hunched against the wind, he started the walk home.

Caitlin Bennett's story was all over the evening news. It was the lead in the papers and on two of the local television stations. Her taunt had hit a painful target.

Buddy saw the first of the headlines on his way home from work. Unable to believe what he was seeing, he bought a paper and read it on the subway. By the time he reached his apartment, he was shaking with rage.

The bitch. She'd called him juvenile! She'd said she wasn't afraid. He would show her what true fear meant, but before he did, he was going to make her sorry in a whole other way.

He tossed the paper on the floor as he entered his apartment, then used it to wipe his feet, leaving the dirty slush from his shoes behind on the pages.

Work had been hell, and it had been all he could do to concentrate. He'd had a bagel for breakfast and nothing for lunch, and he suspected the headache he had was due to too much coffee and not enough food. But he would eat later—after he finished his little ''gift'' for Caitlin Bennett. By the time it reached its target, she would no longer be mouthing off about lack of fear.

To the uninitiated, Aaron Workman's office was a study in chaos, but he knew where everything was and when it was due. The manuscripts stacked on the credenza behind him were rejects, waiting for his assistant to mail them back to the senders.

The stack on the floor beside his chair was new, and had as yet to be opened and read. The stack to the right of his desk was from contracted writers and was made up of overdue line edits.

The stack to his left, which was the smallest, consisted of possible buys. Some needed cutting, and one needed to be added to, but the stories were there. Those were his favorites. Discovering new writers was why he'd taken this job.

Years ago, his first editorial job had been for a small press in Pennsylvania that was no longer in business, but it had been the impetus he'd needed to know he was on the right track. This was his fourteenth year with Hudson House. The company was in good financial shape, and he was as happy as he'd ever been.

Except for the mess with Caitlin. As an editor, it was unusual to have a personal relationship with one of his writers, but he loved her like the sister he'd never had. From the first book they'd worked on together, their friendship had grown. Now he considered her one of his best friends. During the day, he was able to block out his fear for her, but at night, when he was in the solitude of his own home, it was impossible to ignore. The only thing that kept him from coming unglued was the fact that his brother had come to her rescue.

He paused, his hands still on the keyboard of his computer, and smiled as he thought of Mac. He was a fortunate man to have him for a brother, and he was beginning to think that Caitlin agreed. It had been a great disappointment to him when Mac and Caitlin had first met. The two people he loved most in the world had taken an instant dislike to each other. Now he was beginning to think it had been attraction from the start, only they'd both been too scared to admit it.

He glanced at the clock, then back at the screen, and resumed the letter he was typing. As soon as he was finished, he was going to give Mac a call. He'd tried all day yesterday with no results and wondered what was going on. Maybe they could meet for dinner tonight. Unless pushed, Caitlin had no social life at all.

A few minutes later he hit Save and then Print, getting up from his desk to pour himself a fresh cup of coffee as he waited for the letter to emerge.

"Mr. Workman, your mail."

He turned, rolling his eyes at the new stack his assistant set on his desk.

"Does it ever end?" he griped.

She smiled. "No, and you would be sorry if it did."

He sighed. "You're right, and thanks." He set his

coffee cup down and began to shuffle through the stack. "See anything interesting?"

"The usual. Three submissions you asked to see based on proposals. A couple of unsolicited ones."

Aaron waved his hand. "Send them to a reader. I don't have time to go through them first myself."

"Will do," she said, and sorted them out. "Oh, I almost forgot. This is a Priority Mail envelope addressed to you and marked Personal. I didn't open it."

Aaron took it, sipping his coffee as he looked for a return address, then shrugged.

"Thanks, Teresa. I'll give it a look in a couple of minutes. This time I want to finish my coffee without spilling it down the front of my shirt."

She laughed. It was a known fact within the office that Aaron could not do two things at one time without making a mess, which included reading and drinking. More than one manuscript had suffered the consequences of his spills.

As she left, he turned toward the window, taking his coffee with him as he looked out on the city below. Even from the eighth floor, the streets looked filthy. Once lily-white snow was now a slushy mixture piled high at intersections and forming formidable barriers, sometimes impossible to step over, at curbs. If the weather would stay clear for more than two days at a time without added snowfall, they would be able to get out from under, but as it was, the city was barely keeping up with the snow.

Wrinkling his nose at the mess, he took another sip of his coffee and then turned toward his desk. The red, white and blue of the Priority Mail envelope teased his curiosity. More than likely it was a wanna-be writer trying to pull what he or she thought was a cute little stunt by marking a proposal as personal. But its mere presence on his desk taunted him like an unwrapped gift on the day after Christmas.

Grunting at himself for delaying the inevitable, he set down his cup and reached for the envelope. With nothing more for a clue than a New York City postmark, he grabbed the pull tab and gave it a yank.

There was a flash and an explosion, then the feel of searing heat. He heard a scream, unaware that it was his own, and then everything went black.

Caitlin was watering an ivy plant when the telephone rang. Mac was in her office on his cell phone with his office manager. She raced to answer it before he was disturbed.

"Bennett residence."

"Miss Bennett! This is Teresa Lane, from Hudson House Publishing."

"Oh, hello, Teresa. How are you?"

"Oh, Miss Bennett. I have terrible news."

The smile froze on Caitlin's face. After her day

yesterday with four of New York's finest, she wasn't sure she could bear more bad news.

"What's wrong?"

"They said that Mr. Workman's brother is staying with you, is that true?"

Caitlin's fingers curled a little tighter around the receiver.

"Yes...yes...he's here. What's wrong, Teresa?"

"It's Mr. Workman. There was an explosion... he's—"

"Oh God." Caitlin's knees went weak, and she slid to the floor. "Please. Please tell me he's not—"

"No, no, but they've taken him to New York General."

"We're on our way," Caitlin said. She was already screaming Mac's name as she hung up the phone.

He came out of her office with a gun in his hand, stopping her square in her tracks. She didn't have time to absorb the fact that it was the first time she'd known that he was armed.

"What's wrong?"

She grabbed him by the arms, willing herself not to shriek.

"It's Aaron. He's been hurt. We have to get to the hospital right now."

The color faded from Mac's face as his body went limp.

"What? How?"

Caitlin could hardly bring herself to say it.

"There was an explosion at his office. They didn't say anything more."

"Christ," Mac said, then pivoted sharply, running toward his bedroom. "Get changed. And hurry."

Caitlin did as she was told. Now was not the time to remind him that her stalker had promised to bomb the publishing house for putting out her books, or to consider the fact that her interview with the media had most likely been the trigger that had set him off. All she could do was pray that when they got there, Aaron would still be alive.

Fourteen

Detective Amato met Mac and Caitlin at the entrance to the E.R.

"My brother...where is he?" Mac demanded.

"They took him up to surgery about fifteen minutes ago."

"Ah, God," Mac groaned, then slumped against the wall. The thought of losing Aaron was impossible to consider. They were all the family each other had, and although they did not share the same blood, they had a bond forged by years of love and friendship.

"We were told it was an explosion," Caitlin said. "Was it a bomb?"

Amato nodded. "A letter bomb. As bombs go, it was a small one, but large enough to do damage to the person opening it."

Caitlin glanced at Mac, then grabbed his hand. "Aaron's injuries...how bad are they?"

"You'll have to talk to the doctor for that," Amato said. "All I know is he's got flash burns on his face and hands. I would imagine his eyes were impacted, but it's hard to know how much until they get him out of surgery."

The first wave of panic had passed, leaving Mac numb and searching for focus.

"Amato, you said this was an explosion."

"Yes."

"Then why are you here? You're Homicide, right?"

"When the bomb went off, the windows behind where Aaron was standing blew out, sending large shards of glass into the street below. One of them struck and killed a man who was getting out of a cab. That makes it murder."

Caitlin's expression went blank. The urge to scream and never stop was overwhelming. Everything just kept getting worse and worse.

"Dear Lord...because of me...because of me."

Mac grabbed her arm and pulled her to him, his voice shaking with emotion.

"Stop it, Caitie! Don't you quit on me now, girl. I need you to be with me on this."

The panic in his voice was more startling than the news they'd just received. Mac was her rock. He wasn't supposed to come undone. A cold shudder rocked her body, and when she saw the devastation on his face, all she could do was apologize profusely.

"I'm sorry...so sorry."

"It's okay," he said softly. "Just stay with me, okay?"

Blinking back tears, she turned to the detective. "What can you tell us...? About the bombing, I mean."

"Not much. The bomb squad is at the scene now. I'll have a full report in a day or so. Until then, all I can tell you is to be careful of your own mail. In fact, I would advise not opening any of it on your own. Bring it down to the bomb squad and let an expert check it first."

Another wave of disbelief swept over Caitlin, filling her with frustration and a sense of growing anger.

"This is unbelievable," she muttered. "This man, whoever he is, has not only killed wantonly, but has invaded every aspect of my life. If only we knew why, then maybe we could find out who."

"I have Neil and Kowalksi checking into your father's old business associates. Maybe we'll come up with something there."

"Have you spoken to Juanita Delarosa, Daddy's old secretary?"

"Detective Kowalski has been trying to contact her by phone, but we're not getting an answer. If I'm not mistaken, she and Neil are going to New Jersey tomorrow to find out if she's still at the same address." He glanced at his watch and sighed. "I'm sorry, but I've got to get back to the station. If there's anything we can do for you, let us know." Then he gave Mac a sympathetic pat on the shoulder. "Sorry about your brother."

Caitlin hesitated, then spat out the words as if confessing a sin. "He was my editor, you know."

Amato looked startled. This cemented the bombing squarely into the middle of the case. "No, I didn't get that connection."

"It's because of me."

Now Amato was really confused. "In what way?"

Caitlin bit the inside of her lip to steady her nerves. "You saw the story about me in the paper last night?"

"Yes, but I assumed that—"

Mac put his arm around Caitlin's shoulders and gave her a squeeze. "She leaked the story herself."

Amato looked stunned. "Why the hell would you—"

"I believe the explanation would be that she was using herself for bait," Mac said.

Guilt weighed heavily on Caitlin's conscience as she confessed what she'd done.

"I didn't know about the women. I didn't know that he was killing people who looked like me. I just wanted it to be over. I thought if I taunted him enough, he would make a mistake and then we could catch him." A single tear silently rolled down her cheek. "I wanted this to stop. Instead I made it worse."

Amato shook his head in disbelief. "Well, if you'd asked me first, I would have told you it was a damned dangerous stunt, but I have to give you credit, Miss

Bennett. It was also a real gutsy move, and in ordinary circumstances, it would probably have worked. However, I don't think we're dealing with an ordinary man. He's not only crazy and cruel, he's cunning. You be careful. Real careful."

"Yes. I will, but right now, all that matters is Aaron. He has to be okay."

"I'm sure the doctors are doing all they can."

Caitlin nodded. "Please call if you have any news on the case."

"Yes, I will," Amato said, then hurried out the door.

Caitlin turned to Mac, expecting to see hate on his face. "If he dies, it will be my fault."

A sheen of tears glittered in Mac's eyes, but the tone of his voice was hard and sure. "No, it won't, Caitie. Don't ever let me hear you say that again. I told you before, and I'm telling you again now, the only person at fault is the man behind the crimes."

She wrapped her arms around his waist and laid her cheek against his coat.

"I love Aaron," she said. "He's like the brother I never had."

"I know," Mac said, then managed a little grin. "He loves you, too."

"Thank you, Connor, more than you will ever know."

"Let's go tell someone we're here, so when the

doctor comes out of surgery, they'll know he has family waiting for news.''

Caitlin let Mac lead her to the nurses' station, but her thoughts were on what he'd said, not what he was telling the nurse in charge. Family. He'd included her in his family. She hadn't had family in so long that it felt good to think she belonged, even if her feelings for Mac were anything but brotherly.

A few minutes later they entered the surgical waiting area. Caitlin's heart went out to the people who were already there, reminding her that she wasn't the only one with troubles.

''There are a couple of seats against the wall,'' Mac said, cupping her elbow as he led her across the room. ''Now, let's get these coats off,'' he said, and helped her out of hers, then took off his own, draping them across the back of the small sofa.

She sat quickly, conscious of the other people's curious stares, and looked down at her feet, afraid she might be recognized and forced to talk about what was happening.

Mac slid his arm around her and pulled her close against his side. She looked up at him then, her chin trembling, her eyes welling with tears.

''Oh, Mac.''

''I know,'' he said softly.

''He has to be okay.''

A muscle jerked at the corner of Mac's mouth, the

only indication of the struggle he was having with his own emotions.

"Yeah," he said gruffly, and gave her a quick hug. After a bit, Caitlin realized the looks they were getting were nothing more than the curiosity any newcomers would have received, so she settled back, unobtrusively looking around. Out of the fifteen people waiting, it was the only child who caught her attention.

A tiny girl, no more than five or six, was sitting silently on the floor with a coloring book. With a scattered array of brightly colored crayons and a coffee table for a desk, she chose only the red, digging into the picture on the page with hard, angry slashes—an obvious reflection of her mood.

Caitlin watched her for several long minutes, lost in the tender curve of the child's neck, the way her long, curly hair fell across her little pink sweater, and the fierceness of her grip as she marked the page with angry strokes. A few moments later, she realized the little girl was staring at her, as well.

Caitlin started to smile, but there was something in the child's expression that held her back. Instead they looked, one at the other. It was the little girl who made the first move by reaching for a crayon and holding it toward Caitlin.

The offer was obvious and, for her, impossible to refuse. Caitlin slipped to the floor and slid over to where the little girl was sitting, casting a questioning

look at the man at whose feet the child sat. She saw
he was surprised by what the child had done, but he
nodded his permission for Caitlin to come closer.

The look in the child's eyes was haunting. Caitlin
wanted to hold her. Instead she took the crayon,
watching with interest as a new page was turned, offering a new picture for Caitlin to color.

The crayon was black. Caitlin suspected the choice
of colors was telling, but she took it without comment
and began coloring the mane and hooves of the pony
in the picture. When she was through, she laid the
crayon down.

The little girl looked up, seemingly surprised by
what Caitlin had done. Again she picked up the black
crayon and handed it to Caitlin.

This time Caitlin shook her head, pointing to a
bright turquoise crayon instead. By now the child was
frowning, but Caitlin didn't give in. She crossed her
arms and sat back, waiting to see what would happen.

Mac leaned forward to watch, his elbows on his
knees, and happened to see the father's eyes welling
with unshed tears.

The child offered the black crayon again, pointing
to the page.

Caitlin shook her head and pointed to the turquoise
crayon. It was a standoff of major proportions.

The child dropped the black crayon onto the floor
and began coloring the opposite page with the red,
jamming the crayon onto the paper as if it was a knife.

Such anger in such a young child was frightening, and Caitlin couldn't bear to watch, but when she started to leave, the child abruptly grabbed the turquoise crayon and all but flung it in Caitlin's lap.

Resisting the urge to grin, Caitlin quietly picked it up, using it to color the little saddle on the pony's back. When she was through, she laid the crayon down on the table and sat back.

Again the child looked up, the frown deeper on her face. She pointed to the page, indicating that Caitlin should keep coloring. Caitlin pointed to the yellow crayon. The little girl's fury was almost comical, but Caitlin feared her reasons for resistance were anything but.

The child shook her head.

Caitlin pointed again at the yellow one.

The child looked at Caitlin, judging her expression to see if she was as adamant as she'd been before. Whatever she saw convinced her to hand over the yellow crayon next.

And so it went, crayon after crayon. Caitlin colored her picture, using a different color every time until she was through. Suddenly she leaned back and laid down the last one, holding up her hands in delight.

The little girl looked at the page and then up at Caitlin, then back at the page again. Her gaze slid from the page she was coloring to the one Caitlin had done. She looked down at the nub of red crayon, her shoulders slumping in defeat as she slowly laid it down.

Caitlin sensed that something momentous had happened, but she was afraid to move, afraid to guess what was on the child's mind. But when the little girl pointed to the pile of crayons, Caitlin suddenly understood.

All but holding her breath, she picked up a blue one and laid it in the child's outstretched hand, then turned to a new page in the book.

The little girl sighed, staring at the picture as if she'd never seen it before, the crayon awkward in her grasp. With hesitant movements, she slowly leaned forward and began to color—tentatively at first, as if afraid of the marks she made. But the more she colored, the bolder her strokes became, until finally she was using the crayon normally.

Caitlin wanted to cheer; instead, she picked up another color and waited. A few seconds later the child laid down the blue crayon and held out her hand without bothering to look up. Caitlin handed her a green one and sat back with a sigh.

Way to go, baby girl.

Then she felt a touch on her shoulder. She turned. It was Mac, and the look on his face stopped her heart. *God...oh God...is that what I think it is? Please let it be love.*

She swallowed nervously, wishing they were alone, needing to hear him voice what she saw in his eyes.

"Miss?"

It was the father.

"Yes?"

"Thank you."

She smiled. "I didn't do anything."

"You don't understand," the man said. "She hasn't spoken in three weeks…. And that coloring thing…it's been going on nonstop ever since her mother—"

He choked on his words, unable to finish.

"I'm sorry," Caitlin said. "Is she ill?"

"My wife…she was the victim of a carjacking. They shot her in the head and dumped her and my daughter out of the car. She saw the whole thing."

"Dear Lord," Caitlin whispered, staring anew at the child. Now the anger and the red crayon were beginning to make sense. She could only imagine what the child must have felt, seeing her mother covered in blood and being so afraid. She didn't know how to assimilate what had happened to her and so had shut herself off into a world where nothing could intrude. Unfortunately she had shut herself off from the very people who could help her, as well.

"And your wife?" Mac asked quietly.

The man shook his head. "She's brain dead. They took her off the ventilator this morning, and now we're just waiting for her heart to stop."

"Don't you have any family? Someone who could be with her so you could be with your wife?"

"I have parents in Florida, but they can't afford to travel, and what with all the expenses of this...this..." He shuddered, then laid his hand on his daughter's head, trying to manage a smile. "Well, you know how it is."

That was just it. Caitlin didn't. Not once in her entire life had she ever had to worry about money. She'd felt guilt before, but never as much as she did now.

She looked up at Mac and knew he could tell what she was thinking. She turned back to the man.

"Sir? I'm sorry, but I didn't get your name."

"Hank Bridges."

"Where do you work, Mr. Bridges?"

"I work for the Sanitation Department, but I don't know how much longer they're gonna cover for me. I've had to be gone a lot since—"

Caitlin quickly changed the subject.

"What's your daughter's name?"

He smiled. "Katie. She's five."

At the sound of her name, the little girl looked up.

Caitlin tried to smile, but the pain in her heart kept getting in the way. "Isn't that something? My name is Caitie, too."

Katie's eyes widened slowly, eyeing Caitlin with new interest. When she nodded silently and then poked a finger through a loose curl dangling around Caitlin's eye, Caitlin caught her breath.

Suddenly she could feel herself beginning to come

unwound. The stress she'd been under, her near brush with death, the weight of guilt she bore, the not knowing whether Aaron would live or die—all of it seemed petty compared to what this child had endured, but she couldn't stop the rush of emotions.

Caitlin grabbed Mac's hand, which was still resting on her shoulder, and tried desperately to regain her control. But her empathy for the child was the last straw. She covered her face with her hands.

The look on Katie Bridges's face went from curious to startled. She dropped the crayon she was using to stare pointedly at Caitlin.

Mac hurt for her and for himself. After all that had happened, Caitlin's breakdown was inevitable. The problem was, he felt like crying, too. There was too damned much sorrow in the world.

While no one was watching, the little girl suddenly crawled into Caitlin's lap and began patting her face.

"Don't cry," she whispered. "Don't cry. Your daddy can kiss it all better."

"I don't have a—" Caitlin stopped. She'd been about to say that she didn't have a daddy anymore when she realized the child meant Mac. Instead of explaining, she grabbed the little girl's hands and lifted them to her lips, tenderly kissing one little palm and then the other. "Did you let your daddy kiss your hurts?"

The child frowned and then looked down.

"Did you?" Caitlin asked.

She shook her head.

"Why not?" Caitlin asked.

There was another moment of silence, and then she leaned over and whispered in Caitlin's ear. "Because."

"Because why?" Caitlin asked.

"Because he wasn't there when I fell."

Caitlin heard the man gasp and understood his shock all too well. This was the explanation for the behavior he hadn't understood. Her reason for not talking—her anger. He was the only person she knew to blame.

"Dear God," he cried, and lifted his daughter out of Caitlin's lap and into his arms. "Katie... baby...Daddy is so sorry about what happened to you and Mommy, but it wasn't his fault. Daddy was at work, remember? If I had been there, I would have hugged you both and made it all better, wouldn't I?"

Her little face crumpled.

"I would have loved you and kissed you and told you I was sorry you fell out of the car."

"And you would have made the bad man go away, too, wouldn't you, Daddy?"

The child's question, so poignantly asked, had everyone in the waiting room in tears.

"Yes, baby girl. Daddy would have made the bad man go away."

At that point the child started to cry, quietly at first, then in huge, gulping sobs.

"Thank God," the man muttered as he rocked his daughter against his chest. "Lady, I don't know your name, but I know what you are. You're an angel. I'm sorry for whatever reason you have to be here, but I will be forever grateful that you were."

Caitlin got to her feet. "I'm glad I could help," she said. Her voice was shaking. If she didn't get out now, she knew she was going to make a fool of herself. "Mac, I'm going to the ladies' room. I'll be right back."

"Wait," he said. "I'll go with you."

She shook her head, then pointed to the bathroom and phone bank across the hall.

"You can see me go in and see me come out, okay?"

He nodded reluctantly, knowing he had no choice.

"Is she your wife?" Bridges asked when she was gone.

Mac's heart gave a tug. "Not yet," he said. "Maybe in time."

"She said her name was Katie, too. Isn't that a coincidence?"

Mac wasn't going to explain, then thought to himself that if ever a woman deserved acknowledgment, it was Caitlin.

"Her real name is Caitlin, but her close friends call her Caitie."

A slight frown crossed the young man's face as the name settled in his mind.

"Now that I think about it, she looks sort of familiar."

He looked to Mac for further explanation.

Mac sighed, thinking what could it matter.

"Probably. She's Caitlin Bennett, the mystery writer."

"Oh man, isn't she the woman who's being stalked?"

"Yeah," Mac said. "I'd appreciate it if you wouldn't mention that when she comes back."

"Mister, after what she did for me, you don't have to ask."

Before Mac could answer, a nurse appeared in the doorway. Every eye in the room turned toward her, some in fear, some with expectancy. Then her gaze settled on Hank and his child.

"Mr. Bridges, you need to come now."

Hank looked at Mac and then down at his daughter, his face crumpling in heartbroken resignation.

"I guess this is it," he said. "Tell her again I said thank you."

"I will," Mac said. "And I'm very sorry for your loss."

It was all Mac could do to watch them leave. Their lives as they'd known them were coming to an end. He could only imagine what it would be like to love one woman desperately enough to marry, have a child with her and then have to give her back to God and finish life alone. Weary from grief and worry, he sat back down on the sofa and dropped his head. There was nothing left to do but pray that both Aaron and Caitlin would be okay.

A short while later, Caitlin returned to find Mac in the waiting room. When she saw the look on his face, she realized that Hank Bridges's waiting was over.

While her fear for Aaron was sickening, she felt better about herself than she had in months. Bridges didn't know it yet, but he no longer owed a penny to the hospital for his wife's extended care. There was also an extra ten thousand dollars in his checking account that hadn't been there an hour before. Money couldn't heal grief, but sometimes it made the grieving easier.

"Any news?" she asked.

Mac shook his head.

She settled back down beside him, her gaze fixed on the door.

"Caitie?"

"What?"

"What you did with that little girl..."

Caitlin shrugged, refusing to look at him. "I just played with her, Mac. Don't give me credit for something I don't deserve."

"You're making me crazy, do you know that?"

Now she looked. "What do you mean?"

"I thought I didn't like you. You know that, don't you?"

She grinned weakly. "Yes, but I *knew* I didn't like you, which makes me one up, doesn't it?"

He shook his head, a wry smile on his face.

"You never let up, do you, girl?" Then he sighed. "You know that I'm lost on this, don't you? I don't know what to do."

"You mean about Aaron? There's nothing we can do except wait."

"No, I'm not talking about Aaron. I'm talking about you. I'm falling in love with you, Caitie, and I don't know how to stop it."

It was the last thing she'd expected him to say, and yet it was the sweetest.

"Oh, Mac. Why would you want to?"

"You? Me? Together? It couldn't work."

"Why?"

"You're too damned rich."

She couldn't have been more insulted if he'd slapped her. "My money makes me unlovable?"

He cupped her face. "No, baby. Unapproachable. There's no way I could ever match the Bennett fortune."

She knew she was staring, but for the life of her, she couldn't stop.

"Well then," she said, her eyes filling with tears, "I suppose it's a good thing I still don't like you. It saves us both a lot of trouble."

"Caitlin, please don't."

"Oh, shut up, will you, McKee? I have enough on

my plate without having you rip out my heart and then hand it back to me on a platter.''

She stood abruptly, intent on sitting somewhere other than beside this infuriating man, when a doctor appeared in the doorway.

"The Workman family?" he asked.

"Here," Mac said, and tried to judge the expression on the doctor's face as to whether the news was bad or good.

"Mr. Workman came through surgery well," he said. "He suffered a broken nose, a concussion and a couple of broken ribs. His most serious injury is to his eyes."

Caitlin sank down into the nearest chair, too sick to stand.

"I think they will heal in time," the doctor continued. "But they are bandaged completely and will be for at least a week, maybe more. Barring any unforseen complications, I expect a full recovery, but I need to err on the side of caution by telling you he will have some facial scarring from the burns that might need plastic surgery. Right now, it's just too soon to tell."

"Thank you, Doctor," Mac said. "Thank you for saving my brother's life. When can we see him?"

"He's still in recovery," the doctor said. "And we intend to keep him sedated for at least twenty-four hours, so I strongly advise you to go home. It's when we dismiss him that he's going to need help."

But Mac wouldn't budge. "I just need to see him first," he said. "Even if he can't hear me, I need to do this for myself. Please."

The doctor smiled, then nodded. "I suppose it won't hurt," he said. "Come with me."

Mac turned. "Caitlin?"

"You go. Just tell him I love him."

"I don't think it's safe to—"

"I won't budge from this chair until you return."

Mac frowned, torn between the need to see Aaron and his fear of leaving Caitlin alone.

"Really," Caitlin urged. "I'll be fine."

"I'm sorry," the doctor said. "If your wife is ill, she's more than welcome to—"

"She's Caitlin Bennett, and I'm her bodyguard, not her husband."

Understanding dawned. "I'll call security," the doctor said. "They can stay with Miss Bennett until you return."

"Mac, really," Caitlin argued, but he was ignoring her.

"That would be great," he said.

"Let me make a quick call, and then I'll be back to escort you to see your brother."

He left, leaving Mac and Caitlin alone. She refused to look at him.

"Caitie, I didn't mean to hurt you."

Her chin was trembling as she lifted her head.

"Well, you did. It's rather startling to know that

my value as a woman is based on my monetary worth. All this time I thought—''

''You're twisting my words.''

''Oh sure, and you're breaking my heart. Here comes the doctor. Go see Aaron. I'll just sit here and count my money while you're gone.''

He turned away, furious with himself and the whole situation.

Fifteen

Caitlin walked into her apartment without waiting for Mac, leaving him to disarm the security system and lock the front door behind her. The relief of knowing Aaron was going to be okay was wonderful, but her heart was broken. Her father had spent a goodly portion of her growing up years reminding her that there would be men who would pretend to love her to get to her money. She'd been prepared for that to happen since puberty. But she hadn't expected to fall in love with a man whose pride was stronger than his love for her. She wanted to kick and scream and curse at the fates for dealing her another harsh blow.

Instead she stalked into her bedroom, slammed the door behind her and began stripping off her clothes. Damn Connor McKee to hell and back. He had made her feel dirty and shamed, as if the simple act of being born to wealth was something for which she should apologize.

"Stupid, bullheaded, macho, testosterone-loaded male."

She kicked off her shoes and tossed aside her coat.

"Major ass, anal-retentive twit."

Her slacks and sweater went flying.

"Hairy, subhuman, directionally deficient primate."

Out of invectives and insults, she dropped her lingerie into the hamper as she entered the bathroom, then turned on the shower, letting the water warm as she twisted her hair up in a knot to keep it off her neck. Grabbing a clean washcloth from the cabinet, she stepped into the shower and then slammed that door, too, just because she could.

The warmth was welcoming, and the water coming out of the jets was like thousands of tiny fingers kneading her skin. Groaning in quiet ecstasy, she turned her back to the water and closed her eyes, letting it wash over her body in a warm, cleansing spray.

She stood for what seemed like forever before turning her face to the showerhead. But the cleansing she needed wasn't happening. No matter how long she stood there, she couldn't wash away the images of the women who had died, their faces butchered, their battered bodies sprawled lifelessly against the snow.

She inhaled deeply and then exhaled slowly, trying to move herself into a meditative state. Instead she saw Aaron lying in the midst of fire and broken glass, bleeding like the women in the snow.

Her lower lip trembled as she pictured the office exploding and swordlike shards of plate glass flying outward and then down from the tenth floor. Knowing that as it did, it ended the life of a man who had done nothing more sinister than take a cab ride uptown.

Pain rose within her in waves, pushing and shoving like an incoming tide. Knowing it was there and not being able to stop it only added to her feelings of guilt and helplessness.

She opened her eyes. The shower stall was filled with steam, and the bathroom looked as if a fog had rolled in. She had to wash and get out. If she lingered much longer, the paint would start coming off the walls.

As she reached for her washcloth, she noticed color beneath her unpainted nails.

"What on earth?"

Using her fingernail, she dug it out and then rubbed it between her fingers.

Crayon.

A slight smile moved across her face. The smile widened as she started to laugh, but the laugh came out as a sob.

Poor Katie.

That a child should have been thrust into terror at such a young age was obscene. It had taken Caitlin Bennett twenty-nine years to learn that life could and would kick you in the teeth, even when you were down. But Katie Bridges had learned it before she was old enough to go to school.

The floor tilted beneath her feet. She grabbed at the walls, but the room wouldn't stop spinning. She sank to the bottom of the shower stall, her head bent, her hands braced on her knees. Everything within her was coming undone.

The first tears came slowly, burning her eyes and the back of her throat, sluiced away by the shower as quickly as they fell. Then came the harsh, choking sobs that ripped up her throat and echoed within the shower stall like an animal in pain.

Already heartsick about the fight they'd had and mad at himself for hurting Caitlin once again, Mac went straight to the phone to check for messages from Atlanta, figuring the best way to deal with their latest dispute was to give it some time. If he filled his head with work, he wouldn't have to think about what he'd done. But the messages were brief, nothing more than updates on investigations already in progress. It would seem that his office was running smoothly, even without him there. If only his personal life were in such good order.

Tossing aside the cell phone, he kicked off his shoes and began changing his clothes. The least he could do was be comfortable in his favorite sweats. As he came out of his room, he glanced at Caitlin's door. It was still shut, adding to the solidity of the wall he'd put between them.

He paused, laying the flat of his hand against the wood, as if touching her in the only way he had left. Suddenly he heard a strange, painful cry, and he jerked. Had she fallen? Was she ill? Had the killer been hiding in her home, awaiting her return?

"Caitlin? Caitie? Are you all right?"

No one answered.

He knocked on the door and called out again, still getting no response.

Worried, he opened the door and hurried inside, only to find she was nowhere in sight. The door to her closet was closed; the clothes she'd been wearing had been tossed aside like garbage, waiting to be picked up.

He frowned. Caitlin could be distracted when in the middle of her writing, but she wasn't a messy person. Chalking it up to her state of mind, he looked toward the bathroom, wondering if he dared intrude. Then he heard the sound again. The hair rose on the back of his neck. Without thought for what she would say, he bolted inside.

One moment Caitlin was on her knees, the water pounding against the top of her head, and the next thing she knew Mac was between her and the flow, lifting her to her feet and then into his arms.

"Baby...don't cry. God. Not like this. I'm sorry...so sorry."

The tenderness in his voice was her undoing. Instead of making her feel better, it made it that much worse. This was what she'd been missing—a man willing to stand between her and the world, and still love her as she was.

Her cries were breaking Mac's heart. Moving swiftly, he carried her out of the shower, then set her down and began drying her off as he would have a child. All the while, she kept sobbing.

"Caitie...Jesus...don't cry," he pleaded as he turned off the shower and stripped off his own wet clothes.

She inhaled on a sob and went limp.

He caught her before she hit the floor. The lack of expression in her eyes was frightening, almost as frightening as the sounds of her despair. He carried her into her bedroom and laid her down on the bed.

"Caitie, I didn't mean to hurt you. Please stop crying."

"No more," she mumbled, then rolled into a fetal position and closed her eyes.

Mac yanked the covers from beneath her, then crawled in beside her, pulled her to him and covered them up. He was afraid to let go. He wanted to ask her what she meant by "no more," but he was scared of the answer. In a normal world, Caitlin Bennett was not the kind of woman who would take her own life, but the world had gone crazy on her, and he didn't know her anymore.

He thought of Aaron, unconscious in the intensive care unit, of the woman in his arms who was at the mercy of an unidentified killer, of three families who were mourning their women, of a man who'd died because he was in the wrong place at the wrong time, and of a little girl who'd seen her mother's murder. It was enough to make anyone crazy, and so he held her, because it was all he could to.

Somewhere between the time he'd taken her to bed and the next passing hour, Caitlin hushed. Now and then the aftershock of a shudder would rip through her body as a reminder of what she'd endured.

He rose up on one elbow, thinking she had fallen asleep. She was staring blankly at the wall.

"Caitie?"

She didn't respond.

He kissed the side of her face and then her neck, then held her that much closer.

"This will pass," he said. "We will find the man who's doing this and put him away where he'll never hurt you or anyone else again."

She shivered, as if the mention of his existence was more than she could bear, but it was her only response.

Mac's belly knotted. "Talk to me, Caitlin. Call me horrible names. Tell me I'm a fool. Tell me I'm crazy. Just talk to me."

She drew her knees up toward her chest, curling her body in upon itself, and in doing so, pulled herself away from him.

The knowledge that she was both physically and mentally withdrawing was too frightening to let pass.

Mac sighed. He'd been wrong a few times in his life before and realized it later on, but nothing that amounted to the knot he'd put in his own gut today. The thought of never seeing her again was too awful to consider. If the least he had to do was swallow a little pride, then what the hell had he been thinking?

He rose up on one elbow and then laid his face against the side of her cheek.

"I love you, Caitie. Whatever else you may believe, know that I love you. And I was lying when I said I couldn't deal with all your money. It's really because you snore."

He felt her stiffen and he held his breath. Moments later, she rolled over on her back and stared him in the face.

"Say that again."

"What, darling? That I love you. Okay...I love you. Madly. Deeply."

Life was back in her eyes in a big way, right down to the glare he was getting.

"I don't snore."

Thank God...I made her mad. "Oh, that. Well, actually, you do."

Caitlin sat up in bed, naked as the day she was born. Her hair was in damp, heavy tangles, her eyes swollen, her lips puffy from crying.

"Is this your stupid macho way of trying to make up with me?"

Mac sat up, too, afraid to be lying too close should she decide to attack. He nodded.

"Well, it sucks," she said shortly. "You can't keep doing this to me. You make love to me, then you insult me. Then you watch over me as if you really cared about what happens to me, and then you tell me that we have no future because I'm too stinking rich. And *then* you tell me you love me and that I snore." She hit the bed with both fists. "I won't have it. Do you hear me? I won't have it anymore!"

"Would it make it all better if I told you I didn't want to live without you?"

All the fury in her posture went south. Mac reached for her hand, uncurling her anger as he uncurled her fingers, then threaded them through his own.

"Would you forgive me for hurting you if I told you that I'm so scared of losing you I can't sleep at night?"

"Damn you, Connor McKee, you do not fight fair," Caitlin said as a fresh set of tears threatened.

"Don't cry," Mac growled, pointing at her face. "Do you hear me? Whatever you do, do not shed another tear...at least for today. My heart can't take it."

She pulled her hand away, and then clasped both hands against her breasts, afraid to trust his about-face for fear he would slap her down again.

"Yes, well, at least you still have a heart," she

muttered. "Mine, I think, is on the bottom of your shoes."

Mac slumped. He'd smiled too soon. What if she didn't forgive him this time? He'd said some pretty unforgivable things.

"I said I'm sorry."

Caitlin glared. "Easy enough to say. If you don't mind, I think I'll wait and see if it sticks."

Mac nodded. "Fair enough," he said, then reached for her, pulling her down and pinning her between the mattress and his body. "In the meantime, I think I'm going to make love to you."

Caitlin arched an eyebrow as she wrapped her arms around his neck.

"You think? Mister, if you can't do better than that, then I placed my bet on the wrong damned horse."

He grinned. "You still love me, don't you?"

Her eyes welled with tears. "Yes, but don't let it go to your head."

He nuzzled the side of her neck, then raised himself up on his elbows, pausing to look at her.

"It's not my head that's in need, it's my heart. How much do you love me, girl?"

"Enough to make a fool of myself at least one more time."

"I'll take what I can get," he whispered, then stole her breath with his kiss.

* * *

Buddy sat in darkness while the world around him was spinning. Voices came and went in his head like magpies at a feeding, squawking and shrieking but saying nothing at all. His little package had been successfully delivered. That fag Aaron Workman was right where he'd sent him. Caitlin Bennett had to be mourning the injuries to her friend. The guilt to her soul had to be growing daily.

He closed his eyes and slapped his hands to his ears, trying to drown out the noise. It didn't make sense. He was doing everything right, but it was getting harder and harder to sleep. What was the problem?

Suddenly he bolted to his feet, ran into his bedroom and turned on the lights. She was everywhere in here. Sometimes he imagined he could even smell her perfume. It was expensive and exclusive, like the woman herself, but he knew who she really was, and he knew she didn't belong. She'd stolen everything that was his, and he wanted it back.

"It isn't fair," he whispered, his lower lip trembling like a child's.

His gaze centered on the blowup of her photo hanging over his bed. No matter how many times he slashed and marked the surface, he could still see the contours of her face.

"Don't you see? Don't you understand? What you have should be mine."

She didn't answer, and she wouldn't stop smiling.

In a fit of rage, he threw the first thing he could grab. Then he jerked back in shock, staring in disbelief as his alarm clock shattered into pieces all over his bed.

"See what you did!" he cried, pointing toward his bed. "See what you did? It's your fault. It's all your fault."

He spun away, searching for something else to throw when his gaze fell on the surveillance equipment. That was it. That was what he would do. It had been days since he'd listened to the tapes. He settled down at the table and switched on the machine, then sorted through the dates, searching for the one he'd heard last. Ah yes, here it was. Even though only one room had been bugged, he could tell from their conversations that the bodyguard had taken her to bed. He tossed the cassette aside, his eyes narrowing angrily. The bitch. He was in pain, and she was fucking the hired help. What was wrong with this picture?

He found the tape he wanted, popped it into the machine and leaned back in his chair. An hour came and went, and then another and another. He paused long enough to make himself a sandwich, then came back to listen, eating it as he sat, now and then making notes, reminders to himself that there were weaknesses in her life he had yet to probe.

It was some time later when he heard something that made him smile. McKee was talking to Caitlin, asking her something about a woman named Delarosa. Buddy knew the cops were trying to find her.

They wanted to talk to her about Devlin Bennett's past, but it wasn't going to happen unless they got themselves a psychic. One who could talk to the dead.

Feeling better, he turned off the machine, stretching wearily as he headed for the bathroom to get ready for bed. Juanita Delarosa had been a strong woman for her age. It had taken her far longer to die than he would have believed.

He glanced at his watch as he stepped out of his shoes. It was well after one in the morning, and he had to be at work before nine. He wanted to be rested and ready for the day when he walked into the office. It was the best way to make the voices go away.

Aaron was coming to. He had no idea where he was or how he'd gotten there. All he knew was that he hurt and that it was dark. He started to move and then moaned from the pain. Almost instantly, he heard the sound of chair legs scraping the floor and then his brother's voice.

"Aaron, it's me, Mac. You need to lie still."

"Where…?"

Mac touched Aaron's shoulder, giving his brother something concrete on which to focus.

"You're in the hospital. Do you remember why?"

Aaron didn't answer, instead lifting his hand toward his face.

"No, don't," Mac said softly. "You have bandages on your face. But the doctor said you're going to be okay. It's just going to take some time."

"Can't see," Aaron mumbled.

There was a slight hesitation in Mac's answer. "Yeah, I know. Your eyes are bandaged, but it's just until the flash burns heal."

"Burns?"

Mac hesitated again, gauging how much of the truth Aaron needed to know.

"Some, but not too bad. You just rest. They won't let me stay with you until you get out of ICU. But I'll be here as often as possible, okay?"

Aaron's mind was spinning. Burns? The ICU.

And then it all came flooding back in a series of images, out of sequence and out of control. His heartbeat accelerated, setting off a pattern of rapid and irregular beeps on one of the machines to which he was hooked.

Mac started to panic when Aaron grabbed his arm. "Caitie..."

Instantly Mac understood his brother's concern. "She's fine, just worried about you."

"Letter," he muttered.

Mac patted his arm, breathing a sigh of relief when Aaron's heartbeat resumed a normal rhythm. Aaron was remembering.

"Yes, the police already know," Mac said. "Now, I really have to go before they throw me out. Is there anything you want me to do? Anyone you want me to call?''

Aaron thought of David finding out about this through less than personal channels. It was too cruel to consider.

Mac sensed his brother's hesitation and leaned a little closer. "It's okay, buddy. You and I came to terms with this years ago. Is there someone you want me to call?''

Aaron sighed. It was getting harder to focus.

"David...Caitlin knows.''

"I'll tell her,'' Mac promised.

Aaron's consciousness was fading fast, but he needed to say what was on his heart.

"You...love...'' Aaron said, and then he was out.

Mac fought back tears. "I love you, too,'' he said softly.

Leaving was harder than he'd expected. He stopped three times on his way out the door to look back, just to assure himself that Aaron was still there and that the machines were still beeping. As he started through the doors, Caitlin saw him coming and stood up.

"How is he?''

"Good, I think,'' Mac said. "I talked to him a little.''

Delight changed Caitlin's expression. "Oh, Mac, that's good, isn't it? I mean, that he's awake.''

"Yeah, it's good.''

But she could tell that wasn't all.

"What?"

"Do you know someone named David?"

Caitlin gasped. "Oh my gosh! Yes! Poor David! I'll bet he's half out of his mind with worry."

"Why do you know him and I don't?"

"I don't know. I guess because Aaron is my best friend."

"I thought *I* was your best friend," he muttered.

She gave him a considering look. "I don't know just what we are," she said. "And you have to remember that Aaron hasn't hated my guts for the better part of the last few years. Surely you can't be upset about a man in your brother's life?"

"No, of course not. Just concerned about what kind of man he is. Aaron doesn't have to work, you know. His mother's death left him independently wealthy. I would hate to see someone take advantage of—"

Caitlin started to smile. "Ever hear of F & S Securities?"

"The brokerage house?"

"Yes, and David is the *F,* as in Freeh. His brother-in-law is the *S,* as in Sugarman. He's financially sound. Trust me."

Mac nodded. "That's all I wanted to know. Since you know him, the call about Aaron would be better coming from you."

Caitlin shook her head. "No, I think you're the one who should call. Aaron is your brother. David will appreciate the gesture."

"Yeah, I see what you mean. Do you mind if I step over there to make the call?"

"Tell him I said hello," Caitlin said.

Mac smiled. "I'll do that. And thanks," he said.

"For what?" Caitlin asked.

He shrugged. "I don't know.... Just for being here, I guess."

"I would always be here for you," she said quietly. "All you have to do is ask."

Before he could comment, she moved away, leaving him alone to make his call.

Sixteen

Aaron was moved into a private room two days after his surgery. To satisfy her own fears, Caitlin had hired private security to stand guard at his door in case the killer had thoughts of finishing the job, and filled his room with pots of blooming hyacinths, his favorite flower. He wouldn't be able to see them, but the scent was sweet, and there was nothing wrong with his sense of smell.

David Freeh was ever present, deeply grateful to know that Aaron was alive and more than ready to assume the duties of caregiver until the bandages were removed from Aaron's eyes. Even though Mac would have preferred to have Aaron come stay with him at Caitlin's apartment once he was released, it was agreed that he would be safer in another location. They had no way of knowing how much Caitlin's stalker knew about her friends and their habits, but putting Aaron back in the line of danger was not in his best interests, especially since he was unable to see it coming.

Caitlin moved through the days by working until

she could no longer think. Then she would shut down her computer and crawl into bed. She knew it wasn't healthy, going from one form of self-imposed isolation to another, but it was all she could cope with. Mac held her when she was scared and bullied her when she faltered, and, in a strange way, her emotional breakdown forced her to turn loose of her fears. Sometimes she felt she was at a crossroads in her life—waiting to see if she would be run over by a train or a bus—but other times her anger at being forced to hide would emerge. Those were the times when she felt hope, when she could see a time beyond the horror of what was happening now. And in those times she could almost believe she had a future with Mac McKee.

Caitlin hung up the phone as Mac came out of the bathroom wearing nothing but a towel around his waist.

"Who were you talking to?" he asked.

"Aaron. He's being released tomorrow. I told him you would call later."

"Definitely," Mac said, and let the towel drop as he reached for a pair of sweats.

Caitlin pillowed her head in her hands as she leaned against the headboard of her bed.

"Nice," she said.

Mac turned and grinned. "Admiring the view?"

"No. Your sweats. Love that color."

"They're gray, and you're lying."

"Through my teeth."

"I suppose you want me to take advantage of you now?"

"Only if you're up to the task."

He arched an eyebrow, well aware that he was *up* in a most obvious way.

"You be the judge," he drawled, and let his sweats fall on top of the towel as he crawled toward her on her bed.

Caitlin encircled him with her hand, smiling with satisfaction as he groaned.

"You'll do," she whispered.

"I'm going to do you, that's for damned sure."

She sighed as his tongue dipped into her navel. "You're rude."

"I know, but I'm good."

She pulled him up, making him look at her. "I don't want good. I want great."

"I am the greatest," he said.

"That was Muhammad Ali's claim to fame. You're going to have to get another one."

He raised himself up on both elbows, gazing greedily at her face. He loved her so much, and she was making him crazy.

"I'm the best man for the job?"

She frowned, pretending to study the phrase. "I don't know...that sounds a lot like a plumbing commercial."

He slanted a hard, hungry kiss across her lips, stopping only after he heard her moan.

"Still need a recommendation?"

"No... Lord, no," Caitlin sighed, and pulled him down to her.

Two hours later, they had yet to get out of bed. Caitlin was dozing and Mac was holding her close, watching the play of morning light across her face. The scar above her eyebrow was still a deep, shocking pink, although the bruises she'd suffered had long since faded. If only this nightmare they were living would disappear, as well.

He glanced at the clock and then carefully slipped out of bed, careful not to disturb her sleep. Grabbing his clothes, he dressed in the hall and headed for the kitchen. He needed to think, and before that could happen, he needed the kick of caffeine to jump-start his brain.

He ran water in the carafe, then measured coffee into a filter before turning on the pot. Soon the scent of freshly brewing coffee began to make itself known. Mac walked into the living room and turned up the heat before moving to the windows overlooking the streets below.

Snowflakes swirled within the eddys of air between the buildings on their way to the ground, adding inch upon deadly inch to the snow already there. He frowned. Would this snow never stop?

He closed his eyes, letting his thoughts go back to

last night. For him, making love to Caitlin had been something close to holy. Her breath on his cheeks had been soft and warm, the tears in her eyes, tears of joy. She'd come to him without hesitation, wrapping herself around him and pulling him deep into her sweet heat, and they'd both lost their minds. But reality had come and daylight, and he was afraid. So damned afraid of losing her like he'd lost Sarah.

He turned away from the window and strode into the kitchen, quickly pouring himself a cup of coffee. There were so many obstacles between them. She lived in New York. He lived in Atlanta. Her worth was in the billions. He had yet to make his first million. Someone was trying to kill her, and he hardly knew where to begin in keeping her safe. She was aggravating and hard-headed, and he couldn't remember ever being so attracted to a woman in his life. Not even Sarah had evoked the emotion within him that Caitlin did,

He took a slow sip of coffee as he shook off the dread. He had to think positive and stay focused. Somewhere out there in the snow-covered city, a madman was planning his next move on Caitlin, and he had to be ready.

He took another sip of coffee and filched a cookie from the cookie jar before returning to the living room. Washing down the last bite of cookie with another sip of coffee, he picked up the phone. It had been a week since their visit to the precinct, and he was curious as to how the investigation was going. After a brief search for Amato's card, he made the call, waiting for the line to pick up.

"Detective Amato."

"Detective, this is Connor McKee. Haven't talked to you since my brother was admitted to the hospital. How is the investigation going?"

"Had a little kink late yesterday evening," he said.

Mac frowned. "How so?"

"Neil and Kowalski found the Delarosa woman."

"And she wasn't able to help you?"

"She was dead."

"That's too bad," Mac said. "I guess Caitlin didn't know, although I remember her saying she was elderly."

"She didn't die of old age," Amato said.

Something in the tone of the detective's voice sent a chill up Mac's spine.

"What are you getting at?"

"She was murdered, and based on preliminary estimates, a couple of days before we got there. Her house was like ice, and what with the cold weather we've been having, it was difficult to tell the exact time of death. I'll know more after the autopsy."

The skin crawled on the back of Mac's neck. "Are you suggesting that the killer got to her before you did?"

"It's looking that way."

"Her face...did he...?"

"Naw, but he cut out her tongue. M.E. says she could've bled to death from that wound alone."

The devil walks among us.

Mac shuddered, then set down his coffee cup, the phone still to his ear as he strode to the window. A simple winter scene. Snow-covered rooftops, people in colorful coats and scarves. Beneath the purity of the snow lay an ugliness impossible to conceal.

"McKee? You still there?"

"So she wouldn't talk," Mac said.

"Yeah...we read it the same way."

Mac's shock turned to anger.

"Damn it, Amato, this doesn't make sense! You and three other detectives were the only people who heard Caitlin speak that woman's name. How in hell would he find out you were looking for her unless somebody told?"

"Are you suggesting I've got a leak in my department?" Amato growled.

"I'm not *suggesting* anything. I'm just stating the facts," Mac said.

"Granted, my people knew, but so did you and Miss Bennett. How many people did *you* tell?"

Mac's voice lowered, his words slowed, but his fury was impossible to miss.

"I'm going to pretend you didn't say that. There hasn't been a word spoken about those details except in the presence of New York City's finest and in the privacy of her home. Not even my brother knew what was going on, and look where he landed.''

"Look, McKee, I can understand your concerns, but trust me, my people are one hundred percent. They're professionals. They would not jeopardize an investigation like this in any way, shape or form. When I know something more, I will let you know.''

"Fine," Mac said, and hung up, knowing he was going to have to break the news to Caitlin and scared to death of how she would receive it.

He sat down with a thump, gazing around the room in disbelief and trying to remember if anyone had been present when they were talking who could have leaked the name. To his knowledge, no one had been in this apartment since his arrival but Aaron, the detectives and a couple of takeout delivery boys. And Juanita Delarosa's name had never been mentioned in front of any of them, of that he was certain.

It was frightening to realize that the killer was inching his way toward his ultimate goal—Caitlin herself—and Mac didn't know how to make him stop.

Shoving his fingers through his hair, he kicked back in the seat and put his feet up on the edge of the table. This didn't make sense. He'd been a cop. He knew how criminals thought. So if he was so damned good at his job, why couldn't he see what they were missing?

"God help me," he whispered, his gaze wandering

from the pale, celery-green walls to the ornate wain-scoting above.

He stared blankly, his thoughts jumping from one scenario to another, but the longer he looked, the less he thought about Amato and the more he stared at the room. Within seconds he was on his feet and reaching for the phone. Moments later, Mike Mazurka, the security guard downstairs, answered.

"This is Mike. Is there something you need, Miss Bennett?"

"Mike, it's me, Mac, and yes, there's something we need."

"You name it," Mike said.

"I need a stepladder. One that will get me to the ceiling."

"Give me a few and it'll be right there," Mike said.

Mac hung up the phone, adrenaline racing through his system. It was something Amato had said about who Mac and Caitlin might have told that had gotten him thinking. Granted, they'd only talked about it be-tween themselves, but in this day and age, that didn't guarantee privacy. If her home had been bugged, it was his fault it hadn't been found. He was in the security business, and she was being stalked. When he installed her alarm system, he should have checked the whole place as a matter of course, but he hadn't, and his omission might have gotten a woman killed.

Fifteen minutes later, Mac had the ladder in hand. He turned his attention to the room and all the places a listening device might be concealed. While waiting for the ladder to be delivered, he'd checked everything that was within his reach except the room where Caitlin was sleeping. He called himself a coward for hesitating to wake her, but he knew what would result when he did. The longer he could put it off, the better.

"Okay. If I was a bug, where would I be?"

Heating and air-conditioning vents were the most obvious places, so he started with them first. Dragging the ladder across the floor, he set it up and then started to climb. Halfway there, he realized he was going to need tools to take off the vent covers. He climbed down, cursing himself for not mentioning it to Mike when he asked for the ladder.

He was on his way into the kitchen to see what he could find when Caitlin came out of her bedroom. He stopped, waiting for the moment when she would realize he was watching her, and wondering why it had taken him so long to admit that he was in such total love. Then she saw him and smiled, and his heart skipped a beat. After he told her the latest, that smile would be gone.

"Hey there," Caitlin said. "You look like you're on a mission. What are you doing?"

"Looking for a screwdriver."

Caitlin frowned. "There are several in the drawer to the right of the sink."

"Hot damn," he muttered, and hurried into the kitchen.

Caitlin followed, her curiosity piqued. "Why do you need a screwdriver?"

He palmed a flathead screwdriver as well as a Phillips.

"I've got some bad news."

The color drained from her face as she grabbed the back of a chair. "Aaron! He didn't—"

"No, no, Aaron's fine," Mac said. "I talked to him right after you went to sleep."

"Then what?" Caitlin asked.

Mac sighed. There was no easy way to say it. "The police located your father's old secretary."

"Juanita? Wasn't she able to help?"

Mac crossed the room, laid the screwdrivers down and then took her by the shoulders, giving them a gentle squeeze before he continued. "I'm afraid not, baby. She was dead."

Caitlin immediately assumed what Mac had first thought, that she had passed away from old age.

"Oh dear. I'm sorry I didn't know. I would have gone to her services."

"You probably still can," Mac said. "But she didn't die of natural causes. She was murdered...and Amato is guessing less than forty-eight hours before they found her."

Caitlin stilled. "What aren't you telling me?"

Mac slumped. He would give anything not to have

to tell her the rest, but it was her life that was on the line. She deserved to know everything.

"The stalker did it."

Caitlin flinched, but her gaze never wavered. "How do you know? Did he slash her face like he—"

"No, baby."

"Thank God," Caitlin said, and then realized that still didn't explain how they knew who had killed her. "What made them think the same man killed her? This is an ugly world, Mac. Maybe she was being robbed and walked in on the thief. Maybe—"

"No."

Her voice broke. "Then how? How do they know?"

"He cut out her tongue."

Caitlin paled, then sat with a thump, trembling too much to stand. "So she wouldn't talk."

"That was the inference the cops got. I agree with the theory."

Caitlin's eyes narrowed again, her mind jumping to the same conclusion Mac had drawn.

"Who told? Someone in the department had to leak that information."

"I already challenged Amato on that. He swears it didn't come from them, which got me to thinking, which is why there's a ladder in your living room and why I need a screwdriver."

"I don't follow you." She blinked and stood abruptly. "There's a ladder in my living room?"

"We talked about her...about Juanita Delarosa," Mac said.

"Yes, but no one was here."

"But someone could have been listening."

"I don't—" Waves of color flushed her cheeks as her eyes sparked in anger. "Do you think my home has been bugged?"

"I don't know," Mac said. "But considering what's been happening to you, it's something I should have checked when your security system was installed."

"Oh my God," Caitlin muttered, then snatched up the screwdrivers. "Show me!"

Mac was encouraged by her behavior. Mad was healthy, and Caitie was one of the best he'd seen at venting fury.

"Lead the way," he said, pointing to the living room. "I'm starting with the heat and air vents. And while we're looking, talk about anything...the snow...your book... Anything except what we're really doing."

They found it in the chandelier, lying inside a small glass globe beside a pair of dead flies and a spider that had long since fried from the heat of twenty-four candelabra bulbs.

Mac dropped it into her hand and then put a finger to his lips. She nodded, holding it carefully as he climbed down from the ladder.

More? she mouthed.

He shrugged, then took it out of her hand and dropped it into his cup of cold coffee.

"Do you think there are more?" she whispered.

"We'll soon find out," he muttered, and headed for the next room, dragging the ladder.

But after a thorough search that lasted another two hours, Mac was convinced that the place was clean.

"Looks like that was the only one," he said. "Would you please call Mike and tell him I'm going to set the ladder out in the hall? They can come get it at their convenience."

Caitlin hurried to do as he asked, glad there was something positive she could do. When she came back, Mac was on his cell phone, talking to Sal Amato.

"Yes, I owe you an apology," Mac said.

"Where did you say you found it?" Amato asked.

"Living room, in a light fixture. It was the only one."

"It was enough, wasn't it?" Amato said. "And thanks for letting us know."

"Amato...I know this is asking a lot, but would you do something for me?"

"Depends," Amato said. "What's on your mind?"

"For now, don't tell anyone what I found. Let this be just between you and us."

"Now look here," Amato began, "you're—"

"Just for a couple of days," Mac said. "We don't

know where we're going with this, and the tighter the coil, the less likely it is to come unwound."

He heard Amato sigh.

"Yeah, all right," Amato said, and then added, "Have you seen the evening paper?"

"No."

"Be prepared," Amato said. "There's a big story linking the letter bomb to what's happening to Miss Bennett."

"I'm surprised the phone hasn't been ringing off the wall," Mac said. "Thanks for the heads-up."

"Yeah, don't mention it," Amato said. "Take care."

With that, he hung up, leaving Mac to face Caitlin once again.

"Now what?" she asked.

"The evening papers...they've connected the explosion at Aaron's office to what's happening to you."

"Oh, great," Caitlin said. "I'd better call Kenny."

She disappeared into her office, leaving Mac with growing concern. This standoff couldn't last forever. Eventually the killer would tire of killing substitutes and reach for her instead.

He glanced at the front door, certain that he'd locked it after he'd put the ladder in the hall, and then went to check it again. It was locked safe and sound, and the alarm system was set. His shoulders slumped. This wasn't good. Now he was second-guessing himself. With Mike in the lobby and limited access to the penthouse through the special elevator, she should be safe enough here. But he couldn't take that for granted. He'd done that before, and it had cost an old woman her life.

As he waited for Caitlin to return, another fear surfaced. Had he and Caitlin talked about moving Aaron to David's? He couldn't remember, and he couldn't take the chance that they had. At that point, Caitlin came back.

"Kenny is on the job," Caitlin said. "He's the reason I haven't been bugged by a bunch of reporters. All the inquires have been going through him, and nothing has gone out except what is basically public record."

"Good for him," Mac said, then opened his arms. "I don't know about you, but I could use a hug."

"Always," she said, and went into his arms. "Mac?"

"Hmm?"

"Thank you."

"For what, baby?"

"For being here. You didn't have to, and yet you came."

"Aaron is a hard man to refuse," he said, nuzzling his chin on the top of her head.

"Is Aaron the only reason you came?"

"I told myself so in the beginning, but you and I both know it's not the truth. When he told me you'd been hit by a truck, I couldn't think past the last time I'd seen you, laughing at something Aaron had said and then making a face at me.''

''I didn't.''

He smiled. ''Yeah, actually, you did. It was on the balcony of Aaron's apartment. Remember? It was last Fourth of July, and we were watching the fireworks going off over the river.''

''I remember being at Aaron's. I do *not* remember making a face. What had you done to me?''

He laughed. ''So, we're assuming it was something *I* did?''

''Wasn't it always?''

He shrugged. ''Probably. Looking back, I must have been like some little six-year-old boy, in love for the first time and not knowing what to do with all those emotions except insult you.''

''You're forgiven.''

''Thank you, my love.''

There was a moment of silence, and then Caitlin looked up.

''Am I, Mac? Am I your love?''

''Yes.'' Then he cupped her face in his hands. ''What about me, Caitie? Am I yours?''

A quick shimmer of tears came into her eyes, but she quickly blinked them back.

''Yes, Connor McKee, you are my love. More than you know. More than I can say. Even if my money appalls you. Even if someone wants me dead.''

Mac's stomach turned at the thought of her picture winding up on the wall of Amato's office along with the other victims. He couldn't bear to lose her. And then it hit him. If he didn't change his attitude, he would lose her anyway—when this was over. Was his pride worth more than their love? He felt shame for even considering the thought.

"Nothing about you appalls me except what you're going through. I'm sorry for what I said about that. Forgive me?"

Caitlin's heart lifted. "Does this mean what I think it means?"

"If you are referring to the fact that I refuse to live without you in my life, then yes."

Caitlin smiled while Mac's fear increased. Please God, help me keep her safe.

Too moved to say more, he hugged her then, satisfied for now that she was safe in his arms.

"Mac?"

"What, baby?"

"I'm getting really hungry, and there's not a lot of food in the place. Do you want to order in or go out?"

"Order in, I think, if it's all right with you."

"Sure. Do you want to do it, or shall I?"

"Let me," he said. "I need to make another call, as well. It also occurred to me that we might have given away the fact that Aaron's going to David's when he's released from the hospital. He and David

need to know so they can take precautions. I don't
want to put either one of them in jeopardy again.''

"Oh, no...you're right," Caitlin said. "Go call
now! Aaron is going home today, remember? Tell
David to take the guys from the security firm with
him. They can stay on the payroll until...until the
problem is solved.''

"Will do," he said. "But about the food. What do
you want to eat?"

She smiled. "I don't care. Surprise me."

He grinned. "Don't I always?"

She laughed. "Whatever," she said. "I'm going to
take that piece of cheesecake out of the freezer. It
will be our dessert."

"Honey, you're the dessert. But go ahead and thaw
the thing out, just in case you run out of steam."

He could still hear her laughing as he closed the
office door.

Buddy poured himself a fresh cup of coffee and
then went back to his desk. Several calls had come
in while he was out and he needed to return them
before the end of the day.

"What did you find out?"

Buddy looked up, wondering as he did why women
colored their hair. Hers wasn't just red, it was brassy.

"Not much," he muttered. "I've got to return
these calls first, and then I need you to do something
for me."

She nodded. "Yes, all right."

He sifted through the messages, making himself focus on their topics. These days, his mind had a tendency to wander more than usual. Picking up the phone, he made the first call. It rang once, then twice, then an answering machine came on. He left his name, then laid that message aside and picked up the next. He smiled then, his thoughts on everything but his work. It was time to quit playing around. Once Caitlin Bennett was out of his mind and six feet under, his promises would be kept. It wouldn't fix what had been broken, but it was the only justice he could ever have.

Not much longer now, Mother. Soon she'll have to pay.

Caitlin was in the middle of her second piece of pizza when she suddenly jumped to her feet, her eyes wide with excitement.

"Mac! I just remembered something!"

"Are you going to eat that?" he asked, pointing to the pizza she'd left on her plate.

"Yes," she said, slapping his hand away. "There's more in the box, for Pete's sake. Leave mine alone."

"Just asking," he said, pulling out his fourth slice. "So...what did you remember that's so exciting?"

"Charles Abernathy, Daddy's lawyer. He might know even more than Juanita would have known."

"But the police have already checked with your firm. They didn't know anything."

Caitlin was all but dancing. "No, no. Not them. Abernathy was before."

Mac swallowed the bite he'd been chewing and dropped his pizza onto his plate.

"Before what?" he asked.

"Bernstein and Stella have only been representing us a little less than ten years. Before that, it was Mr. Abernathy. Oh, Mac, what if he's no longer alive? I haven't talked to him in years. He must be eighty-five, at least, maybe older."

"Do you know where he lived?"

"I did once, if only I can find it. I know! It would be in one of Daddy's old address books. I think they're in a box in the office closet."

"Finish your pizza before it gets cold," Mac said. "We'll look in a few minutes."

"I like cold pizza," Caitlin called, already on her way out the door.

"You would," Mac muttered, eyeing his slice with regret. Taking one last big bite, he followed her out. If she was right, and the old man's faculties were sharp, they might get the break they'd been needing.

Seventeen

Caitlin leaned over the seat back and patted her chauffeur on the shoulder.

"Uncle John, are you sure we're on the right road?"

"Oh, yes," he said. "I know where we're going. My sister was in the same retirement home."

"Okay," Caitlin said, smiling as she sat back in the seat. "It's quite a coincidence that your sister and Mr. Abernathy wound up in the same place." Then she looked at Mac, savoring the skip her heart made when he winked and reached for her hand.

"Oh, it's no coincidence, missy. I used to bring your father to visit Mr. Abernathy. Later, when Sylvia needed a place to stay, we naturally thought of Glen Ellen Village. Of course she's long since gone."

"My father came here?"

"Oh, yes. Once a month, regular as clockwork."

"Why didn't I know that?" she muttered.

"Your father...he was a very private man," the chauffeur said.

"Yes, he was," Caitlin said. "I think, more than I knew."

"We're here," Mac said, pointing to a large entrance gate and to the facilities beyond. "It wasn't such a long drive after all."

"At the foot of the Catskills, you know. You should see it in the fall when all the leaves begin to turn. A rare beauty it is," John said.

The car rolled to a stop, and the old man got out, grabbing the door before Mac could move.

"Mac, let him do his thing. He likes to be needed."

"Don't we all," Mac said as the chauffeur opened the door, then stepped back, giving Mac room to get out. Once Mac was out, he turned and took Caitlin's hand, helping her onto the front walk, where the snow had been shoveled away.

"You give Mr. Abernathy my best, missy."

"I will, Uncle John, and we shouldn't be long."

"Take your time. Take your time. It's a nice enough day. I'm just glad to be out of the house."

Mac took Caitlin's hand. "Okay, honey. We're off to see the wizard."

"We hope," Caitlin said.

"Don't give up before we've even talked to him."

"You're right," Caitlin said. "But let's hurry. I keep feeling like I'm being watched."

They reached the front door. Caitlin paused long enough to fiddle with her hair.

"How do I look?"

"Good to go," Mac said, and gave the stray lock of hair over her left eye a tug.

Minutes later, they were escorted to the room that Charles Abernathy now called home.

"Mr. Abernathy, you've got visitors," the nurse said, and then motioned for Caitlin and Mac to go in. "He's a little hard of hearing, but sharp as a tack."

Mac gave Caitlin a quick wink, as if to say, I told you so, and then followed her inside the room.

Caitlin had retained a mental picture of the man who'd been her father's lawyer, but this old, withered gentleman wasn't him. Charles Abernathy had been well over six feet tall and portly. This fellow was bone-thin and wizened. In fact, he looked as if his body had crumpled, leaving him in the wheelchair like a discarded piece of paper. She quickly moved to the window where he was sitting and pulled up a chair so that she could face him as she sat.

"Mr. Abernathy, I'm Devlin Bennett's daughter, Caitlin. Do you remember me?"

The old man squinted, staring for a long silent moment at Caitlin's face. Then he suddenly smiled, and she saw the man that he'd been.

"Why, Caitlin, of course I remember you. I was sorry to hear of your father's passing. I couldn't attend the services, you see. I hope you don't think less of me for not going."

She clasped his hands and felt a very faint warmth

from the blood persistently pushing through what was left of his veins.

"Of course not, and I'm the one who should be apologizing for not visiting you. You were one of my father's most trusted friends."

"It's not proper to mix business with pleasure, you know. But Devlin and I did have a friendship that transcended that of lawyer to client. I miss his visits. We used to talk of the old times." His smile withered as his eyes grew dim. "There's no one left, you know, who remembers those times."

"I'm sorry," Caitlin said.

Abernathy shrugged, as if shaking off a bad dream. "Where are my manners? You there...young man. I don't believe I caught your name."

"It's Connor McKee, sir. Is there something you need?"

"Another chair for you. There's one at the desk. Please be so kind as to pull it up by us and seat yourself."

"Thank you, I will."

Caitlin bit her lip, uncertain how to broach the subject of her father's past, but time was not on their side. And judging from the blue cast around the old man's mouth, time was not on his side, either. Oddly enough, before she could figure out how to ask what she'd come to ask, the old man beat her to it.

Once Mac was seated, Charles straightened his lap

robe and then lifted his head, looking Caitlin square in the eye.

"You must have come for a reason. How can I help you?"

Mac smiled to himself. At one time, Abernathy must have been a fierce courtroom competitor.

"You're right," Caitlin said. "I'm in a terrible dilemma."

"I don't practice law anymore, you know. Too old. It's a damn shame when the body wears out before the mind. I can still think, but my legs don't remember how to walk."

"It's all right," Caitlin said. "I don't need a lawyer. I need you and your memory."

He slapped his leg with a smile. "Then you've come to the right place. What do you need to know?"

She hesitated, looking to Mac for guidance, but he only gave her a nod, as if to say the floor was hers. She sighed. He was right. Only she would know what to ask.

"Before I ask you any questions, you need to know why I'm asking. Do you know that I'm a writer?"

"Oh, yes. I listen to your books on tape quite often. I'm especially fond of *Detour.*"

Caitlin hid her surprise. "Why, that's...marvelous. Thank you," she said, then went on to explain. "For the past six months or so, I've been receiving some very disturbing letters from what I assumed was a disgruntled fan. Recently we learned that he's not just disgruntled, he's deadly. He's tried once to kill me and failed, and in what we think is frustration, he's begun killing women who look like me, instead.''

"Oh my!'' Abernathy looked closer at Mac. "Are you an officer of the law?''

"Not now, sir. But I was. I own and operate my own private security business. I'm acting as a bodyguard for Miss Bennett until all this has been resolved.''

"I should think so,'' Charles said, then took Caitlin's hand.

"Your father would have hired more than one bodyguard,'' he said softly.

Caitlin smiled. "Mac wasn't hired, Mr. Abernathy. He's with me because he chooses to be.''

"Ah...so that's the way it is,'' he said, eyeing Mac even more closely.

"Look, Mr. Abernathy, the reason I'm here is that we're grasping at straws. We have no leads as to the killer's identity, but there's some speculation that his motive could be related to my father's past, rather than my books.''

All of a sudden the old man grew still.

"I can't talk about your father's private affairs,'' he said gruffly.

Caitlin dropped her head in defeat, but Mac wasn't ready to quit.

"Please, Mr. Abernathy. You don't understand. He's not just killing women, he's butchering them.''

"He killed Juanita Delarosa so she couldn't talk to us," Caitlin added. "No one knows we're here. I told no one, not even the police, that you even exist. For all they know, Bernstein and Stella have always represented us."

Charles waved away her concerns. "Oh, I don't care about safety. I've far outlived my time as it is." Then he shook his head in disbelief. "Poor Juanita. I remember her well." He looked at Mac with a piercing gaze, quite startling in an old man's face. "Did she suffer?"

"Yes."

He leaned back in his wheelchair and closed his eyes. As they sat, awaiting his next move, a single tear rolled down his face. When he opened his eyes, they were fierce.

"What do you want to know?"

"Did Daddy have any enemies who would be capable of something like this?"

There was no hesitation in his answer. "None that I know of. His enemies were all about money."

Mac laid his hand on Caitlin's arm, begging her forgiveness in advance as he asked. "Did he have any secrets? Something that only you knew?"

Caitlin looked startled and wanted to argue that her father wasn't that kind of man, but then, she hadn't known of his visits to Glen Ellen. Maybe there were other things about him that she hadn't known, things that would matter—things that might save her life.

Abernathy frowned. "I'm sorry, but you've taken me by surprise with that question. It's been so long since I was in the habit of keeping confidences that I..."

He stopped, then looked up, his eyes widening in memory.

"There was one thing that I always thought rather strange, although I can't imagine how it could have any bearing on these murders."

"Anything," Mac urged. "I was a cop long enough to know that one man's garbage is another man's treasure."

Abernathy looked at Mac and smiled. "And that includes information. Am I right, son?"

"Yes, sir, you are. Now, what were you saying?"

"Well, for as long as I could remember, your father had two thousand dollars a month sent to a woman in Toledo, Ohio. There was even a clause in his will that the monies be continued after his death. I did so up until the day I retired, and I distinctly remember giving Julius Bernstein that information myself when he took over your father's affairs."

Caitlin was flabbergasted. "Two thousand dollars a month?"

He nodded.

"How long had that been going on?" she asked.

"Close to thirty years, I'd say."

Mac looked at Caitlin. "Can you think of any reason why he would do that?"

Caitlin shook her head. "No. In fact, I'm shocked."

"Mr. Abernathy, do you by any chance remember her name?" Mac asked.

Abernathy smiled. "Why certainly. I told you it was my body that quit, not my mind. Her name was Georgia, like the state. Georgia Calhoun."

They were all the way back into the city before Mac thought to ask John Steiner if he'd ever heard of Georgia Calhoun. When he asked, the chauffeur tilted his head, as if giving it some thought, then shook his head.

"No, I can't say that I have. Is she a relative of yours?"

"No, sir. We were thinking you might have heard Mr. Bennett speak of her in years past."

"Oh, no, sir," John said. "Mr. Bennett didn't confide in me at all. I just drove his car, you understand."

"It's all right, Uncle John. I confided in you enough for both of us, didn't I?"

Ignoring the blare of a horn and the cabdriver cursing in the lane beside him, John chuckled as he braked for a red light.

"That you did, missy. And I kept your secrets, didn't I?"

Caitlin grinned. "Did you ever. Daddy never did find out that it was me who broke the headlight on his vintage MG. He thought he'd done it. He raged for weeks at his carelessness."

John laughed. "And it took him six months to find a replacement, remember?"

"It broke me from ever driving a car again," Caitlin said.

Mac looked at her with surprise. "You can't drive?" he asked.

Caitlin met John's gaze in the rearview mirror and then broke into laughter.

"Well, let's just say that it would be in everyone's best interests if I never got behind the wheel of a car again."

"You just needed some practice, and this city is no place to learn to drive a car," John explained.

The light changed, and the car accelerated. Mac took Caitlin's hand, threading her fingers through his and then giving it a gentle squeeze.

"Come to Atlanta. I'll teach you to drive."

Caitlin turned. "Are you serious?"

He nodded. "When I leave, come home with me."

"For a visit?"

He hesitated, then smiled. "For starters."

She lowered her voice. "Connor McKee, what are you asking me?"

"We're here, missy," John said.

"Don't get out," Mac said. "You're on the traffic side of the street. I'll help Caitlin out, and thank you for a wonderful drive."

John Steiner turned, giving the pair in the back seat
a nod and a smile.

"Yes, sir, thank you," he said, then gave Caitlin a
calm, studied stare. "You take care of yourself,
missy, and if I were you, I'd be thinking hard about
that visit to Atlanta."

Caitlin blushed as Mac helped her out of the car,
then waved the old chauffeur on his way.

"Why do I feel like I just got caught necking?"

Mac grinned. "Wishful thinking, maybe?"

She punched him lightly on the arm and grinned.

"Inside with you. We need to check on Aaron."

"And I want to get on the Internet and see what
we can find out about Georgia Calhoun."

An hour later, Caitlin was throwing together a
snack and Mac was on the phone with Aaron.

"Yeah," he said. "We're doing all right. How
about you, little brother?"

"I'm probably going to gain fifty pounds," Aaron
said. "David is a lot like Mom. Remember how she
always wanted to feed us, no matter whether we were
hurt, sick or sad?"

Mac laughed. "Boy, do I ever. I could go for some
of those coconut cookies she used to make."

"Caitlin makes some that are pretty close," Aaron
said.

Mac didn't bother to hide his shock. "Caitlin
cooks?"

Aaron laughed aloud, then winced. "Oh, that hurt," he moaned. "Don't make me laugh again, please."

"Sorry," Mac said. "But I've yet to see Caitlin cook anything. She opens cans, reheats and eats peanut butter and pickle sandwiches, but I don't see her cook."

"Oh, that's because she's into a book. In between times, she's great."

"Well, something to look forward to."

"Sticking around that long, are you?" Aaron teased.

"Stuff it, little brother. It was a figure of speech."

"By the way," Aaron said, "thanks for calling David for me."

"Hey, no problem. He's pretty sharp. You'd do well to take some of his investment advice."

Aaron chuckled. "Always thinking ahead, aren't you, Mac? When are you going to let yourself go and enjoy life before it's too late?"

"Enough about me," Mac said. "I've got some computer work ahead of me."

"Better you than me," Aaron said. "Besides, who knows? I may have to learn to use Braille."

Mac heard the fear in Aaron's voice and frowned.

"That's not going to happen," he said. "You heard the doctor. You're going to be fine, but it's going to take patience."

"Of which I have little," Aaron said. "Oh, I've

got to go. David is telling me that lunch is ready. Lucky me. We're having smothered steak, baked potatoes and Caesar salad.''

"Just be glad you're still here to eat it," Mac said. "Take care, and remember what I told you. Stay out of sight until this mess is over."

"I don't have to be told twice. I'll talk to you later."

Mac hung up, then immediately turned to Caitlin's computer. During his stint on the force, he'd gotten pretty good at locating missing persons. He'd even found a couple of perps with outstanding warrants with no more information than old work records. This time he had a name, a city and a state. If only he hadn't lost his touch. They needed a break in this case in the worst way.

Sal Amato was on the way out of the precinct when a FedEx truck pulled away from the entrance. He noticed it with half a thought, then headed toward his car, his mind on lunch and wondering where the hell Paulie had gone. He'd said he would be right behind him.

He started the car, letting the engine warm up as he waited. A minute later he saw Paulie waving at him from the door. He rolled down the window.

"What?" he yelled.

"Lieutenant wants you. He said the tape is back from Quantico."

Sal killed the engine and got out on the run, slipping and sliding through the snow-packed lot as he hurried toward the door.

"Are you kidding me?" he asked, as he ran inside.

"No," Paulie said. "And hurry. The lieutenant says there's something we need to see."

They took the stairs two at a time, both puffing by the time they reached the third floor.

"Has anyone called Neil and Kowalski?" Sal asked.

"I don't know. Franconi just told me to find you."

Caitlin was washing cream cheese off her fingers when the telephone rang. She grabbed a towel, drying her hands as she ran to answer.

"Bennett residence."

"Miss Bennett, it's Detective Neil."

She tossed the towel on the counter and leaned back against the wall, picturing the man's face as she spoke.

"Hello, Detective. Has there been news?"

"Well, we're not sure," he said. "My partner and I have been viewing security tapes from your building that were taken on the day that package was delivered to you."

"Package? I assume you mean the one containing the Rat Tartar."

There was a moment of silence, and then he almost chuckled.

"That would be the one," he said. "The reason I'm calling is, there are several individuals on the tape who we can't identify and we would like you to take a look at them. Do you mind?"

"No. I'd be glad to," Caitlin said. "I'll just tell Mac and then call a cab."

"There's no need for you to take a cab. I'm in the neighborhood. Why don't I drop by and pick you both up?"

"Why, that would be fine," Caitlin said. "When can we expect you?"

"I'm only a few minutes away. I'll come up for you. That way you won't have to wait in the lobby, where you would be... That way you won't have to wait."

"Thank you for being so thoughtful," she said, knowing what he'd been about to say—that in the lobby she would be exposed, to some degree, a target.

"Great. I'll see you in about five minutes."

Caitlin hung up, then looked at their lunch with a sigh. It would just have to wait. Having settled that in her mind, she began searching for the plastic wrap.

"Who was on the phone?" Mac said as he came into the kitchen. Then he frowned. "Why are you putting that up? We haven't eaten yet."

She handed him a piece of bagel that she'd smeared with cream cheese and then laid a piece of bacon on the top.

"That was Detective Neil. He wants me to come down to the precinct and look at the security tapes."

"What tapes?"

"From this building, the day the rat was delivered."

"Good idea," he said. "I just started a search for Georgia Calhoun, but I'll go turn off the computer." He took a bite of the bagel as he started to leave. "Hey," he said. "This is good."

Caitlin smiled. "You don't have to sound so surprised."

Before Mac could defend himself, the doorbell rang.

"Wow, that was fast," she said, then looked down at her feet. She was wearing her puppy slippers. "I can't wear these," she gasped.

"I'll get it," Mac said as Caitlin raced to the bedroom to put on shoes.

"Come in, Detective. Have a seat. Caitlin is almost ready. I've just got to go turn off the computer."

"Wait," Caitlin said as she hurried into the room. "Why don't you just stay here and finish what you started? Everything will go a lot faster if we're working at this from both ends."

"No way," Mac said. "You don't get out of my sight."

Caitlin laughed and pointed at Neil.

"But, Mac, I'll have police protection. Detective Neil has offered to take me to the station, and I have every expectation that if I asked him real nice, he'd also bring me back to the door.''

Neil smiled. ''You have my word on that,'' he said, then looked at Mac. ''I promise, Mr. McKee, that I will take good care of her.''

Caitlin turned to Mac, silently pleading her case.

Mac sighed. This wasn't good. He didn't like the way Neil looked at her, but already he couldn't tell her no. What in hell would it be like to be married to a woman you couldn't refuse?

''Yeah, I see what you mean,'' Mac said giving Neil a hard stare. ''I suppose it will be all right. When you've finished with the tapes, you'll personally see to her return?''

Neil nodded and extended his hand.

''You have my word that I will not let her out of my sight.''

Reluctantly Mac shook the man's hand, then helped Caitlin into her coat.

''Button up,'' he said gently as he fastened the top buttons she always left undone. ''You don't want to get cold.''

It wasn't what he said but the way that he said it that told Caitlin how much he cared.

''It's not this cold in Atlanta, is it?'' she asked.

His eyes widened. This was the first time she'd hinted she might accept his invitation. A slow smile spread over his face.

''No,'' he said softly. ''It's not nearly this cold.''

"I'll be looking forward to that," she said, then kissed him soundly, oblivious to the detective at her back.

Neil stared at the pair, then unobtrusively turned his back, pretending to look at a painting by the door.

Caitlin tapped him on the shoulder. "I'm ready."

He turned, nodded at Mac and then offered her his elbow.

"Ever ride in a police car?" he asked.

"Yes, actually I have," she said as they went out the door. "It was for research on my third...no, my fourth book. Only it wasn't in New York. It was in L.A."

"Interesting," Neil said.

It was the last thing Mac heard them say. Anxious to get back to his research, he headed toward the office, sensing time was of the essence. He didn't want Georgia Calhoun to turn up like the Delarosa woman had.

Sal Amato was still staring at the enhanced still shots lifted from the video he had been looking at for the last few minutes. In all his years on the force, he'd never known this much fear, but if he said what he was thinking aloud, it could cause shock waves that might never end. Finally he looked up.

"Lieutenant, does that guy look familiar to you?"

Del Franconi shrugged. "You tell me?"

"Paulie, what's your take?"

Paulie Hahn was sweating. He kept looking at the picture and wanting to throw up.

"It can't be," he muttered.

"Looks too damned much like him to ignore," Franconi said. "I want you two to do some digging. Find out if what we know about him jibes with the facts, and do it fast."

Sal turned, his eyes wide with disbelief.

"Man, Lieutenant, if that's who I think it is, we're in a world of hurt."

"No, if it's who we think it is, he's going to be the one in pain."

Eighteen

Mac's fingers flew across the keyboard as he stared at the screen. It was all about accessing phone books and social security records. Granted, he was hacking into a couple of places he wasn't supposed to be, but the way he figured it, the ends justified the means.

According to the facts on the screen, there were three Georgia Calhouns in the state of Ohio, two in Toledo, one in a small town on the other side of the state. He printed the information off the screen and then exited quickly, his heart racing as he reached for the phone. Wouldn't it be something if he had the woman located before Caitlin got back from the precinct?

The first number he called was no longer in service. His hopes slipped a little as he dialed the next number, but he reminded himself that this was just the first step. The phone rang once, then twice, then three times. Expecting to get an answering machine, he was elated when a young woman answered.

"Hello?"

"I'd like to speak to Georgia Calhoun," he said.

There was a pause on the other end of the line, and then the woman spoke. "I'm Georgia Calhoun. Who's calling, please?"

"Miss Calhoun, I'm with a lost and found organization, and I'm working for a family who's trying to locate a woman named Georgia Calhoun."

"Oh my! Like on those talk shows where long lost relatives are reunited?"

"Something like that," he said. "But I need to ask you some questions to make sure I have the right person. Will you help me?"

"Why, yes!" she said. "What do you need to know?"

"First, how old are you?" Mac asked.

"Twenty-three."

His hopes fell. This couldn't be the woman Devlin Bennett had been paying. According to Charles Abernathy, he'd been sending money to her for nearly thirty years. This woman wasn't old enough.

"Well, that doesn't fit our parameters. I was thinking that the woman would be in her fifties, at least, maybe even older."

"I was named for my aunt Georgia. Maybe it's her you're looking for?"

Mac's hope rose once more.

"Maybe," he said. "Is it possible for me to talk to her?"

"Oh, no. I'm sorry, but Aunt Georgia died a few years ago."

Damn. Another roadblock.

"I see. Have you by any chance ever heard the name Devlin Bennett?"

"No, I don't think so. Is that the man who's looking for Georgia Calhoun?"

"In a way, yes," Mac said. "Is there anything else you can tell me about her, like where she was born? Does she have any living siblings who might know something more?"

"Mother would. If you'll wait a moment, I'll get her."

"Thanks," Mac said. "I appreciate your help."

A few moments later, he heard footsteps returning. He hoped this woman was as willing to help as her daughter had been.

"This is Grace Calhoun. My daughter says you were looking for Georgia?"

"Well, ma'am, I'm looking for *a* Georgia. I don't know if it's the woman to whom you're related."

"I see. What do you need to know? She's been dead some years now, you know."

"Yes, ma'am. Your daughter told me. I'll ask you the same question I asked her. Have you ever heard the name Devlin Bennett?"

"No, I can't say as I have. It's too bad my husband has passed. He could have told you more than I can about Georgia."

"She's not your sister?" Mac asked.

"Oh, no, she was my husband's family. Stepsister,

actually, but most of the time she went by Calhoun. You should really be talking to Joseph, but I have no idea where he is these days.''

"Who's Joseph?'' Mac asked.

"Her son. But he moved away after she died.''

Mac fidgeted, wanting to hurry her, but knowing she was going to have to tell it her way.

"I see. Look, Mrs. Calhoun, this is a delicate subject, and I want to assure you that I mean no disrespect when I ask, but if she had a son and still went by the name of Calhoun, did she divorce and take back her maiden name or—''

"Oh, Georgia never married,'' she said. "It was quite a scandal at the time. That was...oh, let me see, back in the sixties, I think, and in those days no one here in Ohio, and I mean no one, had a baby out of wedlock and ever admitted to it.''

"Yes, ma'am, but she did?''

"Oh, yes. After a few years, well, it didn't seem so bad. Of course, Georgia never had much money, and Joseph was a sickly little thing when he was small. But he grew up to be a good-looking man.''

"What about the father? Didn't he have anything to do with them?''

Grace lowered her voice. "That was just it, you see. We never did know who the father was. She wouldn't say. Never did tell. I heard that she told the boy on her deathbed, but he left right after she died, so I don't guess it mattered any to him.''

Mac was running out of questions and ideas. None of this made any sense. If this Georgia had been getting two thousand dollars a month from Devlin Bennett, then she would have had some money. Not a lot, but some. This couldn't be the woman.

"Yes, I suppose you're right," Mac said. Then he glanced down at his notes, remembering a question he'd been going to ask when she'd changed the subject.

"Another question, Mrs. Calhoun, if I may?"

"Yes?"

"You said that Georgia was your husband's step-sister?"

"Yes. Their parents married when Georgia was six and my husband was two."

"By any chance, do you remember her maiden name?"

"Let me see…I'm sure I heard Frank speak it before. Frank was my husband, you know."

"Yes, ma'am."

"I know the boy's name was Joseph Raymond. Georgia said she named him after Joseph Cotton and Raymond Chandler. Those were old-time movie stars, you know. Way before your time."

Mac grinned. "Now how would you know how old I am?"

She giggled. "You just sound young, that's all. Am I right?"

"I'm thirty-five."

"Close enough," she said. "As for Georgia's name...where would I...?" She gasped. "The Bible! It would be in the family Bible. Would you like me to check?"

"Yes, please," Mac said.

He wasn't sure how it could matter, but he'd listened this long; the least he could do was hear her out. He waited, hearing bits and snatches of her excited conversation with her daughter as they scrambled to find it. Finally she was back.

"Let's see now," she said. "It would be way back toward the first. There's been a lot of births and deaths recorded in this book since we started. Here it is," she murmured, talking more to herself than to Mac. "Neil. Her name was Georgia Faye Neil."

Mac was assimilating the information as he quickly wrote down the name—Joseph Raymond Neal. Then he hesitated.

"Would you spell that last name for me please?"

"Certainly. N-E-I-L."

Mac made the correction without thought. It was only after he had laid down the pen that the name actually clicked. And when it did his fingers went numb. He couldn't think. He couldn't even find the strength to hang up the phone.

"Mister? Are you still there?"

He shuddered, making himself concentrate. "Would you spell that last name for me again?" he asked.

"N E I L," she said.

"And you said the son was Joseph Raymond. Did he go by Neil or Calhoun?"

"Well, now that you mention it, I believe he did favor the name Neil. It was his legal name, you know, her not being married or legally adopted by my Frank's family."

"Uh, thank you for your help," he finally said, and hung up before she could say anything more.

He tried to get out of the chair, but his legs wouldn't work. He didn't know why it was happening, but he knew who was after Caitlin. Now how could he get her back without alerting the man that he knew?

Amato. He would help.

He grabbed the phone and punched in the number. The man answered on the first ring.

"Amato."

"Detective, this is Connor McKee. I need you to go get Caitlin and bring her to the phone ASAP."

Amato frowned. "I don't know what you're talking about," he said. "Miss Bennett isn't here."

"Where's Kowalski?"

"Out. What's going on?" Amato asked.

"Caitlin isn't there watching security tapes from her building?"

"No. There wasn't anything on those tapes. We discovered that days ago. What the hell is going on?"

Oh, Jesus. "Neil came by here probably two hours

ago. Said he and his partner needed her to view some security tapes. He said he'd bring her back when they were through."

Amato's stomach turned. After what they'd just seen, this didn't sound good.

"Look, McKee, we got the results from that tape back from Quantico. There's something on it I think you should see."

"I don't have to," Mac said. "It's Neil, isn't it?"

"How did you know?"

"Because I just got off the phone with a woman in Toledo, Ohio, who told me something very disturbing. We learned today that for the past thirty years, Devlin Bennett sent two thousand dollars a month to a woman named Georgia Calhoun. He sent it every month up to the day she died. Now, I don't know all of it, but I do know that she had a son named Joseph Raymond. And that he chose to go by her maiden name, which happened to be Neil."

"Oh man," Amato muttered. "This isn't good."

"No, it isn't," Mac said. "Caitlin is somewhere in this city with a man who wants her dead. I don't know why he hates her, but we both know what he's capable of. I'm on my way down there. Have Kowalski waiting."

"I'll send a squad car," Amato said. "You'll get here faster."

"Wait, I've got a better idea," Mac said. "Meet me at Neil's place. I can't believe we'd get lucky enough that he'd take her there, but it's the first place we have to look."

"Good idea. I'll give the patrolman the address."

Caitlin shivered as a cold gust of wind whipped around the corner of the building, stirring up a small eddy of snow and blowing it into her eyes.

"Careful," J.R. said, and took her arm as she ducked. "The street is slippery. I wouldn't want you to fall."

"Thanks," Caitlin said as he settled her in his car and then hurried around to the driver's side to get in.

"Buckle up," he said as he started the engine, then flipped the locks on the door. When she jumped at the sound, he smiled. "Safety first."

"Of course."

They pulled away from the curb, weaving skillfully into the traffic. Caitlin leaned back with a sigh, gazing out the window at the snowy streets.

"Sometimes it feels like this winter will never end. I know you're not supposed to wish your life away, but I am so ready for spring."

"Spring," he echoed, and gave her a cursory glance.

Caitlin nodded and smiled. "Yes, it's my favorite season. When I was a child, we always went south in the spring. We had the most wonderful old house on the North Carolina shore. Mother would bake cookies, and Daddy would pretend he was a bear and growl that he was going to eat them all.'' She sighed. ''It was so much fun. Later, after his business really took off, Daddy didn't go with us anymore. But I have the memories.''

A muscle twitched near the detective's eye as he braked for another light.

''Memories,'' he muttered. ''Yes, we all have our memories.''

As a writer, personalities were always interesting to Caitlin. She looked at him, urging him to share.

''What about you?'' she asked. ''What are some of your favorite childhood memories?''

''Let's see. There was the time when my mother got fired because her boss found out she was an unwed mother.''

Caitlin gasped. ''I'm sorry. I didn't mean to—''

J.R. interrupted her, letting the poison of his childhood spill between them.

''Oh, yeah,'' he drawled. ''I'll never forget the big family dinners we used to have at my uncle Frank's house. Everyone sitting around whispering about me, wondering who the sorry bastard was who knocked my mother up and then abandoned her.'' He looked at her then, enjoying the shock on her face. ''I was sickly as a child. Hard to believe now, isn't it?''

Caitlin was stunned by his bitterness.

''Detective, I didn't mean to resurrect bad memories. Maybe we should change the subject.''

He started to laugh. A slow, deep-belly chuckle that sent a chill up her spine.

"You still don't get it, do you, Caitlin? You are the subject."

He hit a switch, and the siren came on and the red light on the dashboard started flashing; then he accelerated swiftly through an intersection as Caitlin stared in disbelief.

"What are you doing?"

"It's payback time," he said. He took the next right in a skid. "Sit back and enjoy the ride."

"You? It's you who's been sending me those letters?"

He smiled. "Oh, those 'juvenile' little love notes? Yes, it was me."

"And those women? You killed those women?"

He shrugged. "Expediency. Practice. Releasing pent-up hostility. Call it what you will."

Don't react. Don't scream. Whatever you do, Caitlin Bennett, don't let him see you cry.

Caitlin's fingers curled around the door handle as she took a deep breath, ignoring her instinct to panic. As long as he kept driving, she would keep breathing.

"Another thing," J.R. said, chuckling beneath his breath. "You can't open your door until I unlock it, so don't bother to try."

"On the contrary," Caitlin said, making her voice steady when all she wanted to do was shriek. "I wasn't going to jump. Unlike you, I'm not suicidal."

He hit her cheek with the back of his hand.

"Shut up, bitch! You don't know anything about me."

Tears of pain pooled quickly, shattering her vision of the world. She touched the place where he'd hit her, and her fingers came away covered in blood.

Dear God.

She thought of Mac, back in the apartment, completely unaware of the danger she was in, and almost lost it. This wasn't fair. Surely God wouldn't give her a man to love and then let her die before they had a chance to enjoy a life together.

The buildings they passed were little more than a blur. Drivers honked, people shouted at him, some even cursing as he wove through the traffic. But the flashing light on his dashboard gave him free access to the streets. It was everyone else's job to get out of his way.

Caitlin's mind was racing as she thought back to the books she'd written. What on earth would one of her heroines do in a situation like this? Taking a tissue out of her purse, she blotted the split skin on her cheekbone and then took a deep breath.

"You're right, J.R. I don't know anything about you. I'm sorry. I shouldn't have judged."

Startled by her quick about-face, he hesitated before he answered.

"That's better," he muttered. "I'm the one in

charge, bitch, and all the money in the world won't change that fact.''

Money? Is this about money?

"Tell me why.''

"Why don't you just sit still and shut up?'' he muttered.

"I just think I deserve to know why you hate me, don't you?''

When he spoke, his voice was hard and full of menace.

"You open your mouth and scream for help and you're dead. Here. Now. Do you understand?''

She nodded, her heart in her throat.

He shook his head, like a dog shedding water, and then blinked. When he did, Caitlin felt as if another man had just taken the wheel of the car.

"You don't know who I am, do you?''

She shook her head again, afraid to speak.

"Devlin Bennett was my father. I'm the bastard he left behind as he went on to bigger and better things.''

Caitlin gasped. "You're my brother? You're my brother and you want me dead?''

He accelerated, laughing maniacally as the car fish-tailed.

"You don't know anything!'' he shouted. "I'm the firstborn...the one who should have inherited all his wealth. But no. He didn't even acknowledge my existence when he died!''

Caitlin moaned beneath her breath.

"But I would have given you half. All you had to do was tell me," she said.

A muscle jerked at the corner of his mouth. If he was surprised by her acceptance, he showed no signs. Moments later, he took a sharp left turn. Half a block down, he came to a sliding stop. He turned where he sat, staring at her face in disbelief.

"And you know what you would have done? You would have demanded proof. How could I give you proof? That evil son of a bitch who fucked my mother made sure I could never substantiate that claim."

Caitlin was shaking from the inside out. The fact that they had stopped in front of what appeared to be an abandoned warehouse was superseding every sane thought she had. She made herself focus, knowing that once they left this car, her chances of survival would be diminished to almost nothing.

"What are you talking about? All you would have to do is take a blood test. DNA would do the rest."

He grabbed her by the throat, pulling her face so close to his that she felt the heat of his breath.

"No," he said slowly, as if explaining himself to a simple child. "Daddy had himself cremated, didn't he? And he had his ashes strewn all over the Atlantic. There was no way I could prove his paternity if there was nothing left of him to test. Right?"

Tears seeped from Caitlin's eyes as she struggled to breathe past the grasp he had on her throat.

"But I'm here," she said, still choking for air. "They could have tested me."

He turned her loose with a shriek of laughter and thrust her backward. Her head hit the window with a thud.

"You still don't get it! Testing you would prove nothing! Nothing, do you hear? You're adopted! Even *I* knew that."

Caitlin's ears began to roar as J.R. jerked her from the car. Stumbling and falling as he dragged her into the building, she finally started to fight. The struggle was brief. He hit her once, and then the world turned black.

The squad car ran on full alert all the way to Neil's apartment. As it slid to a stop at the curb, another black and white was stopping right behind them.

"Apartment 505, sir," the officer said as Mac reached for the door. "That will be Detectives Amato and Kowalksi behind us."

Mac got out, unwilling to wait, and started into the building on the run.

"Wait!" Amato yelled. "The manager is meeting us with a key."

The detectives caught up with Mac at the foot of the stairs just as a middle-aged woman came out of the apartment on their right.

Amato flashed his badge. "Ma'am, we need you to let us into 505."

She handed him the key. "My husband's not home. The stairs...my knee...I can't take you there. Bring it back when you're through."

Mac took the key out of Amato's hands and started up the stairs on the run. Trudy Kowalksi was right behind him, arguing all the way.

"You're wrong. All of you," she argued. "He's my partner. He wouldn't be involved in something like this."

Mac hit the fifth floor landing barely out of breath and ran all the way to the apartment, jammed the key into the lock and turned.

He'd been praying all the way up that Neil would be inside and Caitlin with him, although he knew in his heart that would be too easy. Neil wasn't going to let himself get caught. Not until he'd done what he set out to do. He waited for the others to catch up and then let Trudy call out Neil's name. He would be less suspicious of the sound of her voice. When no one answered, they used the key.

"They're not here," Trudy said, her voice triumphant.

"I didn't think they would be," Amato said as he huffed and puffed his way into the apartment.

"Where's your partner?" Mac asked as he realized Detective Hahn was not in sight.

"On his way with a search warrant," Amato said.

Trudy turned on the man, her hands on her hips in angry defiance. "A little late, wouldn't you say?"

Mac turned abruptly, spied a closed door at the end of the hall and headed toward it.

"Wait!" Trudy yelled. "I swear to God, I'll testify against all of you if—"

The door swung inward as Mac hit the lights. He grunted as if he'd been punched.

"In here!" he yelled.

Trudy pushed past him in anger, then stopped.

"Oh my God," she whispered. "The pictures. Are they all pictures of—"

"It's Caitlin. They're all Caitlin," Mac said, and wanted to cry. "I let her go with him. I fucking gave her to him like a present. He must have been laughing all the way to the car."

"No," Amato said. "He screwed all of us. Hell, I even had him investigating the murders of the women he killed. Talk about deception. He was the master."

Mac strode to a nearby table and started digging through the stack of papers there.

"There's got to be something here that will tell us where he's taken her." Then he paused, shoved a handful of papers aside and picked up a pair of cassette tapes. They were numbered and dated and marked *Bitch's Place*. Mac's heart skipped a beat. The hate within this room was almost palpable. He turned.

"Start looking, damn it! Help me find Caitie before it's too late."

Trudy looked stunned.

"Those women...those poor, defenseless women. He brutalized and then butchered them." Slowly the tears began to fall. "I guess I should be thankful I'm a short redhead instead of a slender brunette. I might have been one of his victims."

"I got it, I got it! Hey, where did everybody go?"

At the shout, they all turned to see Paulie Hahn waving the long-awaited search warrant in the air.

"In here!" Amato yelled.

Paulie came through the door, a wry grin on his face.

"I see you waited," he said, and then he saw the walls. "Oh man, Sal, you were right."

"Damn it, people, help me find a way to stop him before he kills Caitie, too," Mac demanded.

Amato took charge. "Kowalksi, take the living room. You know what to look for. There's more stuff on these walls than I would have believed possible. We'll start in here. Look fast, people. A woman's life is riding on us."

Mac tore through the papers on the desk as Amato and Hahn began going through the stuff tacked to the walls. He kept picturing the raped and strangled women, their faces slashed like gutted fish. And with every paper he discarded, his hopes fell a notch. The longer Caitlin was in the killer's hands, the shorter her life would be.

It was Trudy who broke the tension when she came running from the living room.

"I found something," she said, thrusting the paper in Amato's hands.

"What is it?" Mac asked.

"Looks like a rent receipt," Amato muttered.

"Yes, but look at the address," Trudy said. "Why would he be paying rent on two places unless...?"

Mac grabbed the paper. "How far is this from here?"

Amato frowned. "A good twenty minutes."

"Not if we hurry," Mac said, and bolted from the room with the others right behind him.

Nineteen

Caitlin opened her eyes and groaned. Her head was splitting, and she had no idea why. It wasn't until she discovered she couldn't move that she remembered J. R. Neil. Staring in disbelief at the ropes around her wrists, she quickly realized her feet were also bound.

God in heaven, he had tied her to rings set in the floor.

"Wakey, wakey."

She gasped. The man's guttural chuckle was like something out of a nightmare.

"Neil..."

"That's 'Brother dear' to you, bitch."

"Let me go."

He stared at her a moment, then threw his head back and laughed.

"Just like that?" he asked, dancing around her spread-eagled body like a moth flirting with a flame. "Let you go? You're madder than I am if you think that's going to happen."

Caitlin took a slow breath, trying to calm the nausea bubbling at the back of her throat. He would like that, she knew. Watching her puke up her guts in pain and fear. Anger pushed through her pain.

Damn him...damn his evil soul. I will not give him the satisfaction of seeing my fear.

She would play it his way. He needed to tell her why. She could tell that this jubilation was part of the game. Like a child who'd just hit a home run, he still had to run the bases so he could hear the cheers. That was fine with her. As long as he let her talk, she couldn't die.

"So *are* you mad?" she asked.

He stumbled, then spun, pointing at her with a daggerlike knife.

"Wouldn't you be?" he asked, approaching her slowly, then straddling her body, aware that intimidation was better at creating fear than pain was.

"Crazy? I don't think so," she said. "It's so sleazy."

He kicked her then, the toe of his boot digging sharply into her ribs.

"I'm not crazy!" he screamed. "This is simple revenge. Your father screwed me. I am going to screw you."

The taste of copper was suddenly strong in her mouth, and she realized that she'd just bitten her tongue to keep from crying.

"That's sleazy, too," she said, frowning as if studying an odd subject. "Screw? You know what, brother? That's such a low-class word. Daddy wouldn't have approved.''

He stared at her in disbelief. Why wasn't she crying? Why wasn't she begging for her life like all the others? He fingered the knife in his hands, reminding himself that he was the one in control.

"Daddy? Fuck Daddy!" he shrieked, and ran the tip of the knife beneath her sweater and pulled upward. It ripped from hem to neck, baring her breasts and belly in one fell swoop.

Caitlin inhaled sharply, her stomach flattening in reflex. It was the only outward response she made to what he'd done.

She looked at her sweater and frowned. "That's too bad. I really liked that sweater. If you'd asked, I would have taken it off.''

J.R. froze. What the hell game was she playing? Taken it off? She would have taken it off? He didn't want a willing participant, he wanted her begging and pleading for her life as he tore her guts apart.

He managed a halfhearted sneer and took a couple of steps backward, then ran the tip of the knife lightly up his fly, giving her a full view of his groin.

"I can make you scream when you come," he said softly.

"No, you can't," she said. "You can hurt me. You can kill me, but you will never make me cry. You're nothing but a coward.''

"Shut up," he said.

"Raping and killing innocent women because you didn't have the balls to face me. All you had to do was tell me who you were. It would have been easy enough for you to prove. I know that Daddy sent your mother two thousand dollars a month for more than thirty years. You could have made your claim on that alone."

His expression fell. "He did what?"

"It's true," she said. "I talked to Daddy's lawyer. It was sent to her up until the day she died. All you would have had to do was speak up. Instead you snuck around, sniffing and growling like a dog, making yourself believe you'd been cheated, when the truth was that the only one who was cheating was you."

"You're lying!" he shrieked, and slashed the knife through her slacks, cutting the belt and waistband in one motion.

Oh God, Mac. I love you. I love you. Forgive me for not saying it enough before I died.

"I do not lie."

He started to pace, spitting out words as if they were bitter in his mouth.

"My mother died of cervical cancer in a goddamned charity ward. There was no money. *There was no money, I tell you.*"

Fear was so heavy in Caitlin's mind that it was hard to think, but if he lost focus on what she was saying, she was dead.

"I have no reason to lie. Your mother's name was Georgia Calhoun, wasn't it?"

She saw the blood drain from his face. "How did you know that?"

"I told you. Daddy's lawyers. They have records of the money. Two thousand dollars a month to a Georgia Calhoun in Toledo, Ohio. The money stopped when she died. Maybe she put it in savings. Maybe she tore up the checks. I don't know. But I know they were sent."

He started to pace, trying to assimilate what she was saying and put it in context against the poverty in which he'd grown up. All those years. That miserable grind. It wasn't enough that he'd been a bastard. He'd been a poor bastard, too. This couldn't be true. Mother had loved him too much to deny him. She might have denied herself, but not him. He couldn't let himself believe it was possible.

And then a memory surfaced. Something he hadn't thought of in years. He'd been eight and running with the wrong crowd of kids. Trying desperately to fit in, he'd gotten caught shoplifting at a neighborhood store. It was only a candy bar, but when the owner called his mother, he waited in torment for her to arrive.

He could still remember the look of disappointment on her face as she made him apologize to the owner. Satisfied that he had learned his lesson, and thinking to take pity on the bastard kid from up the block, the store owner had offered to give him the candy bar. Thinking that he'd come out the winner in a very big way, Buddy had reached toward the treat when his mother caught his hand.

He closed his eyes, remembering the smell of her perfume and the way the sunlight caught and held upon her hair as she knelt in front of him.

"No, Buddy. You must not take the treat. Making mistakes is a natural part of life. You learn from your mistakes, my son, but you should never benefit, too. Thank the man for offering and then we'll go."

He opened his eyes and looked out the window into the snow.

He'd been a mistake. He'd known that from the start. So his mother had practiced what she'd preached. So what? She was dead, and he was here, and a Bennett would have to pay. He turned, looking at Caitlin with a blank, almost innocent stare.

"It doesn't matter," he said. "You still have to die."

"Why?"

"Because I said so."

It was the calm tone of his voice that told Caitlin it was over.

He started toward her, and she closed her eyes, unwilling to watch her own blood spill.

"Open your eyes," he said, as the weight of his body settled upon her thighs.

"No. I choose not to be a part of my own death."

He started to cry, hitting her with his fists as he tore off what was left of her slacks.

"You have to open your eyes or it won't work."

"Then so be it," she said as his hands encircled her neck.

In the distance, she imagined she heard the sound of approaching sirens, but it didn't matter. They wouldn't be coming here, and even if they were, it would be too late.

His fingers tightened with each choking sob he took.

"It should have been mine. It should have been mine."

When she went limp, he rocked back with relief. Justice. It was all he'd wanted. And exactly what he deserved. He looked at her limp body with satisfaction as everything, including sound and sanity, faded away.

"That's Neil's car!" Trudy shouted as Amato slid around the turn.

"Yeah, and if I don't wreck us before we get there, we're gonna nail the bastard," Amato said. "Paulie, you and the two officers behind us take the back. Kowalski and I will go in with McKee."

"You'd better hurry," Trudy said, pointing toward the black-and-white ahead of them. "McKee's already on the way in."

"Shit," Amato muttered as he threw the gear into

Park. The engine rattled and then died as he rolled out of the seat.

They spilled out of the car, Hahn motioning for the approaching officers to follow him to the back, while Amato and Kowalksi drew their weapons and ran in through the front.

Momentarily blinded by the darkness after the glare of sun on snow, they paused in the shadows as their eyes adjusted to the light.

"There," Kowalksi said quietly, moving toward an iron staircase at the far end of the building. "McKee's going that way."

Mac entered the warehouse at full speed, the officer who'd driven the car right behind him. The ground floor was empty, the huge space unbroken except for a couple dozen steel beams that were part of the structure itself.

From the corner of his eye, he caught a brief flash of red and spun toward the sight. Caitlin had been wearing a red scarf when she left. He headed toward the stairs, where the scarf hung like a beacon.

They ran with guns drawn, knowing that at any moment shots could rain down on them from above. Within seconds they were there, taking the steps two at a time. The echo of their footsteps ricocheted from one end of the building to the other, and yet Mac didn't pull back. He would rather die going after her than hesitate and find her already dead.

They reached the top, only to see a series of what had probably been offices. A quick glance down the hallway and the dust on the floors told Mac that none of them had been disturbed—except the last one on the left. He could see the trail in the dust where something had been dragged inside. The door was slightly ajar.

"Down there," he mouthed and hit the door running, kicking it open with his boot, his gun steadied with both hands as he aimed straight before him.

After that, everything seemed to happen in slow motion.

His mind shattered, accepting only bits and pieces of what he was seeing.

Caitlin tied to the floor and not moving.

Neil kneeling over her body with a knife.

Blood on her face.

Blood on his hands.

He heard himself scream out Neil's name, and then everything started coming undone.

Neil jerked and then stood, spinning to face the enemy.

Mac fired, taking absent note as a blossom of red suddenly appeared on Neil's shirt.

He fired again, then again and again, emptying his gun into J.R. Neil's chest, and yet the man still stood, as if his body had been suspended by invisible wires.

"Is he dead?" the young officer asked.

He was saved from answering as Neil swayed and then fell, hitting the floor with a hard, solid thud.

Seconds later Mac was on his knees beside Caitlin, feeling for a pulse. There was none. Grabbing the knife Neil had dropped, he slashed the ropes at her wrists and ankles, then tossed her bonds aside as he searched for hidden injuries.

"Please, God, no," he begged, then slid his hand beneath her head, arching her neck to clear her airway as he began to do CPR.

Moments later Amato and Trudy arrived. Instantly she was on her knees and, without uttering a word, began doing the chest compressions. Over and over they worked—Mac breathing for Caitlin, Trudy working Caitlin's heart.

"Help is coming," Amato said. "An ambulance is on the way."

But Caitlin wasn't breathing and Mac wasn't quitting—not on this woman. Not ever.

Another minute passed as his hopes began to die. Then, suddenly, Caitlin coughed.

"She's breathing!" Trudy shouted, and rocked back on her heels.

"Thank you, God," Mac whispered, rolling Caitlin over on her side and patting her on her back as she struggled to draw air. "Easy, Caitie...it's Mac."

She grabbed his wrist, her fingernails digging into his flesh. Dragging in oxygen through a bruised and burning throat, she tried to crawl into his lap.

"Thank you, God," he said softly, dragged her into his arms and started to cry.

Trudy stood abruptly. Without looking at his face, she stepped over Neil's body as if it were a piece of filth and walked out.

Paulie reached for her arm as she passed. "Kowalksi, I—"

Amato stopped him. "Let her go," he said. "She's got to deal with this on her own."

They turned then, looking at the man on the floor and the woman in his arms. Paulie took off his overcoat and handed it to Mac.

"They always leave 'em bare," he muttered. "I hate it when that happens."

Mac grabbed the coat, pulling it closer around Caitlin as she clung to him in terror.

"It's all right," he kept saying. "Everything is going to be all right."

Epilogue

One week later

Caitlin opened the oven door to check the progress of the turkey, then quickly shut it again, satisfied that all was as it should be.

Running down her mental list of things still left to do, she turned toward the sink to finish cleaning the vegetables. As she reached for a knife, her fingers started to shake. But she took a deep breath, reminding herself that the nightmare was over.

Mac came into the kitchen as she began to dice the celery.

"Everything smells wonderful," he said, then wrapped his arms around her waist and nuzzled the back of her neck. "Including you."

She turned in his arms, allowing herself the luxury of one quick, passionate kiss.

"Hold that thought," she whispered.

"As tight as I'm holding you," Mac said, then laid his cheek against the top of her hair.

They stood for a moment, savoring the silence and the joy of being held, and then Caitlin pulled back, knowing how easily the moment could spin out of control.

"I've got to finish these vegetables. Aaron and David will be here soon."

"Is Leibowitz going to come?"

Caitlin grinned. "No, thank goodness, although I held my breath when I asked him. He's going to L.A. with a new client," she said. "A pretty one, too, from what his secretary says."

"That's good. He's was too damned possessive to suit me."

"Without provocation, I can assure you."

He sighed, unable to put into words what her presence in his life meant to him. She didn't have to tell him who she loved. She'd shown him many times over.

He kissed the side of her face, just because he could, and because he still got cold chills remembering the panic of blowing oxygen into her lifeless body.

"I know, baby. Is there anything I can do to help?"

She pointed to an apron hanging on the pantry doorknob.

"Sure, grab an apron and a paring knife and dig in. You can peel the potatoes for me."

"I'm not wearing an apron," he said, as he picked up the peeler and a potato.

Caitlin stopped to watch, tracing the obstinate thrust of his jaw with her gaze and letting her feelings for him fill her soul.

"I love you, you know."

Mac paused, the potato half peeled in his hand, and met her troubled gaze.

"I love you, too, baby."

"I know," she said, her voice quiet with satisfaction.

"Are you okay?"

She nodded, remembering the nightmare she'd had last night and the panic she'd seen on his face when she'd awakened with a scream.

"Today is a good day."

"Good enough to think about marrying me?"

Her eyes widened. "What did you say?"

"You heard me."

"Are you finally admitting that you love me enough to forgive me for being born rich?"

He grinned wryly. "Yeah, I guess. So...what do you say?"

She wrapped her arms around his neck and planted a kiss square on his mouth.

"I say yes," she said, and laid her head against his chest in quiet joy.

"Would you live with me in Atlanta?" he asked.

She smiled as she looked up. "Of course! I can write anywhere, as long as I know you'll come home to me every night."

His arms tightened briefly, and then he turned her loose.

"Wait," he said, digging in the pocket of his jeans. "I had this...just in case." He pulled out a ring box and took out the ring. "It belonged to my mother," he said. "If it doesn't fit, we can have it sized."

Caitlin stared at the two-carat yellow diamond he was putting on her hand, her mouth open in shock.

"It's beautiful," she said.

"It's an heirloom. Close to a hundred and fifty years old now, if our family history is to be believed. It was on my great-great-great grandmother's finger when she survived an Indian raid, and my great-grandmother was wearing it when she lost her husband and baby to typhoid fever. The women in my family have always been tough. Like you, they were survivors. I wish you could have known them."

"Oh, Mac," Caitlin said, and then started to cry.

"Well, hell," Mac said as he gathered her in his arms. "I meant to make you happy. You know I can't stand it when you cry."

"I *am* happy," Caitlin said. "You just touched my heart."

The doorbell rang.

Caitlin gasped. "That will be Aaron and David. I'll get it. I want to see how long it takes him to notice the ring."

"Sorry, but they already know. I had to have Aaron get it out of the safe-deposit box for me."

She grinned. "That's all right. At least the bandages are off his face and he'll be able to see it on my hand."

She hurried toward the door, leaving him in the kitchen to finish the potatoes. He heard his brother's voice, then laughter and a small, rousing cheer. She'd shown them the ring. He smiled, trying to imagine what the next sixty-odd years with her might be like. They wouldn't be boring, of that he was certain.

She'd come to terms with the lie of Devlin Bennett's life, especially after the last of the research Mac had done on her behalf. Instead of looking for answers in Neil's past, they'd looked in Devlin's, instead.

And the answers had been there, locked away in old hospital files and family journals and diaries they found in an undiscovered safe-deposit box. The secrets. The shame. Hiding the thread of insanity that had run through his family had been Devlin's cross to bear. It had spilled from father to son, passed from mother to daughter, through four generations until Devlin was born.

After witnessing his grandfather's suicide and hearing the whispers of the family past, he'd sworn he would be the last. It would end with him or he would know the reason why.

Mac could only imagine the horror Devlin must have felt when his girlfriend, Georgia, had turned up pregnant and the fight that had ensued when she'd

refused to abort the child. But he had to give it to
Devlin. He hadn't abandoned her without thought.
Even if it was guilt alone that had kept it coming,
he'd sent support for her all the rest of her life, even
after his son had reached maturity. They would never
know what had happened to the money Georgia Calhoun received. Caitlin guessed that it might have
wound up in a church, or given to a home for unwed
mothers. Mac was inclined to agree. It made the horror of what had happened a little easier to bear.

As for Devlin, adopting Caitlin had been the only
way his beloved wife would ever mother a child.
Whether she'd known of his family history or not,
they would never know. It was enough for Caitlin that
she'd been wanted desperately from the start. She had
no interest in finding her birth parents. After what
she'd gone through with Neil, she was all too aware
of the dangers of digging into a past better left un-
disturbed.

"You're awfully quiet, big brother."

Mac turned. Aaron was grinning at him from the
doorway.

"I'm on KP."

Aaron snitched a celery stick from the colander
where Caitlin had left them and began to eat.

"That ring looks pretty good on her finger, doesn't
it?" he asked.

Mac grinned. "Almost as good as the woman herself."

"I did good, didn't I?" Aaron asked.

Mac frowned, not following Aaron's train of thought.

"How so?"

"I could have called a professional bodyguard, you know. She could certainly have afforded a dozen."

Mac stopped, staring at his brother in disbelief as Aaron kept on talking.

"Of course, I wouldn't have wished this on her for anything in the world, but since it was happening, I thought it was the perfect reason to get the bickering between you two over with."

"Are you serious?"

Aaron grinned and took another bite of celery.

"As a heart attack. Remember two Christmases ago when I told you that you and Caitlin would make a good couple?"

"You were drunk."

"I was still right," Aaron said, waving the celery stick beneath Mac's nose as he backed out of the room.

"You did it on purpose?"

"Yes."

Mac grinned. "So I have you to thank for the hell I went through?"

"And for Caitlin. You have to thank me for her, too. God only knows how long it would have taken you two to wake up if I hadn't interfered. I am the best," he crowed, in an imitation of their childhood taunts, when one-upmanship mattered most of all.

Mac laughed. "Yeah, but I won the girl."

Aaron rolled his eyes. "Like I care."

This time, they both laughed aloud.

"What's so funny?" Caitlin asked.

"Nothing," they said in unison.

Her eyes narrowed. She'd seen them in this mood before.

"Get out," she said, pointing toward the living room. "Get out of my kitchen and go do something."

"Like what?" Mac asked.

"I don't know," she muttered. "Just go be men."

"I'll give it my best shot," Aaron said, then laughed at his own wit as he sauntered out, leaving Mac to follow.

The joy in her heart was almost perfect as she went about finishing the meal. Although this wasn't the first Christmas she'd spent in Mac's company, it was her first as a woman in love. Everything smelled sweeter. Food tasted richer. Hearts beat faster. It was the best. Only now and then did a flash of evil tease her mind, but she quickly pushed it away.

Just as she was about to take the turkey out of the oven, the doorbell rang again. Confident that there were three able-bodied men to answer, she continued with the task, taking pride in the golden-brown skin of the bird in the pan.

A couple of minutes later, Mac came hurrying into the room. "Honey, there's someone to see you." She frowned. "Oh, Mac, can't you deal with it? The food is almost ready. We're about to sit down to eat."

He shook his head. "Trust me," he said. "You don't want to miss this."

She took off her apron and wiped her hands. "Okay, let's go see the big surprise."

The man by the door looked familiar, but it was the little girl standing in front of him who she recognized on sight.

"Why, Katie! How sweet of you to come visit me." She knelt in front of the girl and smiled. "Did Santa Claus come see you last night?"

Katie Bridges grinned and nodded, and as she did, Caitlin realized it was the first time she'd seen her smile.

Caitlin stood, then, welcoming the father, as well. "Hank, isn't it? How are you doing?"

The man's eyes welled. "Thanks to you, better than I would have believed possible."

Caitlin felt herself blushing. "Please, don't," she said, uncomfortable with praise for something that had taken no more effort than a call to her lawyers.

He nodded, understanding her reluctance.

"I'll make this quick," he said. "And I apologize for intruding on your Christmas dinner, but we're on our way to the airport, and Katie has something she wanted to give you.''

''Are you going to your family for the holidays?''

''No, ma'am,'' he said. ''We're moving to Miami. Now that...since my...well, it's just better. It's where I was raised, and my parents will be close by to help me with Katie.'' He patted his daughter on the head. ''She's not too keen on the idea of leaving,'' he said.

Caitlin knelt again, putting herself on eye level with the little girl. ''So, you have something for me?''

''I made it myself,'' Katie said, and handed Caitlin a small, flat package.

She tore into the wrappings. ''I love presents, don't you?''

Katie nodded, then leaned back against her father's legs, still needing the stability of human contact to cope.

Caitlin rocked back on her heels as her eyes filled with tears.

''She finished it a couple of days ago,'' Hank said. ''But I didn't know where you lived. I called the paper, and they gave me your publicist's phone number. When I told him why I needed it, he gave me your address. I hope you don't mind.''

Caitlin shook her head. ''Mind? I'm honored.'' She looked at Katie, her heart in her throat. ''It's the best picture I've ever seen. May I give you a hug? Just to say thank you?''

Katie hesitated, then nodded, opening her arms lovingly, as only a child can do, and wrapping them around Caitlin's neck.

Oh God...give me a dozen just like her.

When she pulled back, Caitlin was fighting back tears. "I hear you're moving," she said.

The little girl frowned and nodded.

"Well, guess what?" Caitlin said. "So am I."

Katie looked up at Mac. "Are you going with your daddy, too?"

Caitlin smiled. "Yes, my daddy is taking me to Atlanta with him, just like your daddy is taking you to Miami. Isn't that exciting?"

Caitlin stood then, proudly clutching the picture to her chest as she pointed at the Degas hanging on the wall beside the door.

"Mac, would you please take that painting down? I have a new picture I'd like to hang."

Hank Bridges flushed. "Oh, Miss Bennett, you don't have to do that."

"Actually, I do," Caitlin said.

Mac was so proud of Caitlin he could hardly think as he took down the priceless work of art, carefully replacing it with an acrylic-framed page from a coloring book.

"I always did like that Barney," Caitlin said, as she stepped back to view the purple dinosaur among a brightly colored field of flowers.

"Me, too," Katie said, smiling at Caitlin.

"We've got to go," Hank said. "Merry Christmas

to all of you, and…Miss Bennett, God's blessings on you for the rest of your life.''

Caitlin nodded her eyes filling with tears as Mac stood beside her. The weight of his arm across her shoulders was her anchor to the world. Katie looked back as they went out the door. Caitlin waved.

"Thank you, Katie Bridges. Have a good life.''

And then they were gone.

Mac looked at the picture, squinting judiciously as he gave it a firm critique.

"You know…I like what she's done with the purple. It speaks for itself, don't you think?''

Caitlin burst into laughter as Mac swept her off her feet.

The ring on her finger slid toward her knuckle, but she clenched her hand and held on, just like she'd held on to life.

"Isn't that turkey done yet?'' Aaron asked.

Caitlin laughed despite her tears as Mac set her back on the floor.

"Yes, you big moose, it's done. All of you, come and help me dish up. We're going to eat in the kitchen—where families are supposed to eat.''